Steady as You Go

Cheryl Murnane

B

Enjoy!

Cheryl Murnane

CHERYL MURNANE PUBLISHING

Copyright © Cheryl Murnane, 2015

Date of first printing: May 2015

ISBN: 978-0-9903862-5-4

Print layout by Guido Henkel, www.guidohenkel.com

Printed in U.S.A.

Also by Cheryl Murnane

DURING THE FALL

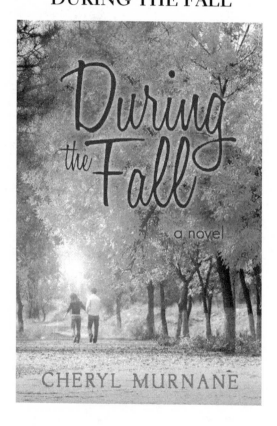

Praise for *During the Fall*

"...filled with beautiful imagery, showing the author's command of
a scene, and how she understands the importance of feeling
through words."

The Author Visits

For the firefighters who risk their lives for all of us

…and especially for Papa! Heaven got a bit brighter when you entered! Thank you for teaching me how to respect the allure of fire!

Prelude

I WALKED THROUGH THE DOOR INTO SACRED GROUNDS, anticipating the freshly poured hot coffee and egg and English muffin sandwich that was always waiting for me by the side cabinet. When I reached for it, the counter was bare – a shock wave raced up my arm. I looked behind the counter and saw two new faces serving the line of hungry, impatient customers; Terry's calm, sweet, dimpled face wasn't there, and neither was Sue's. Then I remembered Sue had left to work full-time at her family's business. I thought, *Terry must be sick.* I recognized Stacy from the afternoon shift.

I proceeded to get in line behind the assembly of unhappy customers. The door opened, and another customer lined up behind me. I turned to see if I recognized the face, but I didn't. We waited while bagel order after bagel order was placed. The new girls were in over their heads, trying to heat the bagels, butter them, and make coffees and lattes, all the while wearing artificial smiles to stop them from yelling back at the cranky patrons.

Stacy clearly wasn't used to the constant flow of breakfast sandwich orders. As more customers ordered, the other girl's smile changed into a look of sheer desperation. They seemed to be responding to the demands of the morning crowd without a good action plan, and the wheels were coming off.

I turned to the guy behind me and said with a chuckle, "These girls are working hard for their pay today."

"I don't recognize the shorter one. She must be new—she has *new girl* written all over her face."

He's a regular, like me.

"Poor thing. The morning rush could eat her up. Tired, hungry people are at their worst before heading off to work," I muttered.

"Well, some of you are! I'm just finishing work. I'm here to grab a coffee to keep me awake for a few more hours," the man replied. He wore a canvas workman's jacket and was dressed in navy blue from head to toe.

I was intrigued. "Oh, what do you do?" I would have guessed he was a mechanic, but his fingernails were too clean, so I ruled that out quick.

"I work for the fire department. I finished a twenty-four-hour shift, and now I have a day off. It's a great schedule. We've been having quiet nights, but last night it seemed every fool was driving too fast and crashing their cars, and we had a couple of elderly people to tend to. It was a busy night. I'm beat and looking forward to a boost of energy."

I liked this guy. He was friendly and relaxed, yet I sensed from the slump of his shoulders and the dark rings under his eyes that something else bothered him beyond being tired. I said, "As a little kid, I always thought being a firefighter would be a cool job. In fact, my wife Maggie's father worked for the department in town years ago."

"Oh yeah? What's his name? I probably know him. It's true what they say—we are like brothers."

"Well, you may know his name, but you never met him. He died on a call a long time ago. His name was Bill O'Brien."

"Oh, man, he was your father-in-law?" He had one hand in his front pocket and ran the other one through his hair. His expression changed. "The guys talk about that fire—it was a big one, massive and historic. It went down as the biggest and most dangerous fire in the town's history, hopefully ever." He gestured for me to move ahead.

Only two more people in front of me before I could get my coffee and head to work.

"So, you recognize his name?" I asked.

"Once a year we hold private ceremonies, more like moments of silence, within the department to acknowledge the fallen brothers in our firefighting family. The guys who served with the fallen members usually tell stories about them in the kitchen at dinner time. It's how we keep their spirit in the fire station alive, and it helps teach us younger guys that a situation can go from bad to ugly in a second. I hope I never have to see what some of my fallen brothers had to see, but I'm prepared if I do."

"Sir, can I help you? Sir?"

The man nudged my shoulder and pointed to the girl behind the counter. I hadn't heard her. I was lost in thought, envisioning the camaraderie the firefighters shared, gathered around a long table eating pasta and telling stories of the great men who came before them.

"I'm sorry. I'll have a medium black coffee and an egg on an English muffin, please. Oh, and whatever this man is having." I pointed to the man behind me.

"You don't have to do that," he said, shaking his hands in front of him.

"Think of it as my way of saying thank you for your service." I smiled.

The man placed his order next, and we waited for the girls to finish them.

"Thanks for the coffee, man." He slapped my shoulder.

"Don't mention it. We're de-facto brothers, I think, right?" I said holding out my hand to shake his. "I'm Tim Barrett. It's nice to meet you."

"You too. I'm Will, Will Driscoll. And yeah, having a family member on a fire department binds people together. I appreciate this." He lifted up his cup and took a sip. "Have a good one, Tim."

"Yeah, you too, Will."

After I left the coffee shop, I walked down the sidewalk. The long New England winter was giving way to spring fever. I side-stepped many people enjoying the warm morning air: quick-stepping commuters, mothers pushing strollers, and a few dogs on leashes pulling their owners along.

I replayed the interaction with the new guy, Will. He seemed to be a cool dude, in all senses of the term, relaxed and unfazed. It seemed fitting that he was a firefighter; he was calm to the bone. I would like to think I gave off the same energy when I met someone for the first time, but I knew the truth. It's not that I'm not calm, it's more that my actions are intentional. I think about how I'm going to act in a situation and predetermine what I will share and what I will say. I am always prepared with an escape plan if things don't run according to my script.

Will seemed the opposite. I could tell he took what life threw at him and responded accordingly with a still, patient demeanor. He reminded me of a surfer—waiting for the ride of a lifetime. I imagined him sitting on his board out in the ocean, feet dangling in the cool water, chatting with the other surfers, waiting and watching for the current to churn up the water to produce the perfect C curl to ride, and then drifting along, gliding on the wave like it was glass before being deposited on the beach. Then he'd paddle back out to sit and wait to do it all over again. While he waited, he would share his recent ride with the other guys.

Even though I had to wait for my coffee and sandwich, my day was off to a good start. Come to think of it, I wouldn't have met Will if there hadn't been a line. Sometimes things happen for reasons we don't recognize at the time and then discover moments—or years—later.

After work, I walked through the door to my house just as Maggie was tying the laces on her running sneakers. I smiled from ear to ear as

I shared my day with her. I kept referring to the guy, Will, who I had met at the coffee shop.

"Wow! I guess he made some impact on you. What is it, Tim — a bromance?" She kidded me and said I was carrying on about him like a teenage girl.

I explained that Will was everything I wasn't and that I envied him. I wanted to be more carefree in life, but I knew I wasn't capable. My dad, who had been in the navy, raised me to respect hard work and always be prepared for what life might throw at me — calculated risks were the only chances he taught me to take, but because of my personality I took caution to the extreme.

I remember once I'd tried to be more casual, wearing loafers without socks, my shirt untucked. I wasn't out of the house an hour before I started complaining to Maggie about how uncomfortable I was; my feet were sticking to the inside of the shoes, and the untucked shirt made me feel unkempt. As we walked up to the doors of the country club, I'd had to tuck my shirt in. That was the last time I can remember wearing loafers without socks and an untucked shirt. It just wasn't my style.

I spoke with Will again in the coffee shop a few days after our first meeting. I was intrigued by him and wished I had a sister to set him up with because Will seemed like a great guy. Terry returned to work, and as usual my coffee and breakfast sandwich were waiting for me on the counter. One morning as I was held up at the crosswalk I saw Will enter the coffee shop, but the heavy traffic prevented me from crossing. By the time I reached the shop he had already left. Weeks passed by before I would talk to him again.

Will

"DAD, CAN I GO WITH YOU? I PROMISE I'LL STAY OUT OF THE WAY."

I was six years old and knew better than to ask, but I always did. I was holding out in case one time he would agree.

"No, son, you can't come. Fighting brush fires is no place for a kid." He patted my head. "I'm not making any promises, but maybe you can come by the station later and help clean the trucks and equipment." My dad was leaving to support his brothers on a fire that was consuming the east side of a mountain.

"All right, Dad." I ran out of the house to my make-believe fire burning up the grass in the front yard. I was prepared with the hose; I turned it on full blast and sprayed every inch of the lawn. My dad appreciated my imagination. It took care of two needs: the lawn needed to be watered, and it kept me from pestering my mother.

~

The type of work I would do when I grew up was never a question. I knew from that early part of my childhood that I would become a firefighter. I dreamed of later becoming the chief. The surprise for my parents was that after living my life on the west coast, I would become one in New England.

After high school I made the move to Massachusetts to attend Salem State College and study fire science. During the years I spent there, to my mother's dismay I fell in love with the New England seasons. I quickly made friends who enjoyed the outdoors as much as I did and I explored, soon finding my way around the area. Surrounded by many hiking and biking trails, I spent more time outside than in. After my studies were done, I would find someone to bike a trail with me or head out alone. Being in the woods helped me clear my head after the tedious task of studying.

I had never felt as alive as I did after moving to New England; the seasons affected me deep within my soul. The weather was a contrast to the pleasant everyday southern California weather, but I felt at ease with the changes, and I was happy to make the move to New England a permanent one. I learned to adapt to living in the cold winter, but in the spring I made a mad dash to get outside and soak up the warmth of the sun and enjoy the longer days.

There were lots of pretty girls at school I was interested in when they came around to talk and flirt with me, but my focus was on studying and working out. I didn't mind having fun, but I was not looking for anything serious. I had spent my childhood around my father's firehouse, and I saw first-hand how families were torn apart when a husband or father died on the job. My father had imprinted on me that I had to achieve my goal of becoming a firefighter before falling in love. Having a girlfriend could lead to marriage, but not all girlfriends would make good firefighter spouses. It took a certain personality to be a firefighter's wife. She needed to be strong and capable on her own in case her husband died on the job, but there was no way I was going to leave someone a widow — not if I could help it.

The most significant death at my father's firehouse was bewildering because it didn't happen in a burning building. Fred was my dad's best friend on the department; they met at the fire academy and were both employed by the same town, at the same station. They formed a close relationship through the many years they spent together on and off the job, especially after they became parents. Fred had a son my age, and on the weekends our families would often spend time together at each other's homes for barbeques.

Freddie Jr. and I would run around the house playing fireman; we rescued our siblings from make-believe scenarios and sprayed water on everything. We had fun together during our childhood years, but in our teenage years, after his father died trying to save drowning victims, Freddie Jr. withdrew from life.

When the fire station had received a call that two people were struggling in the water, my dad and Fred arrived at the pond first. My dad swam out to rescue one of the victims and brought her safely to shore. While paramedics tended to the woman, Fred raced out to bring the next victim in. As they swam toward the shoreline, my dad noticed Fred was struggling to close the distance. My dad swam the short distance to relieve Fred and took the large male victim to shore.

My dad laid the victim on the ground for the paramedics. When he turned back, he saw Fred lying face down in the water. He ran back as fast as he could and pulled Fred to the shore. While the paramedics were busy stabilizing the other victims, my dad started CPR on Fred. Other firefighters began arriving on the scene; they all took turns trying to revive Fred—with no success.

It was later determined that Fred suffered a heart attack trying to save the drowning man. Fred's family had to say hard good-byes to him. The firehouse flags waved at half-mast the day of Fred's funeral, and I watched with respect as the honor guards rotated shifts to stand by the casket – silent soldiers protecting their comrade and fallen brother.

Weeks after the funeral, my emotions began to smooth out, and I began to understand the many risks involved in my father's job. But in my adolescent mind no risk was going to stop me from becoming a firefighter. Instead, Fred's death made me more aware of how short life could be. I needed to appreciate living and experience as much as I could before my time was up. I preferred to live life to the fullest, not like Freddie Jr., who hid from it. The more adventurous my life the better, because when my nerves were pushed into overdrive, I felt alive!

~

After I graduated from college, I spent the summer hanging out at beaches in New England while I searched for jobs. In September I was hired to work in a small-town fire station north of Boston. I started as a probie, which meant I had to learn *everything* that went on in the fire station. I worked hard to gain the respect of my coworkers and prove myself to be responsible. I knew when to shut my mouth and when to ask questions. As the new guy, I rode in the ambulance, rotating duties inside the vehicle every month, from driver to passenger to the EMT in the back. All the videos I watched in college did little to prepare me for the conditions I saw after car accidents or other accidents in general. I learned in my first month that flesh was no match for chainsaws and that broken bones can puncture the skin. Seeing the feeble naked bodies of the elderly would keep me in the gym forever.

I chose to work in a small town rather than the city because of the proximity to the mountains and the ocean. As much as I wanted to be a firefighter, I also loved being active, and having the mountains and ocean close by meant only a short drive to hike or surf. Working the rotation at the firehouse gave me five days off to release the trauma I saw while working. My dad had always made time for fishing on his days off to clear his mind from the job and taught me that I had to keep myself protected from what I saw while working. He said it would shorten my career if I couldn't separate myself from the images in the ambulance.

STEADY AS YOU GO

After I got my job, my parents visited New England. I gave my dad a tour of *my* firehouse. As we walked around he said very little, but his facial expressions and body language conveyed he was proud. When I introduced him to my fellow brothers, he shared stories of five-lane traffic accidents and SoCal forest fires, the type of fires that didn't compare to anything my firehouse saw. I stood next to him, smiling as he spoke. I was proud of my father and felt gratitude for the many years he'd served as a firefighter.

On a tour of my new town, my mother commented that I needed someone to keep me company. She told me I should have a girlfriend, and she looked around for potential ladies. Even though time and time again I told her I had no interest in dating and I was happy playing the field. She was upset that her son was thousands of miles from home and didn't have anyone to share life with. She couldn't understand how the men I worked with instantly became my new family.

I tried to reassure her that I was still young and had plenty of time before I had to settle down. Times were different from when she and my dad were young. They got married when my mother was twenty and my father a year older. They had my sister, Ellen, and then two years later I was born. Their family was complete before they were twenty-four. My mom was old-fashioned. In her mind it was hopeless, at twenty-two, with no girlfriend, my time was running out. All the good girls were taken.

I was young and I wasn't ready to commit to one woman or fall in love, but I didn't let that stop me from meeting women. I wasn't ready to give my heart, yet when I met the right woman, then I would know I was ready to settle down.

~

On my seventh anniversary in the fire service, as I walked through the doors with my new partner, I tripped over his four legs and spring-loaded tail. In all the years that I'd worked in the department I'd commented about the absence of the firehouse dog that accompanied every fireman in the books I had read as a kid, full of pictures of firefighters and their trusty sidekick, the Dalmatian. Our ex-chief had no love or appreciation for dogs and was dead set against having one in his firehouse. It just so happened that his last day and my anniversary were a day apart. I had been researching Dalmatian pups and found a litter with one male pup still available. After a short conversation about the puppy with our new chief, he was in. The house voted on the pup's name; it was unanimous. His name would be Jake — New England slang for a firefighter.

We would eventually train Jake to take part in our elementary school education classes teaching fire safety. During our open houses, when he would show off his many obedience skills, Jake was a huge hit. He was trained to pull the rope that rang the bell when dinner was ready, but his stop, drop, and roll was the fan favorite.

~

Living in New England for eleven years satisfied me. I had everything I needed: my dream job and the great outdoors. I had found the perfect starter home in a wonderful area and lived the way I wanted. Every season offered a new sport to play, satisfying my desire to live an active life. I needed those outlets to release the energy I had accumulated during working hours, witnessing life's less than ideal circumstances, and I appreciated the many ways I could burn off my energy and refocus my mind on my days off by surfing, biking, hiking, or skiing.

Over the years, my mother still expressed her concerns about me settling down, even though I told her not to worry. I was almost thirty and had met many different women, but when I met Melissa I knew she was the one.

Our relationship grew like a wild fire in a dry forest. Within a month I was spending my nights off at Melissa's. When I was working at the station, Melissa would often bring her son, Bobby, by to visit. I knew she was the one who wanted to see me, and I had no problem with that. Melissa and I would sneak away to be alone and talk or make out until our lips ached. Bobby loved talking to my brothers, and they loved having a little dude around to play with and pass the time. Jake loved the crumbs Bobby left on the ground.

I couldn't believe I was falling in love and how she had come into my life out of nowhere. I had been thinking about dating before I met Melissa at the accident scene because my days as a single guy were growing stale. After the impression she made on me, I wanted to know more about her, and being the rescuer that I was, I wanted to help her with Bobby. I could never understand how a man could walk out on his family.

She was *so* good-looking and had an amazing body; she was a devoted, loving mother, and she was brilliant — a real math whiz. It's no wonder her company loved her; she was their financial genius. I couldn't understand what she saw in me, a laid-back firefighter from California looking for the least-resistant path through life. It wasn't that I was unmotivated, more that I enjoyed finding peace and not allowing the little mishaps of life to affect me. Whatever it was, we made a good couple and we knew it.

I could never have prepared myself for the day when Melissa told me she was temporarily moving to Florida. A little more than three months into our relationship, Melissa's mother fell and broke her hip. Melissa had tried to handle the medical issues over the phone and find in-patient therapy for her mother. It became more and more obvious that her mother's health was declining and that her pre-existing immune system issues caused her additional health problems, so Melissa needed to go to her. She explained the situation to me right after she put Bobby to bed.

"I don't want to go any more than you want me to go, but she's all that I have and she needs me. The fall was just the beginning of her decline. I'm taking a three-month leave, with the option to work from Florida if I need to stay longer." She held my hand. "It will go by faster than we think."

"I know. I wish I could go with you, but I can't take all that time off." I sat up and held my head in my hands, trying to think of some way to work this out.

She took a sip of her tea. "Taking Bobby away from you is going to practically kill him, you know. It'll be like his dad leaving all over again. Thankfully he doesn't talk about that any more. I'm afraid he'll never forgive me for moving away from you." She rubbed my back with one hand and took my hand in the other.

"It's only three months before you'll be back." I rubbed my thumb over the back of her hand.

"He won't be able to understand that; he's so young. Time means nothing to him." She rested her head on my shoulder.

"We'll get through it." I kissed her head. We sat watching the fire, listening to the logs hiss and burn. In the back of my mind, I wondered if Melissa and Bobby would come back. I hoped that they were only ugly fears trying to draw me in emotionally. I wrapped my arms around Melissa, holding tight to what I knew was real. She was with me now, and I wasn't going to waste a minute.

Two months later, Melissa called early in the morning from Florida to tell me she wasn't coming back. Her mother's health was not stable enough for her to live alone, and the costs to have her live in a facility were prohibitive.

"Will, I'm so sorry. I can't help this. I feel so out of control." She sobbed into the phone. "I have tried everything possible, but the doctors and I agreed that the only way for my mother to live safely is if someone lives with her. I'm sorry to do this to you — to us."

The ground beneath me felt unstable, like a rope bridge. My fears had come true. The girl of my dreams was not coming back.

"Melissa… I don't know what to say. We have talked many times since you left, and you said that you were trying your best to find alternative care for your mom, but is this really the only option? What about your life back here? Our life?" I hated to sound selfish, but I couldn't let her go that easy.

"Will, I have spent many hours and sleepless nights trying to find another way, but there isn't one. I'm all she has and I need to stay. Bobby has found new friends at his preschool and I'm meeting other moms and new people in my mother's neighborhood. I'll… we'll be all right."

I slumped down to the kitchen floor, not sure what more I could say. I ran my hand through my hair; my breath got loud. I shook my head. "Well, I guess that's it then." I tried to steady my voice, but Melissa picked up on my anger.

"Please, Will, don't do this. It's hard for me too." She started crying again. "I don't want to lose you. I have never been with anyone like you. I feel alive and whole when I'm with you. Bobby's father never made me feel that way. What we had was special. Please don't make this hurt any more than it already does."

"You're right. I'm sorry. It's going to take me time to process this. I expected you home a month from now, and now you're not coming home at all. It surprised me, but listen, everything will be fine, okay? I love you so much." My throat burned and the words got stuck. I swallowed hard. "I need to be at the station in twenty minutes. I'll call you when I can, all right?"

"I love you too. I'm sorry I have to do this."

"Don't apologize. You couldn't have prevented this." I needed to get off the phone. I felt like I was breaking into pieces.

"Be careful at work."

"I will. Love you. Bye."

After we hung up I punched a hole in the wall; so much for the path of least resistance. I had opened myself up to love and got stung. The breakup over the phone, losing the woman I was madly in love with, and the thought of never seeing Bobby again caused an ache in my heart and an emptiness in my soul I had never felt before.

~

I met Tim Barrett at Sacred Grounds the day after my girlfriend, Melissa, told me she and her son, Bobby, wouldn't be coming back from Florida. And while Tim and I made small talk about being a fire-fighter, I'd tried hard to cover up my emotions and my sadness over losing Melissa.

A few days later we ran into each other at the coffee shop again. Tim's client didn't show, so we stayed to drink our coffees and I opened up to him about Melissa leaving me. I told him how sad and upset I felt after my conversation with her. Tim was easy to talk to. I could have never exposed myself to my coworkers the way I did with him—they would have loved teasing me about it.

I explained that I had never experienced anything in life that hurt as bad as losing Melissa and Bobby. I told him unless someone fell into my life like Melissa had, I was done—no more women for me. I couldn't take the heartache. He listened to me vent and helped me through my worst experience with heartbreak. He reassured me that someday when I wasn't looking, I would find another woman.

Maggie

I'LL NEVER FORGET THE DAY MY TWIN SISTER ALISON AND I RODE our bikes home from school to find rows of unexpected cars lining the street and parked in our driveway; we were ten years old. My heart instantly dropped to my stomach as Alison and I looked at each other. We pedaled our bikes as fast as we could. Our pale yellow house with the green shutters seemed to move farther away with every rotation of our tires. We couldn't get home fast enough.

We dropped our bikes and ran through the door. "What's going on? Why are so many cars here?" We were bent over, breathing heavily, our hands on our knees to keep us from falling over. The group of people in the kitchen remained silent and stared at us.

I looked up and saw my mother sitting in a chair, her elbows on the kitchen table, holding a white kerchief in one hand. She turned to face Alison and me and began sobbing. We moved beside her, each of us wrapping our arms around her shoulders.

The walls crept in and the murmur of voices died out. In that moment it was only the three of us in the kitchen. We stood next to our mother, holding her, allowing her to compose herself. My sense of smell grew heightened as I inhaled her musky perfume. A pit grew in my stomach. Years before, I had watched a news report about a firefighter who had died while fighting a house fire in a city outside of Boston. Since then I had always feared hearing the words she was about to say. My father had always assured us that our small town had safe buildings and it was unlikely a fire could grow out of control before they arrived.

It was then I knew my world would never be the same. A ten-year-old could never be the same without her hero and best friend. Ten years of memories shared with my father flooded my mind and I knew they would have to carry me through a lifetime. I would have to learn to trust all over again and try to heal the broken pieces inside me without my father there to coach me.

I knew my father didn't want to leave us. He didn't want to die in the fire. They found him near an exit. He was trying to get out, but he ran out of time. I never felt let down by him, because I knew he'd *tried* to get out. He'd worked to find his way through the dark smoke and hot burning embers to get out safely. *He tried*; that's what I focused on. *He didn't give up.* Witnesses reported that he went back in the building to find his partner Dave; they said something about two in, two out. My dad, Bill O'Brien, was the most committed, devoted firefighter I had ever known. He gave his life to try and save his brother, but in the end they both perished, side by side.

~

I always heard people say I was my father's shadow. I followed him everywhere on his days off. I was either helping him fix things or watching, taking in and absorbing every move he made. He was my hero, my best friend, the center of my life, and I wanted to be just like him. My dad had a tall, slender build and the patience of a saint.

When I was first learning to ride a bike, he worked with me day after day, holding the back of the seat, supporting me so I wouldn't fall. I was too afraid to pedal alone and begged him not to let go, so he followed behind me holding the seat, telling me, "You can do it. You just need to believe in yourself." He would count one, two, three and then tell me he was going to let go. I would scream and plead with him not to. And he never did.

That went on for days. My mother and sister laughed at me, but it didn't help to soften my fear of falling. Alison learned to ride her bike in one day. She fell off and got back on over and over until she could balance and pedal around the neighborhood. I was always the more cautious twin.

My dad finally explained that he couldn't hold on to me forever. I needed to pull away from his grasp, keep pedaling, and balance the bike all by myself. He promised he would run next to me to catch me if I fell. He looked so deeply into my eyes that I thought he could see the back of my brain, his eyes smoldering with confidence that I would stay upright. He encouraged me to trust him, even if I didn't trust myself.

My mother and sister sat on the front steps, watching to see how brave I really was. I walked my sparkling red bike out of the garage as butterflies swam nervously in my tummy. Sweat spread over my palms, and in my head I heard my dad telling me to trust him. Of course I trusted him. *I can do this.* I would do it for him.

As I straddled the bike, my dad held it. Then we moved together, picking up speed, before he let go and chanted, "Steady as you go, steady as you go." And I as pedaled farther away, his words became a faint whisper. "Steady as you go." I felt the wind moving past my face, and the trees whipped by me. The joy of riding my bike without help from anyone filled my chest. Each foot pushed a pedal down, down, down. I came to the end of the road and slowly turned the handlebars to head back home.

Up ahead I could see my family jumping up and down, clapping and yelling out inaudible words. I was doing it! I was riding my bike. I hadn't trusted myself to do it, but I did it because I trusted that my father wouldn't let me down. As I approached them, I realized I had never ridden so fast and didn't know how to stop. I stopped pedaling, took my feet off the pedals, and held them out to the side, away from the bike. It started to wobble, and I lost control of the handlebars and crashed down onto the pavement just a few feet away from my father. He was there in an instant to pick me up and dust me off. He held me in his arms, and when he pulled away from me, he was surprised to see me smiling and laughing, not crying. I didn't care that I cut my knee and scraped my palms. My mom could fix the boo-boos — I had ridden my bike all by myself! I trusted my dad, and he didn't let me down; he never let me down.

~

With his death, I suffered a great loss at a vulnerable time in my life. It was then that I made a pact with myself to enjoy the small things in life because no one knew when their time would be up. Because I'd seen how dangerous life could be, I lived with caution, not wanting to take chances that could hurt me and leave my mother broken-hearted again.

My sister Alison had taken a different oath: throw caution to the wind and live life to the fullest, no holds barred. She missed our father; the steady stream of boyfriends she went through told her story, the complete opposite of mine.

Alison was a risk-taker, more like our father; she lived for the thrill and nothing else. My mother and I spent many hours waiting impatiently by the phone on the nights Alison broke curfew. Then there were the hours we spent in the hospital waiting room when Alison fell off her boyfriend's motorcycle. She was up to any challenge. She had the fiery spirit of a redhead trapped in a brunette's body. My mother joked that as twins we acted nothing alike. Alison's personality didn't match her ordinary appearance, and that saved her time after time with the police.

After many proposals from boyfriends, Alison had chosen to marry Keith, and their lifestyle suited both of them. Keith was part of the extreme sports world and traveled most of the year. Alison's work as an independent artist gave her the freedom to travel with him, and travel exposed her to different inspiring scenes.

~

I fell in love with Tim Barrett because he was so different from the other boys in my life. Tim had direction and purpose. He didn't sit around playing cards or drinking beer until his head pounded and the room spun. I met him during my senior year at college through my friend, Kate.

He devoted his time to carving out his future by making connections with big movers in the financial world; his goal was to own his own investment firm. During his senior year at college, he earned an internship at a prestigious financial firm in Boston and quickly began to make a name for himself as the new up-and-coming money man.

Loving Tim was like being cradled in the safety of my father's arms. His brown hair, soft, loving blue eyes, and tall, strong, lean physique gave me the feeling that nothing bad could reach me. The strength of his personality showed in his broad masculine jaw line that assured me he would be able to handle any problems in life. He was stable and committed to me, which made it easy for me to be myself with him. I hadn't known such depths of love since my father had died. Tim was just the type of guy I imagined myself growing old with. He was cautious, methodical, and devoted.

Our wedding took place on a warm day in June. It was magical and almost perfect. Although we were surrounded by our families and many friends, the only thing missing was my dad. The wedding went down as the party of the year, and people talked about it for months after. The live band and great company kept everyone on the dance floor. Tim and I stared into each other's eyes with admiration while we celebrated our love for each other.

We quickly fell into a routine, enjoying our married life and the comfort we shared. I was married to a wonderful man who supported the choices I made and made me feel confident.

After losing my father I blossomed as a caregiver; I stepped in to fill his shoes and tried to help my mother heal. My job as ER nurse allowed me the opportunity to continue to care for people. I showered my patients with the comfort I sought in life. I was able to offer support to those with illnesses or feelings of dread.

I had my career in motion helping others and after many years of searching, I felt a sense of well-being and peace return to my life. The scars left over from my father's death had healed, and I was moving on, in love with a man who made me feel whole.

Tim

"I'LL MEET YOU THERE IN THIRTY MINUTES," I CONFIRMED OVER
the speaker phone. "I'll be sitting at the table by the window." I
grabbed my keys from my desk drawer. "Yep. Okay, see you then."

I went over all the paperwork for the third time to ensure that it was
all in order and checked that I had plenty of functioning pens. I flashed
back to when I'd started my own investment firm. I had brought two
pens with me to a meeting with a new client. When the client proceeded to sign on the line, we discovered the two pens I'd brought had
dried up. It wasn't the fine first impression I'd been hoping for.

The short walk from my office to the coffee shop gave me time to
absorb the increasing warmth of the sunny spring morning through
my suit jacket. I appreciated being able to leave my overcoat in the
office closet. It was unusually quiet when I walked into Sacred
Grounds. It seemed to be a quiet spell and I saw my favorite table in
the corner by the window was available.

As always, I'd given myself too much time, but I liked to be settled
before a client arrived. I enjoyed meeting clients, new or existing, at
the coffee shop. It was a comfortable backdrop for either the good
news or bad news that I had to deliver. If a monthly report came in too
low, being in a public place almost always guaranteed no yelling, and if
the report was full of substantial gains, there would be a pleasing connection between the aroma of java beans and making money.

I had been coming to Sacred Grounds since it opened three years ago. In fact, I was their first customer. The girls now knew me by name; my coffee and morning sandwich were always—well, almost always—ready and waiting for me. I ran like a Timex. You could set your life by me. I'm likable, dependable and trustworthy, and I rely on those attributes to obtain the confidence of my clients.

While I waited, I set up the documents for my client to sign and laid out two pens—I had three others in my bag. From my table, I watched as customers filed into the shop, craving their morning coffee to kick-start their day. The line grew longer: a few women wearing black yoga pants and tee-shirts, their hair pulled on top of their heads; an elderly couple chatting back and forth about their order; a businessman who appeared to have gotten off to a late start. He impatiently swayed from foot to foot, apparently hoping the line would recede so he could put his order in and get to the office before the boss noticed. I shook my head and smiled to myself, wondering if he owned a watch or if he ever contemplated waking up earlier so he didn't have to feel the panic that grew from being late. I couldn't relate to him.

I looked at my watch again. There were another fifteen minutes before my client was due to arrive. As the bell on the door jingled, I set one of the black pens on top of the stack of papers and moved the other one just above the paper. I lifted my eyes from the paperwork to see if my client had arrived, and I caught Will's eye. We shared a nod and smile. He left the long line and appeared at my table.

"Hey, Tim. How's it going this morning?"

I stood to shake his hand. "Hey, Will. It's good to see you. I'm off to a great start so far. I'm meeting a client to have him sign some documents. Then I'm heading to the golf course to play nine holes with some old buddies. I have to take advantage of these warm spring days. How are you doing?"

"Can't complain, man. I just finished my shift. The sun's out; I'm grabbing a cup of coffee and then I'm gonna mow the lawn and head to the beach for the afternoon. I heard the waves are rolling after the storms over the weekend."

"You surf? I never tried that before. I usually fish when I go to the beach. I prefer the safety of the shore over being in the water." I laughed.

"Ah, yeah. I learned when I was real young, back in California where I grew up. You got to try it. You don't always hit the best waves, but when you do, you get this feeling…" He paused, looking for the right word. "How it feels is indescribable. Well, I guess it feels like flying, except your feet are on a board." Will looked over his shoulder and saw the line was getting shorter. Gesturing with his thumb, he said, "I'm gonna grab my coffee. It was nice seeing you, Tim. I hope the course treats you right. Take care, buddy."

"Thanks. See you around." I shook my head when I thought of myself surfing.

I sat back down at the table to wait. After a few minutes, something caught my attention. Out of the corner of my eye, I saw Will outside the window, bent over to help a little old lady pick up the contents of her handbag that had spilled on the ground. He put everything back in the bag and handed it to her and then offered her his arm. I smiled as they walked away, arm in arm, chatting. What a thoughtful guy he was.

My client arrived, and soon I wrapped up my meeting. My client was satisfied; all was good in my world. I looked forward to the afternoon on the golf course with my college friends. Every spring, we met to play nine holes of golf and work out the winter kinks before the season got started.

It was late morning on a Wednesday, and the highway traffic was thick. It was an odd time of the day for heavy traffic. I drove in the middle lane behind a compact car; I could see up ahead. The lines of cars went on for miles. The left lane was moving faster, and more and more cars were shifting lanes to take advantage of it, yet I stayed comfortably behind the small car, not wanting to weave in and out of traffic. I wanted to get to the golf course safely. Too many times I'd seen drivers pull stunts on the highway that could get them or anyone else killed. They would maneuver their way through the traffic and get miles ahead of me, and yet when I pulled off the highway I would see them a car or two in front of me. They hadn't gained much time with the awful risks they took.

On the course, out of the four of us I was in better form, and it showed in my game. I shot a thirty-three and the other guys were over forty; dinner was on them—losers pay. They didn't know, and I wasn't about to tell them, that I had been to the driving range for the past week trying to straighten out my drive. I enjoyed the mental challenges of playing golf. Every approach to the ball was an opportunity to work on my swing and practice patience with my shots. When spring arrived after the long cold winters in New England, I would spend any free time outside working on my game. Following the rules of golf offered me a feeling of contentment; I always felt better about myself when I stayed inside the boundaries of life.

~

"Hi, honey, I'm home," I called as I walked through the house searching for Maggie. I heard Adele's melodic voice coming through the open patio doors, joined with Maggie's as she attempted to sing along. I shook my head and smiled. I walked outside and found Maggie on the porch painting her toenails.

"Hi, hon, how was your day?"

I kissed the top of her head as she finished applying nail polish to her baby toe. She put her feet up on the chair next to her and wiggled her toes, satisfied with her accomplishment. She settled back in her chair to face me.

STEADY AS YOU GO

"Great. I signed another big company to the firm to manage their investments. If I can get a few more, then we can get started on our family." I playfully wagged my eyebrows up and down and looked at Maggie. The sun dipped in the sky, and the last few sunbeams lit up her face, gleaming through her red hair and twinkling in her clear green eyes. I was crazy about her. I knew I loved her the first time I met her.

My friend Andy, whom I met at Bentley, dated Maggie's friend, Kate. Andy told me about Kate's gorgeous friend and added that she didn't have a boyfriend. After listening to him banter on about her for months, I'd finally agreed to meet her.

Andy and Kate arranged for us to all meet up at the Museum of Science. I'll always remember how radiant Maggie looked the day we first met. I was instantly struck by her natural beauty. A redhead stands out in a crowd. Heads turned as she walked by, and I was proud to be the man walking next to her.

Maggie and I strolled through the exhibits and talked about our childhoods, our families, and our likes and dislikes. She told me that losing her firefighter father when she was ten years old had made an impression on her; she realized she needed security in her life. She wanted a relationship with a man who would be a safe haven, who made safe decisions, one who had a safe job without risks. She didn't want to end up a young widow like her mother.

In our early months together, she told me she was attracted to the stability I brought to our relationship; when she was with me she knew she would be safe and well cared for. Maggie appreciated the calculated way I lived my life, even though my brother Sean referred to me as a control freak.

We dated for four years before we got married.

With her warm, caring personality and the tenderness she showered on people, I knew Maggie would make the most wonderful mother, but I couldn't rush into having a baby until I knew we had a solid foundation and plenty of money saved. Now, after four years of marriage, I realized Maggie was ready, but I needed to secure the future of my investment firm before I started adding dependents to my life. Besides I was only thirty. There was plenty of time to be a father. So, much to the dismay of our mothers, instead of starting a family, we got a golden retriever puppy.

"I'm going to take Clipper for a run. Do you want to join us?" Clipper heard his two favorite words, *Clipper* and *run*, and started banging his tail on the porch to show his enthusiasm. I reached to over to pet Clipper's head, and he stood up, ready to go.

"I'll pass tonight. I have to wait for these to dry." She wiggled her toes back and forth.

"We'll be back," I said, and then I kissed her gently on the lips.

~

Every time I laced up my running sneakers I began the process of deciding which route I would take. I had created four running routes when we'd moved into our house. I could avoid the commuter traffic or run with it; I could run through neighborhoods or stay on main roads. Every run, I tried to fight the desire to plan out my route. Instead, I promised myself, I would allow the path to lead me, knowing I would find the right route for that day. I was trying to practice allowing life to lead me, instead of me leading life. I was learning to accept that some things had to be left to the power of the universe, and running routes was one of the areas where I was content to allow it to govern me. When I ran, nothing could stop the flow of energy I received from the blood pumping through my veins; it was the only time when I felt free from the limitations I put on myself.

I wasn't much of an athlete, although I did compete in track and field during high school. My lean physique made me an ideal competitor in many of the events in the sport, and I held many titles for my school.

As I took to the road that evening, my stamina let me down. I was able to run five miles in thirty-five minutes most nights, but that night I was slacking. Even having Clipper by my side urging me, pulling on the leash and looking up at me while we ran, my time was way off. I had begun to feel the effects of Father Time on my body, even though I was young. None of my friends complained, but I had begun to notice subtle changes; the first was fatigue during my runs. When I started noticing chest pains that would come and go at various times of the day, I chalked it up to stress. I approached my road, happy that my house was around the corner and I would soon be able to drink some water and take a cool shower.

As promised, Maggie had dinner ready when Clipper dragged me into the house. I wished I could have warned her that my timing was off that day; when I walked in she began reheating most of the food.

"What took so long?" she asked as she put a plate in the microwave.

"I don't know. It seemed like I couldn't find my usual pace, and I ran out of energy. I was fighting through it. It's weird—I must be getting old." I chuckled and placed Clipper's dinner bowl next to his water bowl. With a wag, he attacked his dinner as I asked, "No time for a shower, I'm guessing?"

"You look pretty sweaty, and I have to reheat most of this anyway, so take a quick one. I'll wait for you."

I moved in for a hug, but she pulled away and with a playful smile swatted me with a dishcloth. I accepted that I was sweaty and stunk like a gym bag, and I knew better than to try again. I headed to the shower with every intention of getting more than a hug from her later that night.

After dinner the warm spring air clung to the night as the last birds called out from their nests and a gentle breeze blew through the backyard. Maggie and I enjoyed the sunset with a tall glass of lemonade on the porch, Clipper by our feet. We talked about our summer plans and the vacations we planned to take. My parents owned a house on the Cape, where we always spent the Fourth of July. Clipper looked up at us as we laughed out loud, wondering how he would handle the booming fireworks my family set off from the beach.

It was the easy moments I spent with Maggie that made me fall in love with her again and again. Maggie and I had set up our lives in a style that worked for us. We planned our days and experienced few surprises. We were compatible on many levels and felt blessed to have met and to now share our life and visions. I held her hand in mine as bats began their ritual flight overhead. I felt our love as a continuum flowing from her body to mine and from mine back to her. Turning to meet her gaze, I kissed her, an invitation to follow me to the bedroom. Walking hand in hand with Maggie into bedroom, I heard Clipper lay down and moan as I closed the door.

~

Summer came and went too fast, but we were able to enjoy a couple of weeks of vacation at my parents' house on the Cape. Throughout the course of the summer, the changes I had begun to feel while running started spilling over into other parts of my day. My slower running time bled over to fatigue that followed me all day, no matter how early I went to bed or how long I slept in. I never felt rested or full of the energy I had in my twenties. None of my friends seemed to have started experiencing anything like it, so I assumed it was stress from trying to keep my life and Maggie's life balanced. I wrote off my chest pain as a side effect of the stress of owning my business.

Even though my appetite hadn't been affected by my stress, I noticed that my pants began to hang lose. I feared I was morphing into a middle-aged man who'd lost his muscle and looked more like a string bean. I was concerned with my disappearing muscles, but I had no energy to lift weights. I wanted to keep my physique, and I promised myself as soon as I had more energy, I would start lifting again to rebuild the muscle I had lost.

Maggie seldom mentioned the changes in my body because she knew it made me self-conscious, so we didn't talk about it unless I brought it up. When she noticed my fatigue she made me energy-boosting shakes to get me through the day. Few people seemed to notice my weight loss, except the girls in my office, who seemed worried by my new physical limitations. I figured my body would correct itself in time. Otherwise I felt fine.

~

The new year brought huge success to my financial firm. It took a few months but, the marketing campaign my firm launched in the fall paid off. After I'd secured a multimillion-dollar contract with a lucrative company, I called to warn Maggie I was in a really good mood and wouldn't be going to the gym. Instead I asked her to start a fire in the fireplace.

When I walked in the house the aroma of dinner mixed with the snapping sounds from the burning logs settled any lingering stress that remained from my earlier meeting. I was in my palace, and my princess was waiting for me. I set the celebratory champagne to chill in the ice bucket and found Maggie relaxing after her shift at the hospital, curled up in front of the fireplace reading a book, Clipper by her side. As soon as he saw me, Clipper rose and trotted to me, his tail nearly knocking everything over in its wake. He was a devoted dog and always in a good mood.

"Hi ya, boy." I stroked his soft yellow fur, which tickled as I petted him.

"Well, look who's home. What happened today that demanded a fire and champagne? Did you win the lottery?" Maggie said playfully.

"First, let me kiss you, and then I'll tell you everything." I knelt down next her and took her strikingly beautiful face in my hands. I looked deep into her green eyes as I inhaled the soft scent of her sweet perfume, and I kissed her with a deep passion that created a sudden shift in plans. As we kissed, she touched my chest and began to unbutton my shirt, revealing my boney frame. She pulled back and lifted her shirt over her head, exposing the red bra that lifted her round pillow-like breasts.

Maggie leaned into my naked chest, kissing her way up to my neck. I held her, trying to find the clasp on her bra to free her breasts from their confinement. She pulled away and looked into my eyes. I held her gaze as I caressed one perfect breast. Then I began to encircle her nipple with my tongue. She let out a soft sigh.

She reached down to unbuckle my pants and started to kiss the other side of my neck. Suddenly she stopped and became motionless. I eased her pants down from her hips, teasing her nipple with my lips.

"What is that?" Her voice was full of inquiry.

With a nipple in my mouth and my half-naked wife on top of me, I wouldn't have cared if a spider was crawling on me.

"Oh, it's nothing. Keep kissing me."

"No. Tim, there's something there. I don't remember that lump being there before." She reached for her sweater.

"Maggie, I'm sure it's nothing. Why are you getting dressed? Come on. Can't we finish?" I reached for her hands and pulled her close to me.

"Tim, there's a lump on your neck!"

I held her in my arms and reassured her I would look into later. "Maggie, I'm sure it's just a swollen gland. I've been busy, and I'm probably run down. Maybe I'm getting sick."

"That is a sizable swollen gland, if that's all it is. Tim, you need to do something about it. Please call the doctor tomorrow to get an appointment; don't wait too long. I think it could be something serious."

"Maggie, please, don't over react. It's nothing. I've been overdoing it at work and my body is telling me to slow down, that's all."

"The sooner you look into it, the better I'll feel."

I sensed she was worried but I needed to pick up where I left off. I held her in my arms and told her, "I want tonight to be special. The firm and I acquired another large account today."

"The Ribbon Paper Company?" She was smiling because she knew what it meant to the firm. We had acquired the account of an affluent company that would give us recognition as the most prominent and prestigious investors outside of Boston.

"Yes, that's why I brought home champagne. I want to celebrate with you. Honey, this means we are closer to starting our family, and I was hoping that we could practice right now," I said, pulling her sweater back over her head, enticing her with my tender touch, winning the challenge to lure her back to where we left off.

She apparently couldn't stop the thrill rising in her body.

"Fine, but please look into that lump. It seems larger than a swollen gland. I don't want anything to happen to you."

I placed my lips over her mouth and no more words were spoken as we wrapped ourselves around each other in front of the fireplace, celebrating the success of my day.

~

A couple of nights later I woke in the night after a dream. Maggie and I were climbing a hill, and when I turned around to reach for her hand she slid away from me and slowly drifted away, like she was being pulled from me. I was drenched in sweat. I needed to change my t-shirt. I rolled out of bed, careful not to disturb Maggie. As I changed into a dry shirt in the bathroom, I touched the lump Maggie had found. She had been on me to make an appointment with my doctor to look into the lump, but truthfully I was afraid what the doctors would tell me; if it was serious, how would it affect my life and Maggie's? In the dark of the night, worries about the lump began flooding my mind. I pondered the connection between the lump and my endless fatigue, the weight loss, and the more frequent night sweats over the last seven months. Could they be indications of some underlying health problem?

It was becoming obvious that my body was reacting to more than aging or stress, no matter how I tried to fool myself and Maggie into believing that wasn't the case. I'd been writing off the fatigue and the sweats to stress and aging, but I noticed that none of my friends were struggling like I was. It was time. I needed to investigate the changes occurring in my body.

I was able to get an appointment with my doctor the following week. He scheduled me for tests, although it felt more like I had been put through the medical version of a cavity search. I was poked and probed, scanned and touched from head to toe; the serious expressions on the faces of the medical staff frightened me, and I wished I had paid more attention to my symptoms earlier.

When the day came to learn the outcome of those tests, I wished Maggie had let me handle the doctor's appointment alone, because having her sitting next to me in the waiting room increased my nervousness, which in turn increased my blood pressure. Maggie insisted on being in the room to help me translate the test results and she thought I might downplay the doctor's findings in order to protect her from an undesirable diagnosis.

Nervous energy built to an unreasonable level as we waited to be called into the office. I stood and paced the waiting room. I couldn't sit any longer. As I waited an enormous fear grew inside me. I knew something was wrong with me, and I was petrified to hear what it was.

After a few moments an older nurse, who was about five feet tall, came to the doorway and announced, "Tim Barrett, the doctor will see you now."

A cold sensation washed over me, and sweat pooled in my palms. I nervously tried to dry them on my pant legs.

"That's me." I held out my hand to Maggie, and together we walked through the doorway, leaving behind the predictable and comfortable world we would never know again.

We sat in a private office; diplomas and certificates decorated the walls. On the ledge behind the doctor was a photo of a woman and a toddler smiling on a beach; I presumed it was his family. Maggie and I sat next to each other across from the doctor as he delivered the news with an expressionless, stoic face.

He folded his hands in front of him on his desk as he began to deliver the fateful news

I was suffocated by his words as they flew around my mind like hawks circling their prey. "The test results show an elevation in your white blood count… the biopsy revealed…the diagnosis of Hodgkin lymphoma." I sat speechless in the chair trying to absorb the overwhelming news while my world spun out of control.

"What does that mean?" Maggie asked. She reached for my hand and her squeeze brought me back to the room. I sat up straighter in my chair squeezing her hand harder, thankful for her presence.

He explained to us that the form of Hodgkin lymphoma that was attacking my body was at an aggressive stage. "Mr. Barrett, you have different treatment options including radiation and clinical trials, but I must convey to you that you are in a seriously compromised state of health. Your cancer is stage IV-b and has spread outside the lymphatic system and is now affecting your liver. I would highly recommend we get started immediately."

Someone please open a window—I need air. Did he just say what I think he did? Am I going to die?

~

Maggie and I drove home in silence. I'm not sure what kept her quiet. Perhaps she didn't want to say the wrong thing or she was afraid to admit she was right about the severity of the lump. What good would it do now to stuff my face in the fact that I'd made a huge mistake by not taking the signs seriously. I had been too afraid. Afraid that I would discover something that would impact our life.

I was in shock that my body was being attacked by cancer. I felt worse knowing I'd let Maggie down. I held her hand as we drove in traffic. With every car we passed, I thought, *that guy doesn't have cancer. That woman over there will live to see another year pass, and that young guy sitting on a bench holding his wife's hand will be a dad someday and watch his child grow up to accomplish great things.* A small girl ran in a field chasing a ball as her mother watched. Everywhere I looked I saw life, but inside me I felt death.

Then I looked back at the child and thought about becoming a dad. It was too late for that. Why had I waited so long? I had put so many stipulations on having a family; I'd made myself believe everything had to perfect before we had a baby. Now I would never be a dad, but worse than that, I would never be able to share parenting with Maggie. Even if she were to become pregnant, I couldn't imagine her raising our child alone. Maybe having a baby would comfort her, but I couldn't stand to know that I wouldn't be around to watch my baby grow up. I squeezed her hand harder. She turned to me, and I saw a tear fall from her eye.

Telling our parents was the hardest part. My parents should pass before me in the natural flow of life, but in our case it wasn't meant to be that way. The following day Maggie and I brought coffee and bagels to my parents' home. As we ate at the kitchen table I explained the diagnosis. I folded and unfolded my napkin, adding more creases, digging for the strength I needed to enlighten my parents about this news that would shake their world. I told them I would start on chemotherapy, but the odds were stacked heavily against me because the cancer had spread to my liver.

Their response was not a surprise. My mother's eyes filled with tears as she bowed her head. Maggie acknowledged her fears with a grimace. "I know," she said, reaching across the table to hold her hand, squeezing it to show her sympathy. My father rose from his seat, walked over to the window, and stared out at the back yard. Then he turned, saying confidently, "Well, we will find a treatment for you that turns those odds around in your favor. You need to remain strong through this, Tim."

I knew what was at stake. I was in for the fight of my life, and I would fight because I had too much to lose if I didn't. I didn't need my father reminding me.

~

"Can we sit by the window, over there?" I asked, pointing to my favorite table in Sacred Grounds.

"Of course we can." Maggie held my hand and assisted me as I walked to the table and got comfortable in the seat.

"I'll get your sandwich and coffee. Hey, don't go anywhere," she said, trying to make light of the situation.

"You can count on that," I replied. I swatted her ass as she walked away.

We sat at the sunny table where I always conducted my business. It was a treat to leave the house. I had finished my first cycle of chemotherapy treatment a couple of weeks ago and I was in the resting phase now. At first I was able to work in the office, but as the treatments went on I grew weaker, and my exhaustion made it harder to function at work, so I started working from home. I knew that I would eventually have to stop working altogether, and the thought of that scared me. I was confident that my business was in good hands, but my ambition to work still occupied my brain. The thought of doing nothing, just being sick, bothered me.

As I looked around the coffee shop, I wanted to freeze the moment. The bright sunny day was a much needed change from the rain showers that had fallen the past week. Rays of sun shone through the window, reflecting the different tones in Maggie's red hair. She was illuminated before me.

I smiled at her, feeling my heart sink in my chest. These moments together were more and more precious to me. Originally, I was told that I had less than a year to live, but last week they told me it was more likely to be less than six months, because the cancer was aggressive.

My strong, beautiful, supportive wife sat opposite me, full of optimism that a new drug would be invented or a new clinical trial would open up to help cure me. She wore her hope as if it were her backbone. She had shared stories of many cases like mine that had ended in a cure; her patients spoke about their families' experiences with cancer, offering stories of good results from positive attitudes and medicine. She refused to give up on me. I kept fighting my battles for her, but I knew I would lose the war.

I bit into my sandwich just as the door to the coffee shop opened and Will walked in. We caught each other's eye, and I saw the shock on his face. He walked in my direction. I had been trying to avoid Will in the last months when my condition became visibly worse. In the beginning, I had been able to change the subject about my declining appearance. I often wrote it off to having a cold, and when that stopped working, I told him I was under a lot of stress. But today was different. I hadn't seen Will in a long time, and I knew I had lost too much weight and had become so weak that it was obvious that I was indeed sick. I prayed I had the strength to handle the conversation.

I spoke in as strong a voice as I could manage. "Hey, Will, how are you?" I reached my hand out to shake his hand.

"Tim, where have you been? I haven't seen you in weeks. Is everything all right?"

The confusion and concern in Will's eyes were obvious.

"Yeah, it's all right. It's... going." I had learned to only answer the question that was asked and not to offer more information than necessary.

"Will, this is my wife, Maggie. This is Will, the cool guy from the coffee shop I always talk about."

I studied Maggie's face. Right on cue, a sparkle glistened in her eye and her mouth softened when she looked up at Will, a reaction I had seen on many women's faces when they looked at him. I had seen women fall over themselves and trip on their words in reaction to his good looks. It amazed me how women fell apart in his presence, but Maggie didn't falter. She held her composure.

"Hi, Will. It's nice to finally meet you." She stood to shake his hand.

"You too, Maggie." He smiled at her, and I saw an altered expression shine on his face as he held her hand in his.

Will looked back at me and cocked his head. "Are you all right, Tim? You, um, don't look so good."

"Well, I've been putting off telling you that I have... cancer. The prognosis isn't good." I was honest with him, but it didn't make me feel any better.

Will stumbled and held onto the table. Maggie got up to claim a chair from an empty table and offered it to Will.

"Tim, I'm so sorry to hear that." He was clearly stunned. He then turned his gaze to Maggie, who was fiddling with her napkin with nervous fingers.

"I know it's hard to hear. I didn't want to bother you with it. You have your own stuff to worry about. You don't need mine."

I recognized the lost expression on his face; it was just like the look that spread on the faces of other people when I had told them I was sick and the end of my life was looming ahead in the darkness. He was searching for the right words to say. No one can understand that there are no right words, because no matter what emotions they were trying to avoid or cover up with words, their shock was written all over their face.

"No, man, seriously. Whatever I can do to help, please just let me know. You've become a good friend to me over the last year. I can't just sit back and do nothing." He looked at Maggie. "Please, call me if he gets unruly and starts climbing the walls. I can distract him and you can have a rest. I'm sure this is hard on you guys."

"Will, thank you, but you don't need to do that." I had never been one to impose on people, but the cancer raging in my body forced me to rely on people more than I was comfortable with. We had our families' support. I didn't need to put Will out.

"I'm serious, Tim. Take my number and call me if you need anything." He stood up and left the piece of paper with his number written on it before he excused himself. "I won't interrupt your breakfast any longer. Let me know if you need me." He leaned over and hugged me. I'm sure he felt all my bones beneath the thin sheet of skin covering them.

"Bye, Will. Thanks." I smiled and looked at Maggie. I felt helpless after telling Will about my cancer. I reached my thin arm out toward her hand, and she held my hand tight. She smiled at me and nodded. She knew how hard it was for me to tell people I had cancer, never knowing if it would be our last good-bye.

~

During the car ride home, I asked Maggie her opinion of Will. My voice was weak. I was tired from being out all morning; I wasn't used to that much excitement in one day.

I needed to know how Maggie felt about him because I had been contemplating an idea that came when I woke up one night and was unable to fall back to sleep. As waves of fear washed over me, I thought about Maggie and how my cancer would affect her life. After her father died, Maggie had visualized living a life centered on security and safety. Neither of us could have seen this coming, but then I guess that's life, catching you off guard. With my life in peril, I was worried about how Maggie would be able to live after I was gone; she had worked so hard to recover from her father's death, I was unsure how she would respond to losing me. Would she love again, or would she become a young widow who lived in the memory of her late husband?

"He was…" Maggie stopped the car to let a young mother pushing a baby stroller cross in front of us. I looked over at her. Her sunglasses covered her eyes, but I noticed the corner of her mouth turned up just a bit while she thought about Will. She was quiet. I knew her well; she was holding back. She turned to look at me.

STEADY AS YOU GO

"He was very worried about you, which means he has a big heart. He must be a caring man." She nodded, as if she was pleased with her answer.

"Well, yes, he is. He is a firefighter remember. I like to think most of them are caring people, or they wouldn't enter into that field."

"Yeah, I would agree with that. My dad was the warmest, most lovable man and father ever. He was never afraid to show his emotions and hugged everyone he met."

We continued down the main road, passing trees with new flowers and leaves.

"Tim, why are you asking me what I think of Will?"

I fidgeted in my seat. I couldn't let her in on my plan. "Oh, because I always talked about the guy from the coffee shop, and now you finally got to meet him. I was just wondering if he was like you had imagined."

"Yeah, pretty much." She was smiling as she turned into our driveway. "You should think about calling him to get you out of the house when I have to work. It would be better for you than sitting around alone all day."

"Now that there's no sense in trying to hide the fact that I'm dying. I'll think about it."

Maggie helped me out of the car and walked by my side, assisting me inside the house. She covered me with blanket on the couch before she headed out for a run that I had encouraged her to take. I enjoyed having her close to me while she sat on the edge making sure I was comfortable. I could smell a hint of her sweet floral perfume, which relaxed me and put me at ease. I wished I could take the scent with me when I died. I didn't know where I would end up, but the scent and memory of Maggie would reassure me that everything would be all right.

"I won't be long. Call my cell if you need me, okay?" She smiled at me while she tied her running sneakers.

"Maggie, I will always need you." I couldn't continue speaking. My emotions caught me off guard. My throat tightened, and I felt like I might cry. I wasn't sure how I was supposed to welcome death and leave behind my wife, my parents, my brother, my life.

"Oh, Tim. I need you too. I know this is hard for us, but we'll get through it." She came and sat next to me and held me in her arms. I felt a tear drop off her chin onto my cheek. The silence between us spoke at a volume only we could hear. The comfort of her embrace relaxed me, and I allowed myself to be still in her arms.

Maggie had suffered an unimaginable loss at such a young age that caused her to grow up fast and become resilient, but I worried how she would cope with losing me. She never wanted to talk about life without me or make funeral arrangements. She always held hope that a new drug would become available and I would be saved miraculously. While I appreciated her optimism, I needed to know she would be taken care of when I was unable to be there for her. I felt miserable knowing how different our lives had turned out to be from the one we had imagined.

"Go for your run. At least one of us should get some exercise." I released Maggie from our hug and kissed her lips tenderly. She wiped her tears and stood.

"I'll be back," she said as she walked to the door. I heard it open and close. A heavy weight came over me. I curled up like a baby on the couch and cried, thinking, *How can this be happening to us?* Nothing was working out how we had planned. I was supposed to care for Maggie and keep her safe from life's hardships; that's what she expected from me. I was the safety she sought in life, and I had let her down. After my death, she would have to face her life alone without my support. Every night she would have to climb into our bed knowing I wouldn't be joining her and wake every morning to an empty house that echoed the emptiness she felt inside. As I lived, dying a little more each day, I worried she was dying alongside me. My diagnosis was killing her future, and I couldn't be peaceful. I cried until I had nothing left inside.

Will

SEEING TIM IN THE COFFEE SHOP SET MY DAY OFF ON A BAD start. I drove home, thinking that we had never exchanged phone numbers when we first met. I'd had no way of knowing he had been hiding at home, suffering with his family because of his cancer diagnosis. It rattled me to know that not too long ago Tim was a healthy guy, and now he was fighting for his life. Life is tricky like that. Sometimes you never see the collision coming; you can't brace yourself.

It had been weeks since I had seen him around, and I had wondered where he was or what could have happened to him. Numerous times I asked the girls in the coffee shop if they had seen him, and they'd told me that he hadn't been in. I missed seeing him and catching up with him and his life. We often chatted for a while before I headed home from work or he went off to a meeting or the office.

Tim had become a friend. Although we'd spent little time doing things together, an instant bond had formed, unlike any other friendship. From the first time I met him, I sensed he was afraid to live and step out from behind the guarded world he'd created for himself. I joked with him about his childhood and said his parents probably never allowed him to try new things or get dirty. He never denied it but would smile, look away, and change the subject. It became my mission to get him out of his shell and teach him to live life, but every time I'd tried to make plans, he would tell me he was busy.

I stopped at a red light, zoning out. I stared out the window of my truck at an empty wooden bench and thought about my friendship with Tim. After seeing Tim and learning about his prognosis I knew I would lose him just like I lost Melissa, and it opened up the old wounds. I began to wonder how she was doing.

~

The winter I met Melissa started out similar to my first winter at the station. The weather was snowy and icy. It seemed every call was to an accident scene, and I never would have guessed that one of them would change my life. As we were sitting down to our spaghetti dinner, a masterpiece of a meal cooked by John, I heard the tones. First it was an ambulance call; then the dispatcher's voice echoed the call on the loudspeaker in the firehouse:

"A four-car pile-up on Route 28. Multiple injuries, and children are involved."

We dropped our utensils and ran for our gear; being on the ambulance meant we were the first to leave. I loaded into the passenger's seat, my heart beating just strongly enough to remind me I was alive. The adrenaline was building. The firefighters in the engines had to suit up in their boots, pants, and jackets, which took them longer, so we arrived on the scene minutes before they did.

The wreck was unimaginable. In the intersection a northbound car had hit a southbound car head-on. The two cars following behind crushed the southbound car like an accordion, sandwiching the cars into each other like interlocked fingers. We radioed an update requesting backup and the Jaws of Life, warning them to be prepared for casualties and heavy trauma.

We parked the ambulance, and I approached the third car in the accident, hoping to find movement. My partner ran to the first two cars to assess the victims. As I got closer, I heard a women yell, "Help me, help my son!"

Oh no, I thought. *Here's the first kid.*

I approached the car. The driver began to climb out the passenger's window, which had sustained less impact than the driver's side.

"Ma'am, please stay inside the car! We are here to help you."

"My son is in the backseat, I have to get him out!" she yelled, flailing her arms around. From the size of the gash on her forehead I could tell she needed medical attention as blood poured down her face.

I ran over to her and helped her through the window and then to her feet before I looked into the backseat. The glass had been blown out of the back window. Her son, who looked to be about three, was strapped into his car seat. His head hung down, resting on his chest. I didn't see movement, and I feared he was dead. I reached in to find a pulse on the wrist of the arm resting on his right leg. It was faint, but it was there. Adrenaline rushed through my body, keeping me on my toes as I tried to cut through the seat belt that held his car seat in place. I was careful not to rock the seat too much to avoid causing any more damage to his head or neck.

The mother started yelling, "Bobby! Bobby, can you hear me?"

I held her back with my arm and screamed at her, "Ma'am, please sit on the ground and wait for help. I need to remove your son from the back seat!" She wailed and sat down.

"Hi, Bobby. I'm Will, and I'm going to help you. Can you hear me?" I didn't get a response, but I kept talking to him, reassuring him he was going to be okay.

I cut through the seat belt just as our backup pulled onto the scene, and I called for the stretcher and a small neck brace. Two firefighters came running. We pried the back door open, leaving Bobby in his car seat as we placed the brace around his neck. The mother started screaming when she saw blood coming from her son's mouth. A policeman arrived to hold her back, and another firefighter walked over to assess her injuries.

"I want to be with my son—he needs me!" She tried to break free from the policeman, but she passed out in his arms.

I helped load both the mother and Bobby into the back of my ambulance and jumped in for the ride to the hospital. I stabilized Bobby for the ride, and my partner tended to his mother, who was regaining consciousness. I telephoned the ER nurses with an update of our patients' current status and their vitals. I was relieved when the nurse told me they were prepped and ready for our arrival.

After I had Bobby stabilized, I asked Bobby's mother what her name was.

Groggily, she murmured, "Melissa. What's your name?"

I chuckled. "Will."

"It's nice to meet you, Will." And then she passed out again.

We unloaded Melissa and Bobby in the ER and handed their care over to the nurses in charge. My partner went to finish the paperwork in a small room off the ER, and I headed to the vending machine to buy some bottles of water. As I was walking back to the reception area a nurse called to me.

"Excuse me. Did you transport a mother and son from a car accident scene?"

"Is the little guy's name Bobby?" I asked.

"Yes, and the mother is Melissa." The nurse stood impatiently, tapping her fingers together, waiting for my reply.

"Yeah, that was me." I cracked open a water and took a long pull.

"She is asking for you. Come with me." She turned to a volunteer walking past us, took the water bottles from me, and instructed her to give them to the firefighter filling out paperwork near the reception desk. I followed behind the nurse as we walked through the ER doors past empty beds. Through the doors to the ambulance lot, I could see a flurry of activity as more victims from the accident scene were transported in.

"She is right around this curtain, and her son is next to her. Please don't stay long, but say hello. She has been asking for you in her moments of consciousness." She held back the curtain. "I need to assist the patients that are arriving. You may go in." She nodded, turned, and left the way we'd come in.

I stood by the curtain, not sure what to do or say. I looked at Melissa in the bed, a bandage on her forehead and scratches on her face; she also had cuts and scratches on her hands. Bobby was in the bed next her. He began to smile when he saw me.

Thankfully I walked over to his bed. "Hey, buddy. How are you feeling?" The nurses had cleaned him up, and he had no visual signs from the accident.

"Why is my mommy sleeping?" He pointed over to her bed.

"Well, I think she'll be awake soon. She hit her head in the car. Do you remember the accident?"

"I remember you cutting the seat belt and taking me out of Mommy's car." He looked at me with the bluest eyes I had ever seen.

"Wow, really? Your name is Bobby, right? I'm Will." I reached out my hand to shake his.

"It's nice to meet you, Will." He gave my hand a squeeze and moved it up and down two times. "That's my mommy. Her name is Melissa."

I looked over as Melissa began to stir. "Uh, I think she is starting to wake up."

She opened and closed her eyes and then turned in my direction. "Hi." Her voice was thick and sounded like she had just woken up after a full night's sleep.

"Hi, I'm Will. The nurse told me that you wanted to see me." I walked over to the side of her bed.

She rubbed her head, and she clinched her lids shut. "I wanted to thank you for helping save me and my son." She opened her eyes and looked at me; they were the same color as Bobby's.

"I was so scared. It happened so fast! My car slammed into the car in front of me and I was stuck behind the steering wheel. I didn't know how to get out. It felt like eternity, and then I heard your sirens and knew we would be saved." She looked over to Bobby and smiled. "Bobby, this is the man that saved us. Can you say 'thank you' to him?"

"Thank you," Bobby said. He smiled a huge smile, very proud of himself.

"You're welcome. I'm glad I was there to help you." I smiled back at Bobby. Turning to Melissa I said, "Well, I think I should go and let you both rest. It was nice to meet you."

"Thank you again, Will." Melissa was looking at me and smiling. I was able to see past her cuts and bandages to her charming smile that filled my view. I couldn't look away. There was something in her eyes, a look I hadn't noticed before.

"You're most welcome, Melissa." I stared at her and was frozen by the spell she cast on me.

My phone rang, snapping me to. It was my partner. "I'm sorry, I have to go. It's my partner. They must be done with their paperwork. I hope you guys are feeling better real soon." I headed for the receptionist's desk and found my partners there.

"Ready?" I kept walking and headed out to the ambulance.

The cab of the ambulance was eerily quiet but filled with energy as we drove back to the station.

"Okay, which one of you is going to ask first?" I turned to my partners.

"What? Ask you what?" Seth, who was driving, looked around like he didn't know what I was talking about. "Diego? Do you know what he's talking about?"

"I have no idea, man." He nodded at me from the back seat with a crooked smile on his face.

"She asked to see me. A nurse came to get me, telling me the victim was asking to see me. What was I supposed to do, huh? Tell her no? So I went to see her. I don't understand what the big deal is."

Diego had assisted us with Bobby and Melissa, but he wasn't my usual partner. "Brother, she was a good looking woman." He lifted his eyebrows and bit down on his curled index finger. *"Ella es una mujer hermosa."*

"What? What does that even mean?" I shook my head.

Diego always used his native language when he wanted to show his emotions. "She is beautiful." He accompanied the words with a hip thrust.

"Yeah, she is, but I don't know why that matters. You're a sick man, Diego. She wanted to say thank you for saving her. You guys are making more of it than you need to."

I turned to look out the window and thought about how I'd felt when I looked at Melissa just before I left the room. She had a contagious smile, the kind that lit up her face and forced you to smile back. She was a gorgeous woman, but I couldn't act on my feelings because she had a kid, which probably meant she was married.

We returned to the firehouse and parked the ambulance in the garage stall. I checked over the inventory of supplies and replaced the missing items we'd used during the transfer from the accident scene to the hospital. As I restocked the supplies, I wondered who would be picking Melissa and Bobby up from the hospital.

We went out on a couple other calls that night. I kept recalling my chance encounter with Melissa. I couldn't get her off my mind.

We managed to get a few hours of sleep before waking up for the day. We cleaned and organized the firehouse. I was cleaning out the last of the garbage from the ambulance cab when Diego came around the corner.

"*Senora bonita esta aqui.* That pretty lady is here."

"What are you talking about? Let it go, Diego." He was really pushing me this time, and I wasn't putting up with it. "Why don't you go mop the floor and leave me alone to finish?"

Before I could finish telling Diego what I really thought, Seth walked up to me, knocking on the side of the ambulance.

"Hey, Will, you have a visitor. It's that woman from the accident yesterday. She's with her son, and only her son, if you catch my drift."

"Will you two quit it! I think you need more to do." I got out of the ambulance to throw out the trash, and I couldn't believe my eyes. Standing out in the cold in front of the firehouse with the sunshine surrounding them were Melissa and Bobby. I tossed the small trash bag into the larger trash bucket and headed out to see them.

Melissa was bundled up in a hat and a winter parka that stopped at her knees, and Bobby was next to her holding her hand, wearing his jacket, hat, and gloves. Melissa's hat held her hair off her face, and her pure beauty radiated through me. Whatever words Diego muttered about her beauty were more than accurate. She was gorgeous.

"Hi, guys." I closed the distance between us.

Bobby saw me, dropped his mother's hand, and ran toward me screaming, "Will! Will!"

I had no choice but to pick him up or he would have run right into my legs.

"Hey there, big guy. Looks like you're feeling better!"

"I am."

I held Bobby in my arms and looked over to Melissa, who was approaching and smiling.

"I'm sorry to just show up like this, but he has been talking nonstop about you since you left the hospital yesterday. So I borrowed my friend's car to bring him here." I could tell she was embarrassed. "I'm glad you're still working."

"Yeah, no worries, I was just cleaning up. Do you want to come inside? It'll be warmer. I can show this little guy around the station." I tickled Bobby's belly through his jacket.

"Yes, yes. Go inside!" Bobby jumped up and down in my arms.

"Well, I can't very well say no now, can I?" Melissa touched Bobby's cheek.

We walked inside the fire station. Bobby stared and pointed at the fire engines, enthusiasm radiating through him,

"*Vroom-vroom. Wee-ow, wee-ow*—look out!" He jumped out of my arms and ran to the closest engine. His eyes held the same joy as most children's did when they stood next to a shiny red fire engine.

"Would you like to sit in the cab?"

Bobby turned to me with a big smile and began to jump up and down. "Yes, yes!"

With Bobby sitting behind the fire engine's steering wheel, I was able to talk to Melissa. I leaned against the ladder truck so I could keep an eye on Bobby.

"How are you feeling?" My hands were relaxed in my front pockets, my feet crossed at my ankles.

"I'm sore all over, but I'm so glad it wasn't any worse. If we had been in the intersection just seconds earlier, it would have been a different story." She looked at Bobby. "He hasn't spoken about the accident or his bruises." She paused. "All he has been talking about is the firefighter who saved him and his mommy. He's been telling anyone who will listen."

She kept her eye on him while she spoke, a faint smile on her face. I studied her face while she watched Bobby as he pretended to drive the fire engine. I hadn't noticed just how soft her features were or how luminous her blue eyes were. Her hair was off her face, tied back in a ponytail, revealing her true beauty. Her natural elegance was mesmerizing. I'd failed to notice that yesterday.

She turned to catch my eye as I looked her over and soaked up her allure.

"Will?"

Shit. What did she ask me? "I'm sorry, what did you ask?"

"How long have you been a firefighter?"

"A little more than seven years. My dad's a firefighter back in California."

"So you've seen your fair share of accidents. Well, I'm glad you paid attention to your training during Car Accidents 101." She laughed.

"Oh, so you're a joker, huh? Well, maybe if you weren't tailgating you wouldn't have ended up smashing into the car in front of you."

"Well, if that was the case, I never would have met you, would I?"

I saw her cheeks fill with a hint of pink—were we flirting? I couldn't help myself. With her, conversation came so easily. I had never experienced that with a woman before. But I didn't know if she was married or in a relationship. I needed to bail before I took it too far.

"Hey, Bobby, let's go check out the fire pole." I helped him down from the big fire engine and walked him over to the fire pole in the back corner. Melissa followed behind.

Bobby wrapped his legs around the pole, held on with two hands, and tried to climb up. He would move up a few inches before sliding back down. It kept him occupied while I asked Melissa about her life.

"So, has Bobby's dad ever brought him to a fire station? It seems like it's every little boy's dream to grow up to be a firefighter."

She played with her red mittens before answering,

"Bobby's dad isn't in Bobby's life anymore." She turned and looked up at me. "He left when Bobby was just under two years old. I haven't heard from him since." She raised her eyebrows and pursed her lips in a grimace after sharing a private part of her life.

"Oh, Melissa, I'm sorry. So you have been raising him alone for more than a year? Do you have family around here?"

"I don't. My mother's in Florida, and my dad died about five years ago. I'm an only child, so it's just me and Bobby."

"Man, that has to be hard on you." I felt awkward about prying into her life, but at least I had the information I was looking for.

"It hasn't been easy, but I have friends who help, and the company I work for is great."

Bobby slid down the pole to the floor. "Mommy, I need to go potty."

"Okay, honey. Is there a bathroom he could use?"

"Of course there is. Follow me." I led them through the station to the rec room. I pointed to a set of doors and said, "Through those doors, on the left."

Melissa and Bobby came out of the bathroom and walked over to me. Even with a bandage on her forehead, she was gorgeous. I felt attracted to her, and I wondered what she thought of me.

"Well, thanks for the tour of the fire station, Will. I'm pretty sure Bobby will never forget this day."

"Neither will I," I said, bending down to look into Bobby's blue eyes.

I walked them back through the station and said good-bye in the parking lot. I watched as Melissa buckled Bobby into his car seat, and then they drove away. I waved and smiled, feeling a little bit of love growing inside me.

~

I pulled my truck into my garage and thought about how Tim and I had become coffee-shop friends. I could count on seeing him in the shop, getting a coffee or meeting clients. When he hadn't appeared for a month, I knew something was wrong. But I never thought it could be as bad as it was. Cancer—a dirty, six-letter word. It's unforgiving, life changing, and it had my friend in its grasp. I would do whatever I could to make sure his last months and days in this world were the best they could be. It was time to break him free from the chains he wore to keep himself safe.

Tim

AFTER I FINISHED A LIGHT BREAKFAST, I SAT ALONE AT MY KITCHEN table, passing the small piece of paper with Will's number written on it back and forth between my fingers. I had discovered it earlier on top of my bureau when I was getting dressed. A week had passed since he'd given it to me. As I recalled his offer to help, I contemplated calling him. Maggie was working a twelve-hour shift, so she wouldn't be home until after seven. I had a full day to myself and nothing planned. Clipper was keeping me company, but I felt like getting out of the house. My parents and Maggie's parents were busy with appointments and unavailable to take me anywhere.

I dialed the number on my cell phone and waited for him to answer. As the phone rang, my anticipation diminished; on the fifth ring, it went to his voicemail.

"It's Will, you know the drill." Typical Will. His voice sounded so relaxed and cool. My voicemail greeting sounded like a roll call of options and extra numbers to call in case I couldn't resolve the caller's problems.

"Hey, Will. It's Tim. I was wondering if you were around today and felt like hanging out. Call me back when you get this. Thanks."

Asking for help from people didn't come naturally to me, but after being diagnosed with cancer I'd had to learn to rely on people more than I ever had. And, like many other things I had to learn, I'd learned I wasn't alone in this battle. People wanted to help me, and I needed to allow them the opportunity to do so.

I cleaned my dishes and went to the couch to wait for Will to call back. Through my battle I'd started to depend on other cancer survivors and victims for inspiration and strength. I watched Jim Valvano's acceptance speech for his ESPY award many times to help keep me focused on what was important. My cell phone rang as I was listening to Jim talk about cancer's inability to take away his mind, heart, and soul. I looked at the caller ID and recognized Will's cell.

"Hello?"

"Hey, man, how are you?"

"Hi, Will. I'm all right. How are you?"

"You want me to pick you up? I'm heading out to the beach, and I would love some company."

"Really? I would love to go to the beach. It's been too long since I've been there. But I don't want to impose..."

"No way, not at all. I'll swing by and get you in about an hour. Is that good for you?"

"Yeah, that's perfect. Thanks, Will." I gave him my address and began to give him directions before he reminded me that he knew where almost every road in town was.

About forty minutes later I heard a knock at the door and hollered from the couch for Will to come in. I knew Maggie had left the door unlocked before she left for work.

"I'm in here, Will."

He followed my voice and found me trying to get up from the couch, which wasn't easy because it was low to the ground and it was difficult for me to get up from it because my muscles were weak. He stopped in the doorway to give Clipper some love.

"Hey, let me help you." Will came over and helped me to my feet. "You have a beautiful house," he said, looking around.

"Oh, thanks. Maggie did all the decorating. I can only take credit for finding it." We walked through the kitchen.

"Let's get you into the truck."

~

We drove on the highway to the beach. It was a perfect time to get to know Will better. I asked why he hadn't had a girlfriend since Melissa had moved away more than a year ago.

He explained his feelings to me. "I'm not ready to feel that pain again. I know it sounds like I'm a defeatist, but honestly, I love my job and I feel satisfied with my life. I can't imagine finding the time to search for a girlfriend. When the right woman comes into my life I believe I will love again, but I'm not going looking for it."

"I understand what you mean. When I met Maggie, I hadn't been looking for love. She just came into my life, and I knew she was the one."

"In my life, I've thought two different girls were *the one*, but then those relationships fell apart and I was left with a broken heart." Will looked out his window. "Enough about that. We're out to have some fun." He switched the radio on. The Beatles were playing. "You like the Beatles, Tim?"

Before I could answer he turned it up. I thought to myself, *Yeah I liked the Beatles*. My dad always played them when I was younger. "Help" echoed through the cab of the truck, and I laughed at the irony.

When the song ended Will turned the radio off. We talked about his growing up in California.

64

"I was three when my dad put me on a board for the first time. He loves to tell everyone that when I rode a wave to the beach I screamed, 'Again, again!' and at that moment, the surfer in me was born. I haven't stopped since."

"That's cool. Most kids learn to ride a bike, but you learned how to ride a wave." I laughed and stared out the window at the cars driving along with us.

"Would you want to learn to surf?" Will asked me, a little too eagerly for my liking.

"I think it's too late now. I don't have much strength left." Part of me was okay knowing that, but the other part of me — the part that was dying — hated to know I couldn't do or try new things. Knowing I would never experience new things was as if I were already dead.

"So you don't have strength. The best part is the water will hold you up. You don't need strength, you need a board. I'll show you." He looked at me, clearly thrilled with himself. "You're going surfing today, bro!" He turned up the radio, and Jack Johnson's voice filled the cab.

We pulled into the parking lot at the beach. The waves were crashing onto the shore.

"Are you ready to do this?" The glint in Will's eye scared me; he didn't really think I could surf those waves, did he?

"I'm not sure about this, Will?" I answered, more than a bit apprehensive about his plan.

"Come on, you're in good hands. I'm a firefighter. I won't let anything happen to you." He jumped out and tossed a wet suit for me to put on. We got suited up to protect us from the temperature of the cold ocean water.

He carried everything down to the shore and came back to assist me.

I protested, "I thought I would sit in a chair on the beach, enjoy the view and sound of the ocean, and watch you. You really don't have to teach me to surf." I was beginning to think this guy was nuts; what type of person had I invited into my life?

"Tim, you'll be fine. Come on, live a little! What's the worst thing that could happen? I'll be right there, and I know CPR. You're good." He slapped my back.

We approached the edge of the water, and I felt the cool water flow over my feet and pull them deeper into the sand. The sun cast its rays down on me, warming me, as seagulls called out and swam above the ocean. The waves crashed more slowly where we were standing, but further down the beach surfers were catching some big waves, hollering above the surf in delight.

Will collected his board, put it in the water, and instructed me to walk in front of him and hold onto the board; he was behind me in case I fell. When we got out deep enough, a little above my knees, he assisted me onto the middle of the board. Will swam out to deeper water, pushing the board and me ahead of him. I was confused about how this surfing experiment was going to work.

"Um, Will, do you know what you are doing?" I was growing more nervous as we went out deeper and deeper.

"Dude, don't worry. You're gonna surf today." Will turned his head and spit out the seawater from his mouth. He circled in place, turning the board around.

The water was over Will's head, which meant it was definitely over my head. The thought scared the crap out of me. There was no way I could tread water. If I fell off the board, I was a goner.

"Okay, my friend, are you ready for this? Here's an opportunity for you take control of your life. We know death is knocking at your door, but for fifteen seconds you are going to experience freedom like you never have before." Waves crashed around Will as he spoke, and he

66

spit water out, managing to hold the board and continue to talk. "When I say 'go', I'm gonna release the board, and you are going to ride the wave to the shore. You got it?"

"Will, I don't know if I can do this. What if I fall off?" I asked. I lay on my stomach on top of the board and held tightly to the sides with both of my hands.

"No chance in hell. Just hold on. You won't fall."

I watched a wave grow behind us. As it approached, Will gave the board a push and let go. I lay on top of the board, holding on for dear life, and rode the wave to shore. The wind blew through my hair and whisked passed my ears as water sprayed in my face.

I balanced myself and held onto the freedom Will had given me to ride a wave. He was right, I was dying, but that day, at that moment, I felt alive. I was living. I wanted to let go and pump my fists in the air and scream and yell. I felt the rush, filling me with more adrenaline than I had ever experienced. I wanted the world to know I was alive!

The wave rolled past me, and I approached the shore at a slower speed. When I judged that I could stand on the floor of sand below me, I slid off the board and tried to stand up, but I fell into the water instead. Will swam in to help as I sat in the water, little waves moving around me. For once I didn't care how much sand was getting in my suit, in my hair, or anywhere else. I was laughing and enjoying the moment; it was a new experience. I never would have done this a year ago, with or without Will.

"Bro, how was that? Crazy epic, right?" Will helped me to my feet.

"I want to do it again!"

Will brought me back out, and I surfed to shore a few more times before admitting I had no strength left to hold on.

Afterwards, I sat on the beach in the sand. Will offered me a chair, but not today — today I was going to put my feet in the sand and feel its softness between my toes. I was going to hold it in my hands and watch it pour out, like sand through an hour glass. I was *alive*, and I wanted to *feel* life today.

I watched as Will surfed the bigger waves with the other guys. His rhythmic moves as his board glided over the water were mesmerizing. I admired the patience the surfers exemplified as they sat waiting for the right wave to arrive. I thought back over my life and wondered why I had been so focused on working and achieving, leaving little time to enjoy the many pleasures life had to offer. I didn't honor the time I'd had on earth. I took it for granted, always thinking there would be enough time to get to do things or have experiences. But now, as I sat and watched Will and the other surfers, I realized I had let life slip through my hands, just as the sand slipped through my fists.

At that moment I made a promise to myself that for however long I had left to live and for however long my energy would allow, I was going to experience everything I could. I was going to live until the day I died.

After leaving the beach midafternoon, Will and I stopped for a late lunch on the way home. We talked while we waited for our sandwiches.

"Thanks for today, Will. I really appreciate you taking the time to bring me to the beach."

"Don't thank me. It's what friends do."

"I can't wait to tell Maggie about this! She's never going to believe me. Too bad she's coming home late, or I'd ask you to wait for her so you can back me up."

"When she sees the expression on your face and the look in your eye, she'll have a hard time not believing you. Dude, you rocked it out there. I'm so proud of you. I know you aren't a beach person, but I could tell it got under your skin and into your heart. You became one with the beach today, bro."

"Thanks, Will—thanks for everything. You have no idea what today meant to me. You gave me back my life. I know I don't have long to live, but after today, I've decided I'm leaving this world braver than I lived in it, thanks to you. Cheers!"

"Cheers."

~

Weeks after my surfing experience, I called Will again.

"Hey, Will. It's Tim."

"Tim, how are you? I haven't heard from you. I thought maybe Maggie banned you from hanging out with me."

"No. I've just been feeling weak. But I've been resting up for my next adventure. You ever skydive before?"

He laughed out loud. "Oh, boy, what have I started?"

"I found a place about forty minutes from here. It looks really cool. You jump with an instructor, not solo. You up for it?"

"What does Maggie think? I don't want to cause trouble."

I heard hesitation in his voice.

"She's on board. She understands that I want to try new things and live while I can. What's the worst that can happen? I'm already dying. I think it'll be safe. I just have to be ready to jump. The instructor will get me to the ground safely."

"All right then, when are we going?" His voice brimmed with enthusiasm.

"I made appointments for next Monday; are you off?" I suddenly realized I hadn't even thought that Will might be working that day.

"Don't worry about it. I'll pick you up Monday morning; make sure you eat light." Will laughed.

When Monday morning arrived I was ready to conquer yet another fear and take a risk. Cancer was wreaking havoc on my insides, but I was in charge of how I lived on the outside. I had an opportunity for a new lease on life, and I was ready to live it.

When we pulled into the parking space at the skydiving facility, my composure shifted. I wasn't sure if I had the guts to go through with the jump after all.

"All right. Here we go." Will got out of the truck and came around to my side to offer help. "Ready? Are we gonna do this?" He'd clearly picked up on my apprehension. He shook his finger at me. "No backing out, dude. Let's go fly!"

I got out of the truck and walked up to the building. What was I thinking? All the confidence I'd had sitting in the comfort of my house was gone. My palms started to sweat.

"Tim, remember, you're living life, not hiding from it anymore." He opened the door. "We're doing this… together."

I couldn't let him or myself down. I took a deep breath. I had a chance to push myself out of my comfort zone and live. I wanted this. I was scared, but I wasn't going to back down.

We met our instructors and watched a video that fully explained what would happen after we left the room and what could happen to us like dying, if we went through with the jump. I wasn't as nervous as some of the people in the room when the instructor mentioned it. They gave us many chances to back out if we were uncomfortable, but I was going to die either way so I agreed to load into the plane. Soon we were in the air and it didn't take long to reach the jump site. I was strapped to a male instructor who was bigger than me, which helped to settle my nerves a bit. I looked over at Will, who was smiling like a little kid. He gave me a thumbs-up and nodded. Then he pumped his arms in the air; he was ready. His energy was contagious; I gave him a thumbs-up and nodded with a grin. I told myself, *I can do this*.

We stood in the open door of the plane. I received my countdown, and before I could think about what was going to happen I was flying through the air. The cool wind flooded my ears as I looked around at the scenery below and around us. I couldn't get over that the trees looked like tiny plants, and the buildings reminded me of the little houses I used to set up around my train tracks when I was a little kid.

I stretched out my arms and felt as light as a feather floating in the wind. I understood why Clipper loved to hang his face out the car window; the wind on my face was cool and refreshing. I flew like a bird, freer than I had ever been. I wished I could capture the feeling and bottle it to share with Maggie. Never in her wildest dreams could she imagine this feeling.

The sensation of free-falling ended when my instructor pulled the cord and the parachute opened. We jerked slightly and then coasted through the air. The noise and sensation of the rushing air grew softer. We seemed to hang in the air and float above the ground where people went about their ordinary days. I looked at the horizon and saw mountains and high-rise buildings. I watched traffic congest highways as cars traveled to their destinations and I enjoyed being free, suspended above all the distractions that kept me from experiencing life. The day to day responsibilities of being an adult could not rob my clarity to enjoy the moment. Emotions expanded inside of me, making me feel alive. I wasn't moving from task to task. Instead, I was appreciating the beauty around me that I had always taken for granted.

As we approached the ground and prepared for landing, a wash of feelings swarmed my brain. On one hand, I was ecstatic to have had the opportunity to feel the sensations of flying through the air, but a small sense of disappointment loomed at the finite nature of the experience; I knew it was a one-time deal.

I landed before Will did, and as I was unclipped from my instructor, I could hear Will yelling as he approached the ground. I turned to watch him come in and saw how elated he was, his smile was bigger than I had ever seen it before.

"Dude, you did it!" He unbuckled his harness and ran over to me.

"I know—that was amazing!" I sat on the ground. The jump had zapped all my energy.

I stared at Will. He bent over, his hands on his knees, trying to catch his breath, and then he spoke to his instructor. I was happy to have met him. No one else I knew would have gone skydiving with me. All my other friends lived their lives similar to how I lived: two feet on the straight and narrow path. Will embodied everything I wasn't. I was determined to break free from my shell and live like Will until my dying day.

~

During our ride home later, Maggie's name came up. Will asked me what she did for work.

"She's an ER nurse at the hospital in town." I watched the trees along the highway pass out of view.

"Wow, she must see some strange things."

"Well, probably not any stranger than you see."

"I have been to some pretty strange calls, but I imagine the real freaks are too embarrassed to call the fire department. They drive themselves to the ER. People do some bizarre things in their down time."

"Yeah, she's shared some of those stories, but mostly she deals with trauma victims: car accidents, personal injuries, sickness, and heart attack scares."

I again considered my next question, as I had done for weeks, over and over, ever since I introduced Will to Maggie at the coffee shop and noticed the way they had looked at each other. I could tell she thought he was good-looking, as had so many other women in the coffee shop. There was a clear attraction between them. At any other point in life I would have left it at that—a beautiful woman meets a good-looking guy, but one is married so nothing comes of it. But I was dying, leaving behind a beautiful, loving woman who was full of life and unaccomplished dreams. She wanted to have children to share her life and love with. After our honeymoon in Hawaii she had dreamed about traveling to other parts of the U.S. and exploring her family roots in Ireland—things I wouldn't be able to give her. It tore me up inside.

After Will and Maggie's introduction, during the dark moments of sleepless nights, I started to think that Will would make a perfect partner for Maggie. He had a lot to offer a woman, but he hadn't yet found the right one to share his life with. I thought he could bring a new dynamic to Maggie's life that I never could have, just as he had brought me out of my shell and taught me to take chances.

I had reasons to believe that Maggie would protest any idea of a relationship with Will, largely because of his career choice. She had been clear about never dating a firefighter because of the danger in the job. The fears she had about losing a partner as she had lost her dad were too real, so I knew I had to approach this idea from the back door. I had to plant the idea in Will's head and encourage him to act on it; and I prayed he would. I could be at peace over leaving Maggie behind if I knew she would be protected and cared for by a true gentleman. I hated the thought of her being vulnerable to a scumbag who would hurt her.

"Will, do you date?" The words hung awkwardly in the air. I couldn't believe I was asking this.

"Well, what are you getting at, Tim? That's an awful personal question." He grinned. I knew he was joking with me.

"I have been thinking about something for a few weeks. I need to ask you." My palms became moist, and my thoughts spun around my head. "What do you think of Maggie?"

"Um, well." He scratched his head and rubbed the back of his neck. "I don't really know her well, just the stuff you've told me about her. I met her at the coffee shop that time; she's really attractive."

I could sense Will's composure shift. I seemed to have touched on something that made him uncomfortable.

"The doctors haven't given me long to live. I told you that, right?" He nodded but kept his eyes on the road. "I won't be able to experience life with Maggie past this point. Our last moments together will involve doctor appointments and medicine that sucks the life out of me. There will come a point when I won't be able to get out of bed, and she will have to hire nurses to take care of me while she's at work. It's going to be ugly. Yet through it all I know she will continue to love and support me. That's just the type of woman she is." A lump formed in my throat.

"Tim, let's not focus on that stuff. You're still living now. Keep that life going until there's no life to live. I don't want to hear you talking about the end when you still have today."

"No, don't get me wrong. I still have a lot I want to do while I'm strong enough to do it. You see, I'm a planner. I always have been. It's not dying that keeps me up at night, it's leaving Maggie a young widow that hurts me the most. Her welfare is at stake. I've done all the financial planning to provide for her future. Our house will be paid off, and she will only have responsibility for the monthly bills, which she can afford with her salary. She'll get my life insurance. What I worry about at night is her finding another husband." I turned to see the effects of my words on Will.

"Dude, are you asking me to marry your wife?" He was shocked.

"No. Not necessarily... Well," I paused, "not yet."

"What? What do you mean, *not yet?*" He shook his head and looked confused.

"Maggie is the world to me, and I feel that I've let her down by getting sick. I've ruined our chances of having the life we always dreamed of. I waited to secure our future financially, depriving her of having children. I can't give her anything she wants."

"And how does that affect me?" He looked baffled.

"After I die, I want you to take care of Maggie, give her the things in life I couldn't, and be the man for her that I never could. You can show her a different lifestyle than I did. You can teach her to break away from the walls she's built around herself and show her how to embrace the unpredictability of life, not hide from it."

"Man, that's a lot to ask of a friend." He rubbed his neck furiously. "Is this, ah, like your dying wish?"

I watched the cars beside us. "Yeah, I guess you could call it that."

"Wow! That's heavy. And you seem to think Maggie will go along with this? Does she know anything about this?"

"No. And if I know Maggie as well as I think I do, she will protest every bit of it. But you can't let that stop you. Do you remember what I told you about her father dying? Well, she swore she would never date a firefighter, but I know you, Will. I believe you could be the one to steal her heart. If I could pick another man for her, you're it. You have something special inside that someone like Maggie could embrace. And I believe she can offer you the chance to find love."

"Oh, no pressure." He smirked and rolled his eyes.

"No, there is no pressure because it's meant to be. I just wanted to let you know that when I'm gone, you have my blessing to fall in love with my wife."

"This is absurd. You aren't for real! Are you feeling okay? Maybe that jump affected your brain."

"I have all my senses about me. Yes, it's absurd, but it's my wish for you and Maggie to be together."

Will

WHILE TIM AND I WERE DRIVING DOWN THE ROAD AFTER OUR jump, I mentally replayed the thrill of jumping out of the plane and skydiving – floating weightlessly through the air and seeing life from above. Adrenaline still pumped through me. Life was good, and then came the sucker punch, when Tim started in with some ridiculous plan to have me fall in love with his wife and marry her after he died. And the best part was that she didn't even know about it. I didn't know her and she didn't know me, but in Tim's magical world we were to fall in love and live happily ever after. I left it opened-ended with him because it was his dying wish, and I couldn't bring myself to outright deny him.

A week later my phone rang as I was leaving Sacred Grounds. I recognized Tim's number. We had spoken a few times on the phone since the day we went skydiving, but we hadn't seen each other.

"Hello."

"Hi, Will. It's Tim. How have you been?"

"Just finished working. Now I'm looking forward to a few days off. How are you feeling?"

"I have my good days and bad days. Today's a good day."

"That's great." I sensed he wanted to talk about something. "What's up?"

"Well, I was telling Maggie that I missed being able to see you at the coffee shop, so she suggested that we have you over for dinner."

I rolled my eyes. "She suggested it? Or you are orchestrating a way for us to spend time together?"

"Let's just say I'm killing two birds with one stone. Come on, what do ya say?"

"How can I say no? Of course I'll come over. What night are you thinking?"

"Does tomorrow night work?"

"Yeah, I don't have any plans. What can I bring?"

"Just yourself. See you around six."

"Sounds good; see you then." I hung up and laughed to myself. *He's already setting his plan in motion.*

I walked along Main Street and found a sunny bench to sit on. The sun was climbing in the sky, and a slight breeze moved the warm air and took away the chill from the night before. People were mingling about enjoying the spring weather, so I sat to observe for a minute. Traffic flowed peacefully by, and no one appeared to be in a hurry. Children walked beside their mothers, and a few dogs enjoyed the scents on the sidewalk as they ambled down the road. It was a beautiful summer day.

My thoughts drifted away from the sights that played out before me to the conversation I'd had with Tim about Maggie. It had disturbed me for a couple of days. Once I returned to work I didn't have time to give it another thought. But while I sat on the bench in the summer sun I thought about Tim inviting me for dinner and questioned if I'd be able to provide Tim with his dying wish.

I was flattered that Tim thought that I would be good enough for his wife, but it wasn't quite how I had imagined falling in love again after Melissa moved away and broke my heart. I guess life doesn't always turn out the way we imagine it will. It's like surfing. You can catch a wave and ride it, and when it ends it will bring you to the shoreline, but maybe not where you expected to end up.

The following night, I pulled into their driveway and sat in the truck for a moment to gather myself; I had no idea what I was walking into. I stared at the house, a stunning oversized dark gray colonial with meticulous landscaping and a lot of land surrounding it. I chuckled to myself. *Someday it could be my home.*

Two steps separated me from the front door. I climbed them and rang the bell. I heard a dog bark, and next I heard footsteps and Maggie's voice telling the dog, "It's okay." The door flew open. A breeze that carried Maggie's perfume swarmed around me, and a warm wave moved through my body.

"Hi, Will, come on in. Clipper, get back." She held the screen door open, Clipper was behind her.

"Hi, Maggie. Let me hold the door so you can settle Clipper." I smiled at her.

"I'm afraid he's never learned how to properly greet visitors. I'm sorry." She tucked her long red hair behind her ear and looked up at me with a smile.

"No, don't be. He's just excited to see me. Aren't you, Clipper?" I petted him on his head. When he heard Tim call him, he turned. "Oh, I forgot, these are for you." I held out the bouquet of flowers I'd picked up at the florist.

"They're beautiful. How did you know tulips are my favorite?"

I watched as her face lit up and a smile over took her face. She had an exquisiteness I hadn't noticed in the coffee shop. Her red hair and green eyes played off her soft complexion. I had never met anyone as naturally beautiful as Maggie.

"I took a chance. I'm glad you like them. And this is for dessert." I handed her the bag.

"You didn't have to do that. I told Tim to tell you that you didn't need to bring anything."

"It's more a joke for Tim. He told me once how much he loved peanut M&M's. I bought him a couple of bags."

"Oh, he'll love that. Come in. He's on the porch, right through those doors. I'll be out after I put these gorgeous pink tulips in a vase of water."

I admired her body as she walked away—maybe I could make this work after all. Damn. I shouldn't be ogling my dying friend's wife. *What's the matter with me? Tim is crazy to think this arrangement could be acceptable.*

I found Tim sitting in a chair on the patio that overlooked his immaculate, well-manicured yard overflowing with colorful pink, yellow, and white blooming flowers tucked into their edged beds. The beds wound around the natural flow of the curves and turns in the yard. A pergola blocked the direct sun from the patio and the small outdoor kitchen and grilling station, where I imagined Tim cooking during barbeques. A pond in the back corner was accented by a bench and more flowers.

"Hey, Tim! What a yard! This place is beautiful."

"Hey, Will. Thanks. I take no credit for it, but I did write the checks."

We shook hands, and I took the seat next to him.

"I'm just curious. Did you mention anything to Maggie about what we spoke about last week?" I needed to know if she knew about his plan.

"No. I would never—she'd freak out. She knows nothing about the idea, and I want to keep it that way." He looked me square in the eye.

"Okay, I hear ya. I won't breathe a word." I put my hands up for mercy. It was his plan, his to orchestrate; I was merely a player. I figured soon enough Maggie would know, and then we could settle Tim's foolish death wish.

Maggie carried a tray of lemonade and three glasses and joined us on the patio. We sat for a while talking about Tim's prognosis. The cancer was not responding to any of the drugs and in fact was becoming more aggressive. Maggie shared that the doctors offered little hope that Tim would last until the end of the summer. As I listened to both of their comments, I noticed that Maggie still held onto hope that her husband would be cured. Even as a nurse, knowing the odds he faced, she refused to give up on her husband. She said she would do whatever it took to find a clinical study to get him into, and only when his body told them the end was near would she believe it. She sat next to Tim and rubbed his arm as she spoke matter-of-factly.

After we finished our lemonade, Maggie asked if I could grill the steaks while she finished prepping in the kitchen. I followed her to the kitchen. As Maggie found a blue tray to organize the plate of steaks on, I looked around. I noticed how my kitchen definitely lacked the female touch that Maggie had put into hers. Matching towels hung from the bar on the oven door; a candle burned on the counter, releasing the scent of hydrangeas; the walls were painted a soft yellow. I smiled when I noticed the pink tulips in a crystal vase on the kitchen table. There were no empty boxes on the counter, no dishes in the sink — the place was immaculate.

"Maybe I should have you over to decorate my kitchen. Your kitchen looks more like a home than mine," I commented.

"You don't have a girlfriend to help you do it?" She was in the refrigerator collecting the salad and salad dressing.

"No, no girlfriend anymore. It's been a while. My last girlfriend, Melissa helped me organized and decorate, but it's lost the woman's touch."

"Well, maybe someday I can help you get it back to normal." She placed the food on the counter. "Do you mind reaching up in the cabinet above the stove to get the grill tongs? I really need to find a new home for them since I can't reach them up there." She took down plates as she spoke. "I appreciate you helping me. Now that Tim's sick, I don't like to ask too much from him."

I opened the cabinet and reached in to the grab the tongs. Suddenly utensils rained down. I caught most of them in my arms. Maggie raced over to help.

"Oh my goodness, I'm so sorry. I thought I had put them back safely."

Her hands grazed my bare arm as she wrestled to collect the utensils. I was shocked when her touch sent ripples of energy through my body. She stood so close to me that I could enjoy her sweet perfume and the scent from her hair; it smelled like fresh strawberries. I snapped out of it when I realized I was soaking in the scents of another man's wife. *This is ridiculous!* I was not the type of man to fall for a friend's girlfriend, especially not his wife.

"No, I'm sorry. I should have looked more closely instead of pulling." I put back the utensils we didn't need. We finished gathering the food and supplies we needed and then headed back to Tim.

I tended to the grill while Maggie organized the table and set out some appetizers. We talked about my job and that her father was a firefighter too. Maggie shared her opinion about the selflessness that most firefighters possessed, and naturally I agreed with her, but I tried to be modest about it.

I could see Tim looking at me when I spoke to Maggie. He smiled with an almost devilish look in his eyes. I wondered what thoughts were going around his mind. He was undoubtedly thinking about his plan, maybe contemplating how he could make Maggie and I fall in love after he left this world for another one. Every time I saw the look in his eye, it gave me the creeps.

Eating dinner with Tim and Maggie, I saw her personality emerge. She had a warm smile and a sweet, sort of innocent way of sharing her opinions; she had a soft presence. I noticed there was nothing about her that was harsh or argumentative. When she laughed, often at the oddest things, it was infectious, and her face lit up. She was the type of person who made everyone around her laugh just by being there. I realized she was a lot of fun.

I could tell she was a bookworm because she knew random information. She loved the ocean and as a child would vacation with her aunts, uncles, and family on Cape Cod. Maggie told us that she recently read that a sea anemone might look like a flower, but it was actually a carnivorous animal that ate small fish and shrimp.

After thanking her for the lesson on sea anemones, we moved on to talk about when Tim and I went surfing. The fiery redhead emerged. She got the point across that she was not happy that I encouraged his surfing. I caught a glimpse of a sharp edge in her personality. When she became emotional, she was sweet mixed in with a little hot. I liked her style.

"Maggie, I'm sorry it upset you, but Tim had a blast. I was right by his side and was prepared had anything gone awry. I wish you could have seen him. He looked alive riding the waves to shore. It was awesome to see." I smiled at her, hoping to ease her concerns.

"We should do it again this weekend," Tim added with a huge smile, wagging his eyebrows up and down. "What do you say?"

I looked over at Maggie and raised my brows. "Are you in?"

"I can't believe I'm going to say this, but yes, I'm in. But only because I love you, Tim. I would do anything to make your life happier, even just for a day." She reached for his hand, and Tim leaned over to kiss her cheek.

"It's settled! I'll pick you guys up Saturday at nine. We'll spend the day surfing at the beach and hanging out. Oh, and I will get you on a board too, Maggie." I finished my drink and stood to clear off the table.

~

When Saturday morning arrived I was stoked to get to the beach. The forecast predicted a perfect beach day! A light breeze, full sun, and a temperature staying around eighty degrees.

I packed a cooler of drinks. We agreed that Maggie would pack the food because she knew what Tim could eat. I loaded an umbrella, chairs, and my two surfboards into the back of my truck and headed to Tim and Maggie's house.

After we loaded all their supplies, Tim got comfortable in the front seat. Maggie sat behind Tim in the back. "Who wants an iced coffee before we get on the highway? I'll stop at the coffee shop," I offered.

"That sounds good to me! Maggie, you want one, hon?" Tim asked, turning around to look at her.

"Yeah, that would be great."

I pulled into a spot and ran in to order our drinks. On the way out of the coffee shop I bumped into a girl I had gone on a few dates with. I remembered her as being very clingy, and I'd had to end the relationship early, before she got too serious. She grabbed my arm, hugged me, and kissed my cheek. I was balancing the iced coffees in my hands and I tried to back up, but she pulled me in tighter.

"Will! I haven't seen you in so long. You never returned my calls. What happened?" She finally released me and began twirling her long blonde hair around her finger.

"Oh, Stacey! Umm. It's good to see you. I'm sorry I never called, but look, I really need to go. My friends are waiting in the truck. Maybe I'll see you around." I backed away from her as I talked. Luckily, a little kid ran into her, distracting her from the moment. I yelled, "Bye," and climbed into my truck.

"Who was that? It looked like she was very happy to see you," Maggie asked before I'd even closed the door.

"Oh, her. She's a… an old friend. Here you go." I doled out the coffees.

"She seemed like more than a friend. It looked like you couldn't get away fast enough. Heartbreaker?" She teased me.

I turned around just as Maggie was taking a sip of her iced coffee through the straw. She looked up at me. The light coming in the side of the truck lit up her features. *Man, she was gorgeous.*

"No, not me. I just know what I'm looking for in a woman. If it's not there after a few dates, there's no use in leading anyone on. I guess I forgot to tell her that, but I think she gets it now."

The waves, larger than the last time we were here at the beach, were the perfect size for teaching Maggie to surf. However, I was not so sure about having Tim out there. We unloaded the truck and found a nice spot between the shoreline and the softer sand to set the umbrella in. As we set up our area, I pulled my shirt off over my head and caught Maggie's eyes with mine. When she saw me watching her check out my body, she quickly began to dig for something in her bag. Her cheeks flamed. I looked over at Tim to see if he caught the interaction between Maggie and me. I was relieved to see that he was turned away, looking down the shoreline as families secured their spots, setting up their gear.

"It's gonna get crowded today," Tim said.

"It's a perfect beach day. Tim, do want to show Maggie your moves before it gets too crowded in the water?"

"I think that's a good idea. I feel like I have the strength for it now." Tim rubbed his hands together.

"Let's hang ten." I grabbed my board, and Tim and I walked into the water to show Maggie how he surfed.

After a few rides Tim was ready to head back to the beach. It took a lot of his strength to hold onto the board, but he kept himself balanced on it and looked as thrilled as the first time he rode. Maggie met Tim as he walked back to our spot.

"Wow! Tim, that was impressive. I'm so proud of you." She had taken off her cover-up, and I got a full view of her body. Her green bikini exposed enough of her that I could tell she was a runner; she was toned and in great shape. She was a nurse and knew the importance of eating right and exercising, and her body was the proof that she kept herself healthy.

"Did you see me out there, Maggie? Oh, man, it's so freeing to be able to ride a wave; a feeling that I never knew before." Tim was radiant. Seeing him in that mood brought me joy too. None of us knew when his last day would come. If I could offer him an escape from reality, I was more than happy to do it.

"Okay, you're next. Let's go, lady!" I pointed to Maggie.

She looked surprised. "Oh, no, that's okay. You don't have to do that, Will."

"I know I don't *have* to do it, but I want to. I want to teach you to surf. Come on. Just a few waves so you can feel like a surfer."

"Go, Maggie. I'll be fine here," Tim encouraged. "When are you ever going to have the opportunity again? Go!"

She didn't budge. She looked at each of us, a frightened look on her face.

"It would make me so happy to see you out there trying something new, Maggie. Go have some fun."

I was tickled that Tim was insisting, proving he really did have a new appreciation for life.

"Okay, fine — if it'll shut you two up, let's go." She headed toward the water.

It was my mission to get her to surf on the short board I'd also brought, but the long board was easier to learn on. Maggie and I walked down a little farther from where I had taken Tim. I was hoping she'd catch a more powerful wave she could really ride, but not so powerful that it would knock her off. I liked the way the surf was breaking farther down the beach.

She kept peeking at me from the corner of her eye. I wondered what she must be thinking. I got the sense that she was nervous.

"Are you okay with this? I don't want you to do it if you're not. I just thought it would be fun for you to try it."

"No, I'm okay. Well, maybe… Yes, I'm nervous, but I'm really wondering why you came into Tim's life. Don't get me wrong. You're a nice guy and all, but I think it's a little weird that you and Tim met at the coffee shop and now have this friendship. It seems like you've known each other for years." When the wind blew her ponytail in her face, she twisted it and tucked it up into a knot. "And now you're teaching me to surf!"

"My coworkers are like family. I've met other friends since I moved here, but my job is really my social connection. I'm there a lot. Tim and I have a connection that I don't share with anyone else. It is weird; I do agree." I stopped, holding onto the board. "When I first met Tim I picked up some sort of a lost-kid vibe, like he'd spent most of his life doing the right thing and taking life pretty seriously. I don't think he'd allowed himself to have fun and take chances. I thought it would be fun to wake him up and show him how to free himself beyond his limitations. It's in my character to want to help people, I guess."

"Well, thank you, because you did it. You've taught Tim to loosen up a bit. I never thought in a million years I would see him at the beach surfing." She laughed, and her whole face lit up. Her smile was killer. "Or myself, for that matter."

"All right then, are you ready to surf?"

We swam out with Maggie on the board, and me on the side. Between getting hit in the face by waves, I coached her about how it was going to go down; I would be on the board with her a few times for the smaller waves, and then she could do it alone on the bigger waves. I could have let her try it alone, but I couldn't pass up the opportunity to hold her close to me. I'm a guy, after all, and she had an amazing body.

I pushed her out just behind the small breaking waves and climbed on the board to sit behind her. I told her to stand. Once the board was stable I stood behind her, inching my way forward. I held her body close to mine with one arm so she could feel the way I moved on the board for balance as the wave carried us toward the shore. I had to shake the sensual thoughts from my head. Holding her body so close against mine drove me wild. We rode to the shore, and I let go of her. She turned around and flashed the biggest smile.

"I gotta do that again!"

We surfed together a couple more times, and then it was her turn to do it solo. I swam out with her to make sure she got up okay. She stood, and as the wave took her away, I yelled, "Steady as you go." Her head whipped around and she lost her balance. The wave knocked her off the board.

I swam over and grabbed her arm, hoisting her up on the board.

"You fell off! What happened? You were doing so well."

"What did you say? What did you say as I was leaving you?" Seawater poured down her face. She looked like she'd seen a ghost.

"Uh, 'steady as you go'. I wanted you to think about balancing yourself on the board and not fall off, which is what happened." I laughed.

"My father always said that to me. Those are the words he would use to encourage me to try to something new, but to be safe. No one else has ever said that to me." She looked at me with confusion in her eyes. The waves rolled past us.

"I'm sorry to upset you. I had no idea. I just wanted you to be safe." As we moved closer to shore, the waves crashed around us. "Do you want to try again? You're missing some good ones."

"Yeah! And now that I'm expecting it, will you say those words again? I think they'll help." That smile that lit up her whole face returned; every time I saw it I felt weak.

"Yup. Up you go." She hoisted her upper body on the board and I grabbed her legs to help her straddle the board.

A wave was building behind us. "Ready? Steady as you go!"

She surfed away from me. She looked strong, and she had great form. I swam to the shore and caught up with her. After she rode onto the beach, she turned around and jumped into my arms.

"Thank you! That was awesome!"

I held her wet body close to mine, overpowered by the sensations. Thank God I had Tim's blessing, because it was a sin to think about what I wanted to do to that married woman.

We spent the whole day at the beach. By the day's end, Tim was exhausted. Maggie and I packed up the beach gear, allowing Tim to sit and relax. As much as I enjoyed being with Tim, I also enjoyed getting to know Maggie. She was entertaining. Her easy-going nature made it a pleasure to be around her; I could see why she and Tim would be attracted to each other, but I couldn't see how Tim thought I would be able to fill his shoes. First of all, she was madly in love with him. And, I was not Maggie's type. One thing was for sure — she was my type. If Tim's dying wish was for me to take care of his wife and charm her in hopes that she would fall love with me, well, I was up for the task, ready and willing to do what I had to.

Tim

THE SUMMER DAYS GREW SHORTER, AND MY HEALTH BEGAN TO decline faster than I was prepared for. I made the decision to stop chemotherapy because it only caused me to feel sick and did little to stop the attack of cancer in my body. I planned to live out my final months or weeks free from the drugs that poisoned me. I was rail thin with limited energy and began to sleep most of the day.

I was glad that I had taken advantage and tried new things, like surfing and skydiving, when I felt well enough. I looked back over my life, and I wouldn't have changed a thing. I loved my life and had accomplished more than most people, except for being a father. It pained me to leave this world without the chance to have a child to carry on my legacy or leave a remembrance of me for my parents and Maggie, but I couldn't help that now. I knew Maggie was young and healthy and would someday have children. I'd always thought it would be with me, but it wasn't in the cards, and I needed to learn to make peace with that.

I was pleased with my plan to have Will take care of Maggie after I died. He was a remarkable man with good morals, and I was confident that he would make a great match for Maggie. I had to keep my wishes from Maggie, as much as it hurt me to do so. She would never hear of me choosing another man for her, especially a firefighter, but I knew Will on a different level than that—he was looking for love, real love.

He was finished playing the game, ready now to settle down with the right woman. I could imagine Maggie and Will together in life. They would make a strong couple. I needed Will see that and hope that Maggie would see the depths of his appeal, beyond his career.

~

In late August, Maggie went to visit the horse farm, owned by a friend from her book club.

She walked into the family room while I was resting on the couch. "I won't be long. Lauren's mare had a foal last week and I would love to see it."

"Yeah, you should go. You'll enjoy it. I know you love to ride and haven't had a lot of time lately to go. I'll stay here. I'll be okay."

I assumed Maggie was looking for some time on the farm to contemplate what was happening in her life, just as she'd done after she lost her father. Just before Maggie's tenth birthday, her father had taken her and her sister Alison to a local horse farm for riding lessons. Maggie took to it quickly and enjoyed the horse's movements and the freedom of riding and the power of controlling such a large animal, Alison lacked any passion for riding, which was unusual for her because she was more fearless than Maggie. Maggie told me that after her father's death she would often beg to be dropped off at the horse farm to tend to the horses and muck their stalls. It was the only place she could go and escape the despair and emptiness she felt after her father's death.

"I called your mom to tell her I was going to be out for a while and asked her to stop by to check on you. She said she would come by later in the afternoon and bring dinner." Maggie sat on the edge of the couch holding my hand, which had lost most of its strength and muscle.

"Thank you for arranging that. You're so sweet." I rubbed her thigh with my other hand. "Now go and have fun. I'll see you later."

"I love you. See you later." She stared into my eyes.

"I love you more than you'll ever know, Mrs. Barrett." I felt a soft expression take over my face. Maggie placed a quiet kiss on my forehead and headed to the door.

Clipper's tail thumped against the couch. "Well, it's just you and me, buddy. Come up here." The love Clipper showered on me reassured me time after time that my family and I would be okay. Nothing settled my anxiety better than a wet kiss from my dog. We settled in for a nap.

My mother came through the door at four o'clock carrying bags of food.

"Hi, Mom, I'm in here." My voice was weak.

I had been lying down and sleeping most of the afternoon. When my mother walked in, I repositioned myself on the couch.

"How are you feeling? Do you need anything?" Once a mother, always a mother. My mother wore that title better than anyone else I knew. She was proud to be a mother and shared amazing amounts of love with me and my brother, Sean. Somehow she made both of us feel like her favorite; I could never figure out how she did it.

"I could use a drink, if you don't mind." Walking had become a chore for me as cancer depleted my energy. I tried to save my energy for important trips, like using the bathroom or moving from the couch to the chair or my bed. Other than that, I had to rely on my family to serve me; which grated on me in the beginning. I had now become used to it because it took too much energy to fight. I learned that it was easier to say yes when someone offered to help me.

My cell phone on the end table rang just as my mother walked into the room. "Do you mind handing that to me, Mom?" I looked at the number and recognized it was Will.

"Hi, man. What's up?" I tried to sound strong.

"Oh, hi, Tim. I'm glad I got you." Will sounded winded and distracted, not the cool Will I was used to talking with.

"Is everything okay, Will?" I was worried.

"Yes and no." He paused. "Tim, there's been an accident involving Maggie. I'm with her right now. We are taking her to the hospital to have her checked over. Can you meet us there?"

I thought I was going to pass out. *Maggie was in an accident? What?* My ears couldn't believe what they were hearing.

"I'm with my mother. Hold on." I turned to my mother. "Maggie's been in an accident and she's going to hospital. Can you drive me there?"

"I can't drive your standard car, and I don't have mine. Dad dropped me off and went to do errands. He's planning on coming back later."

I heard Will saying something on the phone. "What, Will?"

"Forget I called, I'll figure something out. I shouldn't have bothered you; I know you can't drive. I'll have her home to you as soon as I can. I don't think she broke anything, but we need to be sure."

"Will, what happened to her?" My heart pounded inside my chest.

"She was riding a horse and fell off when he spooked. She'll be okay, Tim. I won't leave her side," he reassured me.

"Okay, keep me posted."

Hours ticked by without news from the hospital. Unable to do anything to help Maggie, I felt useless. My mother and father had offered to drive me to the hospital when my father arrived, but I was worn out and knew that Will was with her. My parents tried to get me to eat, but the little appetite I had was washed away by my worry.

A little after seven we heard a car pull into the driveway. Laughter filled the otherwise silent neighborhood. I would know that laugh anywhere — Maggie was home. My mother went to the door to greet her.

"Come in. How are you, honey?"

I got up from the couch and slowly made my way into the kitchen. Maggie had a bandage on her forehead and walked with a limp. Will held Maggie by the arm and escorted her to a seat at the kitchen table. Clipper stood by waiting for attention from Will.

"Oh my God, Maggie, are you okay?" I wanted to run to her, but my legs wouldn't allow that.

"I'm fine. Please don't be worried."

I could tell that she was embarrassed.

"It looks a lot worse than it is, Tim. Lauren reported that Maggie had hit her head pretty hard on the ground, but there's no concussion. The impact caused some muscle aches and soreness. She should be fine in a few days." Will looked down at her. "She's a trooper, this one." He rubbed her shoulder. "She fought us about going to the hospital, but her friend Lauren convinced her it was the right thing to do."

"Maggie, are you sure you're okay?" I asked worried. I hoped she wasn't trying to protect me.

"Yep. I'm fine. Well, I'll be fine when the aches go away. I'm just thankful that Will was there. He really helped to calm me down, and it was comforting to have him in the ambulance. Luckily, there were enough men at the station, so he took the night off to bring me home." She looked up at him with gratitude. I observed an exchange of emotional looks between them and began to wonder if Will had told her about my idea. He couldn't have, he wouldn't have, not after I'd told him not to.

"Well, I'm just glad you are all right and I have you home now." I sat down next to her.

"All right, I did my job. I'm out of here." Will pet Clipper and turned to the door.

"Oh, Will, won't you stay for some dinner?" my mother asked.

He looked at me and then at Maggie, trying to decide the best answer. I imagined that as a bachelor he didn't have to go home for dinner.

"Will, you should stay. This way my parents can get to know you." I nodded and smirked.

"I guess I'll stay then. How can I help you, Mrs. Barrett?" Will asked as he and my mother headed toward the cooking area with Clipper in tow.

The evening was perfect. I had Maggie safely home, and my parents got to know Will a little, so when the time came for him to make a move on Maggie they wouldn't wonder who he was or if he had an agenda. My mother asked about his family back in California. She asked how many siblings he had; he told her just one, an older sister named Ellen. My mother asked about his mother and father and what they did for work. It was like my mother was digging for information, poking away at him, asking question after question. She seemed satisfied with his responses and began to enjoy his company more and more.

I looked at Maggie next to me. We sat across from Will, and her eyes were penetrating him. I could tell from the look on her face she was intrigued by what she was learning about this man. Her eyes were wide and she was smiling, not a full smile but a smile that declared, "I'm pleased." I reached for her hand and held it as tightly as I could.

The more Will opened up about his life and his family, the more he exposed his softer side. He was a firefighter, but tenderness ran through him, it was revealed when he spoke about his love for his sister and his parents. He was aware of the dangers in his job and his father's job. He'd known at a young age that he would become the man of the house if anything ever happened to his father. He was thankful nothing bad ever had.

He shared his love of animals, especially dogs. He didn't own one because he understood how much time was required to care for them, but he was proud to be the firefighter who brought the firehouse dog, Jake, to the station. He told us that he looked forward to the day when he could get a dog of his own. He smiled and rubbed the belly Clipper offered at his feet.

The evening flew by. I stayed up later than I had in months. After everyone had left, Maggie and I were in our bedroom getting ready for bed.

"I really had fun tonight. Will is an interesting guy, isn't he? I can see why you became friends with him. He is so easy to be around, like a lazy summer day. You don't want it to end." She grabbed her pajamas and walked into the bathroom.

I sat on the edge of our bed, thinking to myself, *This is going to work. I can die peacefully knowing Maggie will be taken care of.* It's all I really wanted out of life at that point. My death was inevitable, but dying with the understanding that someone respectable would watch over my wife allowed me the peace I needed to leave her behind. If I couldn't be the one to love and protect Maggie, I knew Will was the right guy to share his life with her. I just hoped she would come to believe it.

I curled up in bed, looking forward to sleep. I became too tired, too easily these days, becoming aware that my remaining days were dwindling. I slept more and ate less. I didn't want to upset Maggie or my mother by talking to them about my feelings; I knew I could count on Will for that. He had become the friend who handled my illness with ease. He never seemed affected or judged me when I spoke openly and honestly about my feelings or my worries and fears. He just allowed me to speak. When I was mad, he let me vent. It was therapeutic to be around him. Having him at my house this evening with my family reminded me that I needed to spend more time with him and release the bombardment of thoughts that ran wild in my head.

I needed to leave this world in peace and to be honest about my feelings. If I could work out my thoughts and be brutally honest with Will, then maybe he could help me find the courage to share my true feelings with Maggie, instead of protecting her from them. I knew she was going through many of her own overwhelming thoughts; I didn't feel right adding my own to hers. I listened to her, though she seldom complained, and I reassured her everything would be fine. But I never shared the dark, scary feelings about dying that racked me. She was the love of my life. I felt that I had to protect her from my thoughts and fears about leaving her behind.

I planned to call Will and ask him over for lunch. I needed someone to talk to about my final days, and we had to discuss the details of how I expected him to take care of and love Maggie. I was hoping that the time they had been spending together was helping them get to know each other better, so that Maggie would know she could turn to Will for support after I was gone. I also had to thank him for helping Maggie at the farm. If I had been well, it would have been me that she had called, but I was thankful that Will was the one to respond to her call.

Maggie

THE MORNING AFTER MY FALL, I WOKE UP STIFF AND ACHY. I stretched my arms over my head, trying to release my muscles, but it didn't help. I left Tim sleeping in bed and headed downstairs to take care of Clipper and have some coffee.

Clipper finished his breakfast and curled up on his bed, basking in the sunshine in the family room as I drank my coffee and thought about Tim's declining health. I had never imagined that falling in love with Tim would lead to the hopeless despair I'd felt when my father died. I thought I had made the right choices to protect myself from ever feeling that way again.

I knew I had to prepare myself for my new life, one without Tim. Tears built in my eyes. Clipper came and sat next to me with his head resting on my leg; I loved that he knew just what to do to help me feel better.

"It's okay, boy, we'll still have each other when Daddy's gone." I rubbed his head and tried to breathe through my emotions to stop the tears.

A breeze moved through the room from the open window, carrying the scent of clean, fresh early-morning air. As I inhaled it deep into my lungs, I forgot about my aches for a second. The air cleansed away all my negative thoughts and gave me hope that I would be okay.

I made Tim breakfast and carried it up to him, something I did more and more often, because it was easier than having him get out of bed. He was sleeping when I walked in, but I opened a shade to spread light into the room. He stirred a little, and I rubbed his back to wake him.

"Hi, honey, I brought you breakfast. Do you think you can wake up and eat?"

He moaned and rolled over to face me.

I pushed back the tears that threatened me when I saw him in vulnerable positions. I wasn't used to seeing Tim out of control, but time and time again I told myself this wasn't about me. I had to be strong for Tim. He didn't need to see my weaknesses.

"Come on, honey, wake up."

He opened his eyes and stretched an arm over his head. He was losing so much weight that his arms were as thin as mine. He was disappearing in front of me. I helped him eat and got him ready for the day. Then I set him up in the family room with a movie and told him I was running a couple errands and would return as quickly as I could. Clipper was by his side. I knew I had a couple hours before he would need me again.

As I drove to the store, I thought about how wonderful Will was yesterday when I fell off of the horse. I'd been riding for years and had never been thrown before. When the tractor backfired, my horse bucked and kicked out. I wasn't prepared and fell off. Lauren told me I was out for almost a minute and she was worried I'd hit my head too hard. She overreacted and called 911, even though I told her I was fine and that she was being paranoid. When Will got out of the ambulance and walked up to me, I was sitting on the rock wall feeling sore, but more so embarrassed.

"Hi." My cheeks burned.

"Hey there, Maggie. What's going on? Are you trying out for the rodeo?" He smiled at me. I couldn't help but notice how handsome he was as he laughed at his own joke.

"No. I fell off the horse and apparently hit my head. Lauren wants me to go to the hospital, but I think I'm fine." I felt humiliated.

"Let me check you out. I'll tell you what I think."

He touched my head, asked if it hurt anywhere, and looked into my eyes. He asked me to walk and stayed by my side to catch me if I fell. I felt secure with him next to me; he was tall and his body was muscular.

In the end he and Lauren convinced me to get checked out at the hospital, so I reluctantly went.

I'd decided to show my appreciation with a gift basket for him and the firefighters who'd helped me yesterday, I pulled into the parking lot at the fire station. I carried the basket and walked slowly to the main doors. A man sat at a desk behind the glass. I told him I was there to see Will.

I was escorted down the hall to the kitchen area and chuckled when I saw Will cooking at the stove. The man behind the glass told me Will was busy and couldn't meet me at the door, but I'd never expected to see him cooking.

"Will, you have a visitor," his coworker announced.

"Smells good in here," I called out.

He turned around, and a huge smile spread over his face.

"Maggie! What are you doing here?" He put the spatula down and came over to me.

"I wanted to say thank you to you and the other guys who helped me yesterday. Here's a basket of goodies." I handed off the heavy basket with relief.

"You didn't have to do that, but thank you! We'll enjoy this! How are you feeling? Here, sit down." He pulled out a chair for me.

"I'm still achy, but I'll be fine. Thanks again for helping me. I know I could have called, but I wanted to thank you in person." He sat next to me, and I turned my chair to face him.

I looked around the fire station kitchen. It looked like it could have been in someone's home. There was a television on in the corner and a long table with plenty of chairs. The cabinets were dark, the counters a light cream color, and sunlight lit the room from behind lace curtains. It was a very comfortable room.

"Hey, it's my job. I'm really glad you're okay." He touched my arm, and I felt a change in my composure.

"I also wanted to thank you for helping with Tim. Taking him on outings has given him a chance to embrace life. He's really enjoying it." I smiled at him.

"No problem, he's a great guy. I love exposing him to life on the edge. I'm surprised he's up for it." He got up to check on the food cooking on the stove and stirred the pot.

"Well, he knows now that he missed out on a lot. He forgot to live while he was planning for his future. So I guess he's making up for lost time." It was so easy to talk to Will. He didn't cut me off or interject his opinions; he just allowed me to say what I was thinking.

"It must be hard for him… you know, knowing that he is dying." He returned and sat next me.

"He is coping with it. He has no other choice. He tried to fight it with drugs, but it had already taken over. He's very pragmatic."

"How are you doing?" He looked me in the eye.

I was taken aback at the sharp turn in the conversation. Although I was comfortable talking about Tim, I didn't know if I could talk about me and my feelings.

"Um, well… To be honest, it's really hard on me, but I don't focus on that because I'm not the one losing my life. Tim has it a lot worse than I do."

"Does he really? Do you really believe that?"

I didn't know how to answer him. I knew I was suffering over losing my husband, but I couldn't allow myself to talk about it because I felt that Tim needed all the support right now.

"Maggie? Do you talk to anyone about how *you* feel?" He touched my hand, and again something shifted inside of me.

"I'm sorry, I was just thinking. Yeah, I talk to my friend Molly. We work together at the hospital. She is supporting me, and I talk to her a lot. For now I just want to keep Tim's spirits up and keep him comfortable. He's my focus. I'll deal with my emotions at another time."

"Well, please know that if you need someone to talk to or anything else, you can count on me, okay?" He looked me in the eye. When I stared into his dark brown eyes, I sensed support in them.

I smiled. "Thank you. You're a very kind person."

"I like you and Tim. You guys have become good friends. I can't imagine this is easy for either of you. So whatever I can do to help, please let me know."

"Well, thank you. We enjoy your company, too." When the tones sounded, followed by the dispatcher's voice, I jumped as if on cue. Will stood.

"Sorry, I gotta go. Don't forget what I told you—anything you need, anything at all, call me." He smiled, turned off the burners and as he ran off I thought about how handsome he was, inside and out.

I drove home daydreaming about Will's good looks, aware how helpful he was toward Tim. I realized I always felt better when he was around; his positive personality gave me hope that my life would be okay.

I walked into our house and found Tim asleep on the couch. It didn't look like he had moved. Clipper came to greet me, and I petted him. I sat on the edge of the couch hoping Tim would sense my presence and wake up.

I watched him sleep. Although he looked so thin and sick, he seemed peaceful. A tear rolled down my cheek. I would miss him when he was gone. I had already started preparing myself that he wasn't going to be with me forever, and I pledged myself to cherish all the moments we had left together.

When I leaned over and kissed his cheek, he opened his eyes.

"I'm sorry. Did I wake you?" I touched his cheek with the backside of my hand.

"That's okay. I have all day to sleep." He smiled. "Did you finish your errands?"

"All done. Actually, I went to see Will at the fire station. I brought him and the other guys who helped me yesterday a gift basket to thank them."

Tim's expression changed. He was wide awake.

"Really, you went to see Will?" He seemed really interested in the fact and looked happy about it.

"Yeah, I just wanted him to know I appreciated his help. He's such a nice guy." My phone rang, and as I got up to answer it I noticed a devilish smile on Tim's face and a glint in his eye. I wondered what that look was about.

Will

I HAD JUST RETURNED FROM A RUN AND I WAS STRETCHING my legs on my porch when I heard the phone. I got to it on the fourth ring.

"Hello."

"Hi, Will, it's Tim. I hope I didn't catch you in the middle of something?"

"No, not at all. I just got back from a run." I was still breathing heavily, out of breath.

"Oh, I miss those days." He was silent, probably recalling the feeling of the runner's high, missing the ability to move like that. "Well, I was wondering if you had time to come over for lunch today."

"Actually, today is a great day for that. I need to go to the market anyway, so I can grab us some food and head over."

"Thanks, Will. I need some company. Maggie is working, and she has dinner plans, so it'll be a long day for me. I appreciate it."

"No problem. I'll see you in a few hours." I took Tim's lunch request before hanging up.

I pulled into Tim's driveway just as the visiting nurse was leaving. *Good timing,* I thought to myself. Visitors would help break up Tim's long day and entertain him while Maggie was gone. A part of me was upset that Maggie wouldn't be home today; I really enjoyed her joyful company.

I knocked on the door as I entered and called out, "Hi, Tim, it's just me."

"Hi, Will, I'm in here." I found Tim sitting under a blanket on the couch in the family room.

"Are you cold? Do you want some tea?"

"No, I'll be all right. I just caught a chill during the check-up with the nurse."

"Well, this soup should help warm you up." I collected a tray from the floor next the couch and placed the soup and crackers on it. "I got you lemon-flavored water because they didn't have lime." I put the water and napkins down and settled into the chair to the left of the couch.

"What did you get?" Tim asked while he waited for his soup to cool.

"I got a turkey sandwich and a bag of chips. Nothing too interesting."

"Thanks for coming over on short notice. I wanted to thank you again for the other day. I was really worried about Maggie, but knowing that you were with her helped to calm me down."

"Oh, it was nothing, just part of the job."

"Will, have you given it anymore thought about what I asked you a couple months back?"

I practically choked on my sandwich. I didn't see that coming up so soon. He usually waited to the end of our talks to bring up deep stuff. How could I answer him? Should I tell him I was falling in love with his wife? That she was the last thing I thought about in bed at night and the first thought in the morning? Should I tell him that I wished I would bump into her at the coffee shop like I used to with him? I wanted to scream, *You have nothing to worry about. I am already in love with your wife!*

She was everything I had been waiting for in a woman, but she was taken, and her husband was dying—her husband, who just so happened to be a very good friend of mine.

"Um. Yeah, I guess I have." *Safe answer.*

"Well, what are you planning on doing?"

"Tim, come on. It's not like I can force her to love me. She is going to hurt and grieve for a long time after your death. I need to respect that."

"So, are you saying that you will take care of her and get her to marry you?"

He was so stoked I thought he was going to elevate off of the couch.

"Tim, I'm saying don't worry about Maggie. I will make sure she is taken care of. I will check on the house and check in with her. Between her parents, her sister, and me, you'll have nothing to worry about. Okay?"

"No, Will, you don't get it. I don't want another man making a move on her. I don't want a slime ball to take advantage of her kindness. She's going to be weak and vulnerable for some time. I don't want some idiot using that as a motive to get to her."

"But wait," I jumped in. "You approve of scheming behind her back and telling me to take advantage of her, to seduce her into loving me?" I was confused by what seemed like his irrational thoughts.

"The difference is that you aren't a slime ball or an opportunity seeker. You're my friend, and I can trust that you will take care of her and give her the things in life that I couldn't. You're a good man, Will. You deserve happiness." He stopped to take a breath.

"You have lived your life searching for a woman to share it with, and I can tell by the way you look at Maggie, she evokes emotions in you. You feel something for her. I could tell the first time you saw her at Sacred Grounds. Many times I saw women say hello to you, and you would politely say hello to them, but with Maggie it was different. She stopped you in your tracks. When you turned to say hello to her it was different from any other hello I ever heard you say to any woman. For a brief moment, she triggered something in you, and I saw it. It was that moment that I knew you were the man I would ask to love my wife after I was gone."

He was right. Maggie lit something deep inside me, a part that I had snubbed out after Melissa left. I had been working at the fire station and hiding away from any meaningful relationships since she moved. I couldn't allow myself to be vulnerable to the kind of pain I'd felt when she left me; there was no way I would willingly put myself in that position again. Every girl I'd met since Melissa became a fling, a one-night stand, an empty relationship from the start. But when I saw Maggie, she brought back feelings of desire again. She reminded me what it felt like to love. The sensation that I felt when I met her was powerful. She was like a drug. I knew immediately that just seeing her wouldn't be enough. But she was my good friend's wife, and I would not act on my feelings.

"You never mentioned that before. You could tell I was intrigued by her?" I shrugged my eyebrows. "I guess I need to work on my poker face."

"That's just it, Will. You were so captivated by her that you couldn't hide your emotions."

"Tim, I know how you feel about Maggie's well-being after you die. I promise you I will do whatever I can to help her and make sure she's doing okay, but I can't make her fall in love with me. No one can do that."

"That's all I can ask then. Thank you, Will." He held his gaze on me.

~

A few weeks later, I was answering a call for an accident that involved a little kid who had been riding his bike without his helmet fastened. When he fell off, he hit his head on a rock on the edge of someone's property. He had a deep gash on the side of his head that needed stitches.

As I worked to stop the bleeding on the little boy's head, I found myself hoping that Maggie would be working at the ER that day. After we pulled up to the hospital entrance, I unloaded the gurney from the back of the ambulance, pushed it to the open doors of the ER, and filled the nurses in on his vitals and condition. When I looked around and didn't see Maggie, my heart felt a bit heavy.

"Is Maggie Barrett working this shift?" I had to ask the young nurse next to me.

"Yes, she is preparing the room for the patient."

"Oh, okay." I smiled. My day was going to get a lot better. I went to the desk and checked in with Seth to see how much of the paperwork he had to finish.

"Take your time. There's someone here I want to see." I nudged him.

I paced near the desk as he finished writing his report, but I kept an eye on the room they'd taken the little boy into. When Maggie came out from the room down the hall, she looked my way. I gave her a small wave and smiled.

"So, you're flirting with the nurses now. Nice, Will. Real nice." Seth seemed generally disgusted. I didn't know why. Half the guys at the station flirted with the nurses; they were the only women we saw during our long shifts.

"What's the matter? She is my friend's wife." I walked over to her. She looked different, more relaxed, wearing her scrubs, but they didn't prevent me from noticing her curves.

"How's the little guy doing? He was really scared in the ambulance." I tried to peek in the room but couldn't see much except the side of the gurney.

"Why am I not surprised to know you are the firefighter he was talking about?" she said, looking at me out of the corner of her eye. She wrote something in his chart and then placed it into the holder by the door.

"What are you talking about?" We walked over to the nurses' station.

"When we got him in there, he asked for the firefighter who helped him. He wanted you to come into the room while he was getting stitched." She smiled at me.

"Oh, I was right out here. You could have come for me. He's a cute little dude. How's he doing?"

"He'll be sore but feeling better in a few days. His mom is with him." She rested her arm on the counter. "You like kids?"

"I like well-behaved kids," I said with a smile.

"Oh, I see. He must be a good kid then, because whatever you said to him won him over." She tucked her hair behind her ear and I caught a hint of lavender. She smelled refreshing compared to the antiseptic smell of the hospital.

"Do you like kids?" I asked her.

"Yeah," she smiled. "I wanted to work as a pediatric nurse when I first became a nurse, but it didn't work out that way. So I'm here in the emergency room." She looked around the area. "It's okay though, because whenever a child comes in and I'm on, the doctors ask me to assist. They know I can settle kids down and comfort them. So it works for me." She shrugged her shoulders.

The more I learned about her, the deeper in love with Maggie I fell; she was a remarkable woman.

"How's Tim feeling?" I had to change the subject because I was beginning to lose focus. All I wanted to do was stare at her and drink in her beauty.

"Oh, boy. I try not to think about that when I'm here." She rested both arms on the counter.

I was sorry I had asked; it was obvious that it upset her to talk about it.

"He's not good. He's becoming weaker. We had to put a hospital bed in the family room to make it easier to care for him. The hospice nurses are coming every day now. They spend hours with him, trying to help him get comfortable." She shook her head and rested it in her hands.

"I'm so sorry to hear that. I haven't spoken to him this week. The last time we talked it seemed like his health was stable. I didn't want to bother you guys, so I haven't called."

My coworker motioned for me to come. I held one finger up.

"Oh, I understand. It's hard to know what to do in these circumstances. I see you have to go. I won't keep you."

"No, it's okay, Maggie. I'm sorry to upset you here at work like this." I put my hand on her arm. Her skin felt soft and warm like soft flower petal. I wanted to rub it and feel more of it under my hands.

"I'm not sure how much longer I can work and care for him. I think I'm going to need to take a leave of absence."

"I can help you. I finish my shift tomorrow morning and then I am off for the next five days. Just let me know what you need and I'll do it." I lifted her chin up and looked into her eyes. "Okay?"

"You don't have to do that. I'll manage." She wore half a smile, and her green eyes were dim.

"Maggie, you don't have to go through this alone. I want to help both you and Tim. You guys are my friends, and that's what friends do."

She rolled her eyes. "All right. Will you go by the house tomorrow and sit with him? I know it would mean the world to him to have you there."

"I can do that. What about at night? How are you getting along then? That must be hard."

"Tim's mother comes by two nights a week, and I hired a nurse to cover another two so that I can sleep for work. The rest falls on me. We have really nice conversations, and it's extremely peaceful in the hush of the night." She smiled at the thought.

"Well, count me in for the other three nights. I can sleep on the couch near Tim and take care of anything he needs. You should get sleep, Maggie. It will help keep you focused and healthy."

"Tim was lucky to meet you. Did you know most of his friends stopped calling when he started getting physically weaker? But not you. You've stuck around and have been by his side through this whole ordeal. You're a special man, Will." She smiled at me. A sparkle glistened ever so softly in her eyes.

I felt my heart skip. "Tim's the special one. A person doesn't get the chance to meet too many in their lifetime." I smiled at her. "I'll see you after work tomorrow. And don't worry about planning dinner. I'll have it ready when you get home." I rubbed her arm and told her I had to go.

When I got into the ambulance for the drive back to the station, Seth asked, "Who were you talking to?"

"A friend. A special friend."

The ride was too short, and it intruded on my thoughts. I felt whole when I was with Maggie. I was thankful for Tim's blessing to fall in love with her because I would have hated living with guilt. I didn't know how I could make Maggie understand Tim's dying wish. I could only hope that he would tell her his plan before he passed away.

Tim

I KNEW IT WAS WEDNESDAY BECAUSE, EXCEPT FOR THE VISITING nurse, I usually spent the day alone. Maggie continued to work. No one knew when the end was coming, and she needed to reserve her time for when I truly needed her by my side. But on her days off she took care of me, going overboard to make sure I was comfortable and trying to feed me as much as possible. She said it would give me energy, but I doubted it.

The sunlight bleeding through the curtains stung my eyes when I opened them. Will was sitting on the couch next to my bed. I remembered then that Maggie had told me he was coming by to hang out and take care of me. No matter how sick I felt or how sick I looked, Will was the only one of my friends who took the time to check in on me, treating me like nothing had changed. Some of my coworkers had called to check in, but I would never forget my true friend, the one who stayed by my side through all my suffering.

"Hi, Will." I could hear that my voice was weak and groggy.

"Hey, Tim. Can I get you anything?" He got up and came to stand next to my hospital bed.

"Just some water, please."

After I took a sip, Will began talking. "Do you remember when we ran into each other at Sacred Grounds and talked about which hockey player was more talented, Bobby Orr or Wayne Gretzky? Well, I decided that the only way to settle the bet was to read about them, so I got these books from the library. I thought, since we have all day, I could read to you. Then you'll finally realize that Wayne Gretzky is the all-time best hockey player to have played in the NHL."

A cough broke up the laugh I attempted. "Please don't make me laugh. I think I'm at a disadvantage here. I have little strength to argue for Bobby Orr. He is and will always be the most talented NHL player."

"If you can't talk, relax. I'll start with Gretzky. You won't have to argue for Orr because by the end of this book, you'll agree that Gretzky is the best."

I lied in my bed and listened as Will read about Gretzky growing up as a child in Brantford, Canada. I drifted in and out of sleep while Will read. He could have been anywhere on his day off, but he chose to spend the day with me. I enjoyed his company, and I was humbled by his choice.

In the late afternoon, I awoke to the sounds of pots and pans hitting each other. I could smell the aroma of oil and garlic and hear them sizzling in a sauté pan. I thought, *after spending most of the afternoon reading to me and serving me lunch, now he's cooking dinner. This guy is amazing.*

When Maggie came through the door around six, I was resting in the other room. Will had dinner ready for us. He'd made plain pasta and chicken for me and a seasoned batch for himself and Maggie.

"Wow, Will! This is more than you needed to do, but thank you very much. All I wanted was for you to hang out with Tim and get him lunch. You've gone above and beyond." I could hear her gratitude for Will in her voice; it made me smile.

"No need to thank me. I have the time to help, so I will," I heard him reply.

When I felt her hand on my arm I opened my eyes. "Hi, honey." My voice was heavy.

"Hi, darling. How are you feeling?" She rubbed my forehead with her hand. Her cool touch relaxed me.

"Always better when you're here." I held her gaze. I was a blessed man to have such a stunning and strong woman for a wife.

"Can you believe what Will did? He made us dinner! Now I don't have to spend time cooking. I can take care of you instead and we can talk." She ran her hand over my head and stroked my cheek. "Will is a special friend to you. He's a remarkable guy." She kissed my cheek. "I'll be right back," she said before turning to go our bedroom to change out of her work clothes.

My wishes were falling into place. She was discovering the real Will—a loving, generous man who shared so much. My plan would be easier than I thought.

I no longer had the strength to sit at the kitchen table, so Will brought the kitchen to me. He and Maggie ate off TV trays, and I sat up in bed. Maggie fed me bites when I got too tired to feed myself. They told me the story about the little boy who fell off his bike and how they'd met in the ER.

I looked at each of them while they chatted. I could detect a bit of chemistry between them. I could tell from the way Will looked at Maggie that he had already fallen for her. A yearning was in his eyes, and his body language was different when he talked to her. I had been in enough bars to notice when a guy had the hots for a girl, and Will's feelings for Maggie were written all over his face and expressed in his body language. Most guys would kill their best friend for falling in love with their wife, but in my case it was just what I wanted—and needed.

After we ate, Maggie headed to the bathroom, and I said, "Thanks for dinner, Will. I know it really helped Maggie out and that she appreciated it." My voice was weaker. Every day it was getting harder to talk. The cancer was taking everything away from me.

"Yeah, no problem. I'll clean up while you two relax." Will took away the plates. When Maggie returned she climbed in the bed next to me. I held her close, closed my eyes, and inhaled her perfume. I relaxed and fell asleep.

I woke up with a chill to the sound of laughter; Maggie was gone from my side. I could hear her and Will in the kitchen. My body ached after lying down most of the day. I needed to get up and walk around. When I walked into the kitchen, they practically jumped out of their chairs to reach to me.

"I'm okay. I just wanted to walk around a bit." I held onto Will's shoulder.

"Please tell me the next time you want to get out of bed. You're in no shape to do it alone," Maggie scolded me, tucking her arm around my waist. They assisted me to the kitchen table.

"I just wanted different scenery, that's all." I sat in the end chair, appreciating our kitchen. It had badly needed to be remodeled when we bought the house. Maggie and I worked endless hours designing the layout and decorating it so it would be perfect for her: dark cherry cabinets, light granite countertops, and soft yellow walls. This room, her favorite room in the whole house, was full of great memories and love.

I, of course, loved my office the most. My desk faced the window overlooking the neighborhood. The tall trees would be covered with snow in the winter, and in the spring the branches would offer a safe place for mother birds to build nests for their eggs.

Maggie and I had made a wonderful home together. I wondered if Maggie would continue to live here after I died, or if she would move into Will's much smaller home. I hoped that she would stay here, and that she and Will would have a family to share it with, like we'd planned to do.

"Do you need anything, Tim?" Will refilled his glass of water.

"I'll have some water, please. Maggie told me you are sleeping over tonight. Don't you have anything better to do than hang out here?"

Will carried the glasses to the table and sat next to me, across from Maggie.

"When will you accept that I want to be here? Everything else can wait. Maggie needs help at night so she can sleep and function at work. Besides, I'm used to late nights and getting by on little sleep. It's part of my job." He tapped his glass to mine. "Cheers, buddy."

"Cheers." As I swallowed a sip, I thought, *I'm the luckiest guy to have a friend like Will.*

We sat at the table for an hour, sharing stories about Maggie and I finding our house and remodeling it. And then I needed to get back to bed. Will and Maggie assisted me into bed and then they set up Will's bed on the couch. Will went to the bathroom around the corner from the family room to clean up before bed, leaving Maggie and I alone.

"Thank you for arranging for Will to keep me company today. I really enjoyed having him here and not being alone."

"You're welcome. And don't worry. You won't be alone anymore. Will and I have worked out a schedule so that someone will be with you every day. I'm going to make sure you are as comfortable as possible." She tucked in the sheets and fluffed my pillows as she spoke.

I reached for her hand. "Maggie?"

She stopped moving and looked into my eyes. "Yes."

"Did I tell you today that I love you more than the number of stars you can count in the sky?"

She sat down next to me. "No, I don't think so. Go on." Her face lit up, and her smile was gentle. Her love radiated toward me.

I gathered as much strength as I could and poured my feelings out to her. "Having you in my life has brought joy and a contentment that I never knew I could feel. I love you with all that I am, and I will always love you. You are my life. After I'm gone, please love again. Don't be afraid to try again. I want you to have the life I couldn't give you. We were cut short too soon, but there will be another love for you. I don't want to leave you thinking you will be alone. Please be open and ready to find a new life, because *our* life is fading. I want you to live and experience all the things we talked about doing, like having children and growing old together. I love you, Maggie."

Tears ran down her cheeks. I knew she hated to talk about life after I died, but we couldn't avoid it much longer. I knew the end was coming sooner then we could have once imagined. She needed to know how I felt about her carrying on without me. I took a breath and continued.

"Just because I'm dying doesn't mean you are. I want you to go on living, enjoying yourself and your life. I don't want to be watching over you from Heaven, worried because you are alone and sad. Do you understand? I want you to find love again. I need to know that you will do that."

"Do we have to do this now? Tim, you're the man I love and I will always love. Please don't talk about other men, not now while I still have you." She wiped her tears with the back of her hand.

"I need you to know how I feel and what my wishes are; I don't want you to feel guilty about moving on in life and loving another man." I held her hand. "I will stop now, but please don't forget what I told you."

She kissed my lips and said good night.

Will

I CAME OUT OF THE BATHROOM AND STOPPED IN THE HALLWAY when I heard Tim talking to Maggie. I listened as Tim labored weakly to urge Maggie to love again after he died; he was clearing the path for her to love me, and I couldn't help but smile. His warm, nurturing, and encouraging words came from his heart, offering everything she needed to hear so that she could find it in herself to be open to love again.

She met me in the hall and broke down in my arms—I was the one to comfort her. I held her close and inhaled her scent as she wept in my arms and released the emotions that she had been hiding since Tim was diagnosed. Her fears about losing Tim were becoming a reality. It all hit home when Tim spoke about her moving on in his absence.

When she was finished pouring out her tears, she pulled back from my embrace and looked in my eyes,

"He told me to love again after he dies. How can I think about loving another man when the man I want is dying in front me?"

I wiped her tears away with my thumbs "Maggie, Tim cares very deeply about you. When we are together he shares his deepest thoughts and emotions with me, and the most important one to him is your happiness. He's not telling you to find someone tonight, but to continue living long after he's gone. He doesn't want his death to be yours."

"I understand that, but I don't know how I will feel when he's gone. What thirty-year-old can imagine herself living without her husband, loving another man? I need him. He brings stability to my life."

"All I can say is you don't need to figure this out tonight, tomorrow, or next week. And, all Tim is asking is for you to go on living after he is done dying." I smiled a reassuring half-smile, hoping she could understand Tim's request.

"Thanks, Will." She pulled me into another hug, and I got high from the lavender scent of her moisturizer.

"I think I'll head to bed and try to put this behind me." She pulled back but held my hands and squeezed them. "Thank you for everything you've done. You have been a great friend to Tim and now to me. I don't know how to repay you."

"You already have by allowing me to help you." I squeezed her hands and then let go. "Get a good night's sleep. I'll see you in the morning."

"If you need me or if Tim needs me, please come and get me, okay?" She stood at the bottom of the stairs.

"Okay, but I'd rather you slept through the night."

"Good night." She left me standing in the hallway. I took a big breath and realized I was a goner. I was in deep, in love with another man's wife. How had I allowed it to happen?

What if after all this, after allowing myself to feel such deep emotions toward Maggie, after opening myself up again, what if she never returned that love? What had I done? I'd let my guard down, and now it was too late to run. Tim needed me, counted on me, to be around for him. I'd basically given up my days and nights off to help Maggie because the fact was I was madly in love with her.

Tim's voice pulled me from my inner self-inflicted argument. "Will?"

I walked into the family room. "Is there something I can get you?"

"Yes. Some paper and a pen from my office."

I opened the door and switched on the light in Tim's office; I looked around at the room that reflected his inner character. Prestigious awards from financial companies he had worked for were framed on a wall. Another wall displayed framed pictures of family, friends, and Clipper, reflecting Tim's life. The last wall featured sports paraphernalia; I chuckled when I saw the autographed picture of Bobby Orr. I guess there was no way I would win that war. We would have to agree to disagree.

Tim's office space was organized and meticulous, very much like him. I looked out the window in the wall that faced the street. I couldn't see beyond the shadows from the moonlight; they fell like a blanket on the neighborhood while everyone slept. I wondered if Tim and Maggie felt it too—that the better aspects of our strengths were exposed, but our true, deep emotions hid from the light in the shadows, safer there than if spoken. I found a pen and pad of paper and headed out the door.

We were all connected by this disease, each one of us with something to lose. We were being stripped of the lives we knew and the futures we had envisioned. I believed I would come out the winner if Maggie allowed me to show her how complete I could make her life, but if she rejected me, then we all walked away losers. I was prepared to fight for her. If winning her took my whole life, then I would give my lifetime to the effort, until I could hold her in my arms as my wife.

I closed the door behind me and walked past Maggie's bedroom door, wondering if she was asleep or tossing and turning. Then I backed up and stood outside the door, listening to the silence in her room. That reassured me, and I continued on down the stairs.

By the time I returned, Tim had fallen asleep. I left the pen and paper by his side and climbed under the blankets on the couch.

Tim

THE NUMBERS ON THE DIGITAL CLOCK CAST A GREEN HUE IN the room illuminating the paper and pen next to me. My breath was shallower and more labored, and my muscles were weak from lack of use and because my body couldn't absorb adequate nutrition from the small amounts of food I could consume. The number of days left to me was shrinking. The life I loved living was coming to an end. Before I could die peacefully I needed to write a letter.

Clipper was sleeping by the side of my bed while I thought about what I wanted to write. I wrote during the night when I couldn't find sleep. My already weak hand shook with the ache I felt over expressing my feelings to Maggie. I needed to let her know how I felt, and I knew my words would impact her and her life as she read them. I poured my feelings into words that I had never imagined I would have to write to my wife, but there was no other way. When she read my dying wish in *my* handwriting, it would reassure her that I meant every word I'd written. She would realize that I had been serious during our talk earlier when I'd asked her to love again.

I felt blessed to know that if I had control of nothing else in my life, at least I could prearrange for her and Will to be together. I looked over at Will, peacefully asleep on the couch. A coincidental meeting between two people at a coffee shop had brought him into my life and created a connection neither he nor I could have seen coming. I envisioned the life and love that he and Maggie would share; I hoped the heartfelt letter would find its way into Maggie's heart and that she would follow it to Will's.

The next morning I asked Will to place the letter in an envelope and put it in a certain file in my office. I never shared with him what I'd written.

~

On Will's third and last night off, my health plummeted. I knew it would be the last night I was alive. He gave me medicine for the pain and he woke every hour to check on me, giving me gentle massages to help ease the lingering pain. He reassured me that he wouldn't leave me and kept telling me how I strong I was. But what I wanted was Maggie and my parents. At three-thirty in the morning, I requested he get Maggie from bed and place a call to my parents; I realized I was entering a stage closer to death.

As I lay in bed, I heard Maggie and Will's voices as they descended the stairs.

"I don't know, he asked me to get you."

"Well, is everything all right?" Maggie sounded worried.

"His breathing has become slow and labored, and he was talking about playing at his grandfather's house in the woods. I don't think it's a good sign. We should the call the nurse."

"The number is near the phone. Can you call? I want to sit with him."

They were getting closer.

"Yes, of course. Do you want me to call his parents too? He asked for them."

"Thank you, Will. I am so relieved you're here. I'd be a wreck right now if I was alone."

"You'd surprise yourself, but I'm glad to be here. Go sit with him. I'll be back in a few."

Maggie sat by my side, holding my delicate hand in hers. "Tim, are you okay? Can I get you something?"

I struggled to form words; I tightened my grip on her hand the best I could. She leaned in and kissed my forehead.

"It's okay, Tim, I'm here now. Will is calling your parents and the nurse. Don't talk if you don't want to. I'll just lie next to you."

Maggie curled up next to me, her head on my shoulder. I inhaled her lavender scent to try to settle my nerves. I would be leaving all this behind soon, I knew. I fought to take a breath. I had to calm down my nerves, vibrating inside of me. *It will be okay*, I told myself. *I have all the love inside of me that I can take with me. I shouldn't want more.* This was the way my life was meant to be, the end coming sooner than I had planned, but I had lived a great life. I had more than most people did; I had a loving family, and I *knew* love. I knew what it felt like to experience love deep in my soul. Those were the things I wanted to remember as my life faded away.

I heard Will's voice enter the room.

"They're on their way. Do you want to be alone with Tim, Maggie? I can make coffee or fix you something to eat."

"No, you should be here too. Come sit next to him." Maggie patted the open spot on the other side of me.

Time passed, all of us waiting together. No one spoke; the three of us filled the room with love and emotion until my parents arrived.

"Oh, Tim. We're here. It's Mom and Dad."

I felt Maggie get up and make space for my mother to sit next to me. When Will rose, my father took his spot. Maggie released my hand with a kiss, and I felt my mother's warm hand wrap around mine. She stroked the back of it as she spoke.

"You are the bravest person I know, Timothy Barrett. You have fought this nasty disease with more dignity and grace than anyone else I know."

Spoken like a true mother—her son was the best at everything right through his dying day.

"I love you—we love you. Your brother is on his way. If you can hold on, I know he'll want to say good-bye."

I tightened my grip; I would wait for him. My baby brother was the greatest brother in the world. Yeah, we fought and had a competitive relationship, but it was based on the huge love we had for each other.

The admiration Sean had for me growing up gave me the confidence that I could do anything. He always cheered me on and tried to get me to do things I wasn't comfortable with. He was the brave son and I was the cautious son. I had three years on him, so I was always his protector and playmate growing up. As we got older the competition between us was ridiculous, everything from grades to sports and then colleges and jobs. There was nothing we didn't compete over, but we knew, because of the way our parents raised us, that we were both good people and equally loved by them.

He married his college girlfriend last year. They settled thirty minutes north of Maggie and me. I knew I was fading, but not too fast; I would make sure he could make it to say good-bye.

Maggie excused herself to make a pot of coffee, and Will followed her out to the kitchen. In the quiet hush of the night, I heard a woman sobbing, in the distance. I understood it was my wife in the arms of another man, and he was comforting her; a job that had been mine not too long ago. It pained me deeply to know I couldn't be there for her. As her husband I should be soothing her and wiping her tears, but that would become Will's job now. A job he would no doubt do instinctively and with love.

The crying subsided and the aroma of coffee filled the house; peace had been restored for the moment. When Maggie's voice was strong again, I heard her ask Will to call the hospital and tell them she wouldn't be in for a few weeks. He stepped out of the house to make the call on his cell.

My brother arrived in the early morning hours, and my family drifted through a million emotions that day; there were moments of laughter, mostly from the stories my family shared about their favorite memories of me, followed by moments of sadness and tears, which I also shed. As stories were shared and the clock ticked away the last minutes of my life, my house bulged with love, as if it would explode from the emotions everyone shared.

After my parents and brother had their time alone with me, Maggie's mother and stepfather came over in the afternoon to pay their final respects. Will suggested that he go pick up food to feed everyone, and Maggie's parents, my parents, and my brother went to prepare the kitchen for Will's return, giving me another chance to talk to Maggie alone.

I spoke slowly, my words slurred; I was hanging on by a thread and needed to tell her how I felt about her one last time.

"My hours with you are getting shorter. I love you, Margaret Barrett. I love you with all my heart." My voice was much weaker than my emotions wanted it to be. I wanted to yell it to her, to the world. I wanted everyone to know I was madly in love with my wife.

"Oh, Tim, you're the best husband I could ever have asked for. You have taught me so much about living, and now you are teaching me about dying. You are brave, just like your mother said. Not a day will go by that I won't think of you and miss you. I don't know what Clipper is going to do without you. I love you." Tears fell from her eyes as she kissed my cheek, pressing her lips against my skin for a long time.

"Everything is in order. Take care of yourself, Maggie, I mean it. Don't cry for me, but live because *we were*; we were and always will be linked. Crying will not undo anything. You must grieve, but don't live in grief. And please love again. You are much too beautiful a person not to share your life with someone."

"Tim, if I find love again, I do, and if I don't, I will live with the memory of your love 'til my dying day—the day we will be together again."

I felt a tear rolled down my cheek, not sure if it fell from my eye or Maggie's.

Our last words to each other were, "I love you."

She sat by my side, holding my hand into the evening. She didn't speak, she just stroked my hand with her thumb.

Hours later I took my last breath and everything turned dark.

Maggie

I BECAME A WIDOW ON SEPTEMBER TWENTY-NINTH AT SEVEN sixteen at night. I was thirty years old. During the days when I'd had been honest with myself about the reality that Tim was going to die, I had imagined that as a widow I was going to feel alone. I envisioned myself with no one to share my darkest fears or my love and devotion with. I couldn't have believed that my grief would come on so soon or hurt so intensely.

After Tim took his last breath, I held him in my arms not wanting to admit that he was gone, but then reluctantly I resigned myself to the truth. I placed a kiss on Tim's mouth, stroked his fuzzy hair, and crept away from his bed after eight p.m. I had been surrounded by his family, my mother, and Will, and with the nurse standing off to the side, but I needed to be alone to absorb the sharp turn my life had taken. I walked into my bedroom, opened Tim's closet, found his gray Bentley sweatshirt, and with a heavy heart wrapped myself up in it and plunged into our bed.

I heard birds calling from outside my window the next morning. As they roused me from my slumber, I shot up and screamed Tim's name out. Like I'd done so many times before, I reached over to his side of the bed, but it was empty and cold. Then it hit me, like a rolling wave. It was real. Last night had actually happened. I ran into my bathroom and threw up.

I heard footsteps enter the bedroom and sensed someone come up behind me. My head was resting on the rim of the toilet as I waited for relief.

His whisper struck me with the tenderness of a rose petal. "Maggie? Are you okay?" Will asked. He must have heard me call out Tim's name. I wondered, *How can he still be here? Yesterday was his last day off. He should be going to work.*

His warm hand rested on my back. I couldn't face him. Seeing the sadness in his eyes would make it too real. I worried I'd get sick again. But too late — even without looking at him, my stomach emptied itself. How could I keep getting sick? I'd hardly eaten yesterday.

He tucked my hair behind my ear and wiped the sweat from my forehead with a cold facecloth. He closed the lid and flushed the toilet. Then he knelt down beside me. He wiped the soft facecloth over my cheeks and looked deeply in my eyes with a soft, caring expression,

"Can I get you something?"

"Please… tell me it isn't true." My lips trembled, my body shook. I felt raw like my nerves exposed.

"I wish I could, but I can't. He put up a great fight 'til the end, but the cancer had already taken over before he had any chance to win the battle. Come on, let me help you back into bed."

I stood to rinse my mouth and began to shake. He lifted me into his arms and carried me back to my bed.

"Everyone went home late last night, but they are coming back later this morning to be with you. I told them I would stay with you overnight so they could rest. I'm going to get you some toast and a drink. Do you want coffee or juice?"

"Um, I think just water. I don't think I can stomach much right now. Wait — aren't you supposed to be at work?"

"I called the station yesterday and told them I needed to take some time off, so I'll be around whenever you need me." He smiled and held my hand. "I'll be right back with your breakfast." He turned to leave, but before he reached the door I stopped him.

"Will, did they come and take… Tim's body?" After the words left my mouth my lips started to quiver and more tears fell.

He walked back to the bed and sat next to me, wiping away my tears before they fell onto the comforter.

"Yes, Tim's father placed the call to the funeral home and started making the arrangements based on Tim's requests and what you had discussed with him earlier."

"I don't know if I can walk into that room again. I mean… it will never be the same for me in there. The last memory was too sad."

"Well, maybe it's like horseback riding, right? The sooner you go back in, the easier it will be. Would you like for me to walk you down? I assure you, being there won't be as bad as you're thinking it will be."

I realized Will was the perfect person to be with me now. After all the horrible and emotionally draining things he'd seen and experienced at work, he'd learned how to put tragedy and emotions behind him and answer the next call for help.

"I don't know if I'm strong enough right now. I don't think I can handle it." I caught a chill and wrapped my arms around my body.

"Let me get you something to eat and then we'll see how you feel. We don't need to rush it, okay?"

I nodded and rolled over.

Will returned with toast and water, but also surprised me with a cup of herbal tea. He sat quietly on the edge of the bed with his hands folded, rolling his thumbs slowly over and over themselves. We didn't speak. I was numb. The room was quiet, but outside the birds chirped and sang songs of joy as they started their day. Night turned into morning, and the sun started rising. The skies looked clear, lightening to a soft blue.

As I ate the toast, I stared out the window at the morning sky flashing back to the day of my father's burial.

I wanted to wear my bright pink dress and couldn't understand why I wasn't allowed to; my grandmother had insisted that I tone it down and wear my navy blue dress. Everyone in the house was already on edge, so I just agreed. My mother walked out from her bedroom and met me in the hallway wearing a black dress and a black hat with a small veil attached. I understood then that standing next to her in my pink dress might express happiness instead of the sadness that her black outfit conveyed.

As my mother, sister, grandparents, and I stood at the gravesite I looked at my family crying and saw some of the firefighters from my father's work wiping their eyes every so often. I found it easier to look to the sky; no one was crying up there. I stood for I don't know how long, staring at the clear blue sky. Every once in a while a bird would fly by, breaking my concentration, and the words being spoken would come clear. I wanted to block my ears with my hands, but I had already been corrected by my grandmother for doing so. Focusing on the clear blue sky allowed me to block out everyone's emotions and the words people were sharing about my father.

As I lay in bed, a new widow, I experienced the same loss I'd felt as when my dad died. I looked to the sky, but this time it didn't offer the same protection as it did when I was ten. Instead, it made me cry to think I'd never look at a clear blue sky with Tim ever again. There was no escaping the emotional roller coaster I had to ride. I set my tea cup down with my hand trembling and it rattled against the tabletop. Will saw I was heading into a tailspin, and he gathered me in his arms. I cried and cried. He repeated, "Let it out" and "It will get better." He stroked my head and held me snug against his chest.

I was thankful that Will stayed to keep me company; in his muscular and protective arms I found a feeling of comfort. I knew Tim's parents were grieving together, as were my parents; and I knew they would be with me soon enough. For now Will was all I had.

I pulled away. "Look what my tears did to your shirt. You're soaked. I'm sorry."

"Don't worry, it'll dry. That's the least of my concerns right now." He brushed off his shirt and offered me more toast. I took it, knowing I needed all the energy I could get. After I finished my tea I asked Will to take me downstairs.

"Lying here is not helping me feel any better. I might as well go downstairs and get it over with."

I was still wearing Tim's gray sweatshirt, but I changed into clean purple yoga pants. Will followed me, carrying the plate and tea cup. I walked down the stairs slowly holding the railing, trying to delay the sensations waiting for me in the family room. I paused at the bottom. Will placed his hand on my lower back and balanced the dishes in his other hand.

"It's okay, you can do it. I'm right here."

Clipper trotted up to me. *Why is it that a dog can change your mood in an instant?* I leaned down to hug him. My face lit up for just a second before tears started falling again.

"Oh no, what happened?" Will asked.

He placed the dishes on the table in the hallway. I buried my face in Clipper's fur and bawled like a frustrated baby.

Will looked at me with a sympathetic expression. "What's wrong?"

"It's Clipper. I haven't seen him since last night. I didn't think he would affect me like this, but seeing him reminds me that Tim will never see him again. Clipper must be confused about Tim not being here." A waterfall of tears poured from my eyes. Will took me by the shoulders, backed me up, and set me down on the stairs to cry it out.

"When my grandmother died, I was sixteen," he said to me. "She was my father's mother. She had lost her husband in a car accident when I was a baby, so she was a young widow too. After my grandfather died she came over to our house every Sunday for dinner, and over the years we made memories together and had so many laughs. Anyway, I can remember being sad at the oddest times after she died. Something on television or a song on the radio or a holiday decoration would make my heart ache for her. I talked to my mother about it, and do you know what she told me?" He didn't wait for me to answer. "She told me that all the things that saddened me were actually great opportunities to recall the love that I had for my grandmother and I just had to change the way I looked at it. Not right away, but in time I was able to understand what my mother meant. Slowly, I moved through feeling sad to feeling joyful about the happier times with my grandmother." He lifted my chin so that my eyes met his. "So what I'm saying is that Clipper makes you sad now, but in a few days or weeks, maybe even months, when you look at him you'll think about how much Tim loved him. He will be a connection to Tim and remind you how lucky you were to have had Tim in your life."

I looked up at him, this man who came into my life out of nowhere, a man who became friends with my husband and stuck around to keep me company and coach me through my grief—what type of man does that? I could see why Tim enjoyed his company.

"Do you think I will ever run out of tears, that they'll dry up? I can't believe I have any left in me." I mustered a smile, and he wrapped his arm around me.

"Somehow I think our bodies keep making 'em for as long as we need to cry them." He squeezed me close. With a chuckle he said, "Let's go test them in the family room."

134

I walked into my family room. Instead of tears falling from my eyes, a smile spread across my face.

Everything was back in its place, nothing left to remind me of Tim ailing in his hospital bed or the scene that had played out the night before "What happened? Where is everything?" I stopped shaking as I walked around the room.

I turned to Will for an answer.

"I couldn't let you replay what you lived through last night, so after everyone left I took the bed apart and put the room back together the best I could. I tried to remember how you had it set up. How'd I do?"

He reached his hands out and smiled. I walked up to him and gave him the biggest hug; I think I caught him off guard because it took him a minute to return my embrace.

"Thank you. You did better than good." I clung to him; he had become my rock, my anchor. I couldn't imagine how I would have gotten through this without him.

The brief calm that I experienced with Will in my family room was the last bit of calm in my life for days. A couple hours after Will led me into the room that I thought would be a hurdle, my mother and John, my stepfather, arrived and Alison came shortly after. A while later Tim's parents, Betsy and Edward and his brother, Sean brought coffee and muffins for everyone. The flurry of people arriving at the house allowed Will the chance to go home and shower and change. Before he left he stopped me as I was coming out of the bathroom.

"I'm going to head home if you're okay, but I won't leave if you need me to stay. It's just that I feel a bit like an extra now that all your family is with you." He stood with his shoulder against the wall, his hands in his pockets.

"Oh my God, Will, please don't ever feel unwelcome. Whether you like it or not, you're family now. After all you have done for Tim and lately for me, your presence here has even more purpose. I understand you probably want some time alone to process, but please don't be a stranger. I will never forget what you did for me this morning. No one could have helped me through it like you did." I moved in to hug him. "Thank you."

"You have my number if you need me, right? I'm going to try and take a nap, but call me if you need anything." He put his hand under my chin. "You got it?"

"Ten-four."

His eyes were hypnotic. My nerves settled just by looking into them.

After he said good-bye to my family, he headed out the door. My broken heart ached a little bit more as I watched him leave, because I didn't know who would console me like he could or when I would see him again.

~

My step-father John, and Tim's dad, Edward, were responsible for organizing the funeral to Tim's liking based on the letter he left with his father. My step-father took over for Edward when it became too much and he needed to walk away to take a break. I was so apprecia-tive that they handled everything from the flowers to planning the mercy meal.

After we ate lunch I talked to my mother in private in the family room as she held me on the couch smoothing my hair out like she had when I was a little girl. I felt safe in her arms like nothing could harm me as she explained the road ahead of me.

"These early days will be a blur, you won't remember how you got through one day to the next, but I think you have it harder than I did, Maggie. I had you and your sister to get out of bed for in the morning, you guys were a wonderful distraction. You need to promise me that you will give yourself time to grieve, but that you also will call me if you are stuck in your emotions and can't get out of bed. You have Clipper to focus on. He's going to need you to feed and exercise him."

As she talked, my eyes wondered around the room and they stopped when the sight of a photo made my stomach flip. I got up out from my mother's safe embrace and closed the distance to the photo of Tim and me from our honeymoon in Hawaii. We were smiling wearing lei's around our necks, the sunset cast a yellow and deep orange sky; I looked out the window of my family room to the blue sky. It didn't compare to the colors in the photo.

I didn't realize I was coming undone until my mother's arms were once again surrounding me, "How am I going to go on without him, Mom?" Tears ran down my cheeks.

"Maggie, listen to me, you can't wonder that now, it's too soon. Honey, look at me," she held my face in her hands, "it's one day at a time and sometimes it will be hour by hour or minute by minute. But I guarantee you this, you will get through it. You may never get over him, I wouldn't expect that, he was your husband."

She led me back to the couch and sat opposite me, "in time it gets different, and it will get easier. You're young, you have so much left in life to experience and places to travel. You see how full my life is. I loved your father with all my heart and at first when he died I never imagined I could love again. I thought, 'how could I, what would people think?' But then I met John and he filled the emptiness in my life that your father's death left behind. Be patient with yourself; remember what your father always told you, 'steady as you go.'" She was pleased with herself for recalling his words. "Steady as you go. That's what he always told you." She pulled me close.

I laid down on the couch and she covered me with a blanket. "Rest here awhile. You could use a nap. We're all in the kitchen if you need anything."

"Thanks, Mom."

I fell asleep holding onto the photo of Tim and me on our honeymoon. My dreams were all over the place, most blurry visions and voices that seemed to be in slow speed, talking like drones. Then *boom!* an explosion and my father appeared in front of me wearing his firefighter's helmet, jacket, and boots. I yelled, "Daddy! Daddy! No, don't go in! No!" I jumped awake and my sister was by my side; my heart beating fast, sweat rolling down my forehead.

"Let me guess, a nightmare about Dad dying." She hugged me.

"Alison, I haven't had one of those in long time – like a really long time."

"Maggie, you're processing a lot right now; losing Tim is like losing Dad all over again. I'm afraid there's bound to be more where that one came from."

"How could this happen to me again? First Dad and now I lose my husband. It's too much for me take." I scooted down under the comfort of my blanket.

"You'll get through it, just like you did with Dad, with help from everyone that loves you." She smiled at me and only I could tell what my twin was thinking, 'we're tough, us O'Brien girls.'

I couldn't believe how long I had slept; the sun had passed by its high peak and began to dip in the late afternoon sky. I hated to think that everyone would leave me and I would be here in this giant, memory-filled house all by myself. I got up and walked into the kitchen with Alison and everyone stopped talking when they noticed me in the doorway.

"It's okay, carry on." I walked over to the table.

My father-in-law motioned for me to take his seat just as my mother-in-law poured me some tea and offered a muffin to accompany it.

"Is everything all set for tomorrow?" I looked around to see who had the answers.

My stepfather began talking,

"We need to be at the funeral home by eleven. The wake hours will be twelve to three and then five to eight. Will that be too much, Maggie — can you handle that?"

I was not listening. "What? I'm sorry, I didn't hear you."

My mother interjected, "Yes, Maggie will be just fine tomorrow, won't you, Maggie?"

I circled the chamomile teabag around in my favorite purple mug and watched the ripples. With a big sigh I said, "Yes, I'll be ready for tomorrow."

God, I hoped I would be.

After awhile, talking about the upcoming days became too much for me, and I went back to the family room. I was curled up on the couch saying good-bye to my sister when there was a knock at door. My mother-in-law opened it. I heard excitement and some commotion. Alison and I walked into the kitchen holding hands, and a wave of peace rolled over me. Will had returned.

Will

AFTER TIM DIED, HIS FATHER TOOK ME ASIDE AND ASKED IF I could stay with Maggie for the first couple of nights. He thought it would be best for him and his wife, Betsy, to try to sleep at their home, to prepare for the following few emotionally exhausting days.

Was Tim's dad in on the plan?

I agreed. I was more than happy to help in any way that I could, and there were two extra bedrooms so I could sleep in a real bed. I chose the bedroom closest to Maggie's so I could hear her if she needed anything. I hit the pillow and sleep took me away fast. I hadn't slept deeply for the past four nights and my body caved to sleep's call.

Maggie's scream woke me in the middle of the night. I ran to her room; my job as her new caretaker had started.

Over the course of the following days, I watched as the woman I had fallen deeply in love with grieve for her husband. I would be patient and allow time to pass before I made Maggie aware of my feelings for her. She knew I was a caretaker, but for now she didn't need to know I was out-of-control in love with her.

I stood on the sidelines during the day watching Maggie lean on her family for support. They all needed each other to heal and move forward, and I didn't want to get in the way of that. But at night she leaned on me for support when she had nightmares or couldn't sleep. I was glad to stay with her — I needed to be near her.

~

Leaves drifted off the oak and maple trees littering the ground as I made my way to Maggie. She was standing at the graveside next to the casket with her head hanging down between Tim's father and her mother. I stood next to Terry from the coffee shop, a few feet behind Maggie. My heart ached for her — for the pain she was experiencing, but also because I wanted to be near her, to be the one comforting her. As the final prayer ended, I noticed her shoulders begin to shake. I knew instantly she was crying. Her mother tightened her arm around Maggie's waist, and Edward wrapped his arm around her shoulders. The three of them stood supporting each other like a solid wall nothing could penetrate.

After hugging Maggie good-bye and shaking hands with the family, I waited until everyone had filed away to the limos and their cars. The sun heated my suit coat, penetrating down to my skin, and I absorbed the warmth on the chilly fall day. Birds chirped in the distance and a slight breeze kicked up moving the leaves on the trees, wrestling with the fallen ones on the ground.

I stood over the flower-adorned casket that held the body of my good friend. No — my best friend. I had known Tim for over a year and yet I knew him on a deeper level than almost any other person in my life. I'd watched as cancer took his life and stood witness as his soul left his body. There had been many other times when I was present as a person left this world, but it had never been someone I cared about as I had cared for Tim.

"Hi, buddy. The inevitable has happened. Part of me can't believe it, even though I was there with you 'til the end." I noticed my cheeks were getting wet. "Tim, I learned so much from you in the short time that we knew each other. I've always loved life, but you gave me the best gift by asking me to teach you how to love and embrace it. You were a changed man after your diagnosis. It really made me proud to watch the way you accepted your fate and started living instead of dying.

"You're a respectable man. If you're watching over me right now and can hear me, please don't worry about Maggie. She's in good hands. I have already fallen in love with her, and I want to thank you for your blessing that allows me to have feelings for her and know I don't have to feel guilty about them. In time I will act on them, but now I need to let her grieve for you and I need my own time to grieve for your absence in my life. I will miss you, buddy, but you'll never be far from my thoughts." I placed the single yellow rose the funeral director had handed me on top of the casket and walked away.

~

I spent the two nights after the burial at Maggie's and then I had to leave her to go back work. I really missed her and wondered how she was getting along. Alison offered to stay with Maggie, and catch up later with Keith on his BMX tour in Europe, but Maggie encouraged her to leave with him. They left the day after Tim's burial.

Assuming no one had exercised Clipper in a while, on my day off I decided I would drive by her house and take him for a run. I pulled into her driveway and the house looked vacant, but as I approached the door I heard a voice inside. I tapped lightly on the door and heard footsteps approaching. I saw the curtain move and Maggie's face appeared. She smiled. Her eyes looked warm.

"Hi, Will, come in." She held the door open. Clipper was by her side.

"Hey, just who I was looking for!" Clipper rested his head in my open palms. I scratched his head.

"I just got off the phone with my mom. She's been calling every hour to check on me — it's getting to be too much. She also told me

Alison and Keith are exploring the art world in Europe in their down time. Alison is in Heaven!" She smiled.

I moved into the hallway and grabbed Clipper's leash from the hook. "That's wonderful."

"You weren't kidding about being here for him, were you?"

"I figured no one had exercised him and I need a run, so I can bring him with me and help you out." I attached the leash to his collar. "I don't suppose you might want to join us?" I was hopeful she might say yes.

"Thanks. I don't think I have the energy to run, but maybe I could start out walking with you and I'll turn back when you pick up speed. It might do me good to get some fresh air." She grabbed her deep blue fleece jacket and we walked outside.

It was a beautiful fall morning. We strolled along her neighborhood as Clipper inhaled all the wonderful scents on the ground. The sun was out and the air was mild. I allowed Maggie time to get comfortable and as we approached the end of her street she began talking.

"It's so weird being inside the house without Tim there. Let's face it—I knew he was going to die and I would be alone. But now that he's gone it's like there's a chance that when I turn around he'll be standing there. Sometimes I swear I hear him call my name, and I turn, hoping he's come back." She paused. "I'm crazy, right?"

A squirrel ran by carrying an acorn in his mouth, and I held onto Clipper's leash.

"I don't think you're crazy. I think your brain is trying to comprehend what it has just experienced. The idea that one day you have a husband you can touch, hear, and see and the next day he's gone—it's too huge a concept to process. Your brain is responding just like everyone's does. In time, you'll create new habits and feelings and you'll think about Tim but know that he isn't here anymore. Does that make sense?"

"Yes. Thanks." Her hands were tucked up into the sleeves of her jacket. "I know I've said it before, but I'm really lucky to have you here to help me through these tough days. Tim and you had sort of a crazy friendship, and by default, I guess you've become a friend to me too." She bumped my hip. "Thanks for being here for me. I really appreciate it."

"You know, Tim and I had a lot of time to talk before he passed away. He asked me to look after you, not that I wouldn't have anyway. I'm a sucker for a damsel in distress — it sort of comes with my job. I'm a helper, it's how I'm wired, and I can't change it. I'll be here for you as long as you need me to lean on."

I wanted to continue, to tell her I never wanted to leave her side and that lately she was all that I thought about. Being with her had filled my life. She was my match made in Heaven and I wanted her to know it, but I was too smart to tell her. I knew it would scare her away; she was too fragile right now.

"He did that for me? He never told me, never said a word about it, but that sounds like Tim — always setting up plans and preparing for what might happen. He couldn't let life unfold naturally. Then he got cancer and knew he had no say in what happened. Isn't that a tough way to learn a lesson?" She was quiet for a while. "Did he say anything else?"

We turned down another road and Clipper barked at kids riding on their bikes.

"He often told me how much he loved and cared for you and said that he was worried that you would be alone when he died." I couldn't tell her everything — that he'd given us his blessing to fall in love, that he wanted me to be the guy she moved on with in life. I knew she couldn't hear that now.

I noticed a few tears spill from her eyes.

"Hey, I didn't bring you out here to upset you more. Do you think you could pick up a jog and see how you feel? Maybe the endorphins will kick in and help you feel better? What do you say?" I nudged her shoulder. "You need to do something with all that emotional energy swirling around inside of you."

"I guess it wouldn't hurt to try. I'm feeling more energetic now that I'm out of the house, breathing the fall air. Let's go — I'll race you." She exploded and ran fast, catching me off guard.

"Let's get her, Clipper!"

I jogged behind her, Clipper trotting beside me, letting her burn off her emotions. What better way than running? After a few minutes I ran faster and closed the gap between us.

"Hey, speedy! What are you, a show-off?"

I ran by her side, and when I looked over at her she was smiling.

She finished the run along with me. As we approached her house I could tell she felt lighter. The endorphins were doing their job.

"Thanks, Will. How do you always seem to know what I need?" She unlocked the door, and we walked into the kitchen.

"I don't know. Maybe because I've paid attention to what you say and how you act." I unhooked Clipper from the leash and placed it over the kitchen chair. "It isn't hard to read people; you just need to watch and listen."

She took a container of water from the refrigerator, and I grabbed two glasses from the cabinet. She moved nearer to me. When I turned around she was closer than I'd gauged, and we bumped into each other. We froze. I was holding the glasses and she holding the water, her hand was gently touching mine. I looked down into her bright green eyes. Warmth radiated throughout my body; I felt blood pumping through my veins. I held back from kissing her, though that was my instinct. It was too soon. She held my gaze and smiled; I wondered if her body was feeling like mine did.

"Sorry, I didn't see you behind me." I was lost in her eyes.

"No, it's my fault. I was looking at Clipper instead of where I was walking." She licked her lips and looked down. She placed the water on the counter, took the glasses from my hand, and poured water into them. She handed one to me.

"Thank you."

I was unable to move.

I looked at her while I drank the water. God, she was amazing — the most amazing woman had ever met.

Maggie

I MET WITH OUR ATTORNEY AFTER TIM'S DEATH AND IT SHOULDN'T have come as a shock to me that Tim had taken care of everything, just like he'd told me. I really wouldn't need to return to work; as the attorney told me, I was set for life. The house was paid off, as was my car. The life insurance policies that Tim and I took out when we were first married would provide enough money to retire on. Tim's business still needed to be sorted out. However, there was no way I could sit around and not work. I might as well have died with Tim. So I changed my schedule to work three days a week; the distraction was just what I needed.

I returned to the hospital in the beginning of November and the nursing staff and doctors fell over themselves to welcome me back. The last time I had seen most of my coworkers was at Tim's funeral, and I wasn't prepared for the emotions bubbling up when I saw them now. I felt like everyone was staring at me, the new widow.

My dear friend Molly came over to hug me. We met during our first week at the hospital about six years ago and struck up a deep working relationship that had spilled over into our days off. We enjoyed many of the same things like running, spending a day shopping, and having lunch to give us energy to shop some more. We both agreed on the importance of our families in our lives, and through the years we shared many happy and sad times. I was there for her when her father

died, and she was my confidant when Tim was sick. Only she understood the depth of my fear of losing him.

I relied on my family to help me sort through some of my emotions
over losing Tim, especially my mother, who could relate to me the
most, but I saved the deep anger and frustration, the "why me," for
Molly. I wanted to spare my family from my fears and allow them to
focus on helping Tim through his.

During one of our therapy shopping trips to the mall after Tim was
diagnosed, we watched a young mother and father fussing over a
newborn. I broke down.

"I always thought I would have that with Tim, but now his life is
going to be cut short. What am I going to do without him?" Tears fell
from my eyes; I had to sit on a bench.

"Maggie, come here." Molly gathered me in her arms and gave me
a reassuring squeeze. "I know you thought that you and Tim would
have children. I'm sorry it isn't going to work that way, but maybe in
time you will have kids, just with someone else." She looked me in the
eye. "Your mom moved on, right? Look how happy she is with John.
She once thought she would never marry again because no one could
be as loving and devoted as your dad, but she found love again."

"Yes, I remember telling you that. I can't believe you remember."
My tears stopped. I often had moments like this; tears would fall from
nowhere, little bursts of emotion from my fears and worries over what
would become of me after Tim died, but after a few minutes I'd feel
stronger again.

"I remember everything that is important, and I will always be here
to remind you. I don't know what your future holds, or mine, for that
matter. I would like to find a boyfriend, for starters! One thing I do
know is you're the strongest woman I know and you will emerge from
this tragedy an even stronger woman. One day that scene over there,"
she pointed to the mother standing over her husband as he cradled

their baby in his arms, "will be you. Don't give up on love because Tim got sick; you're too young to stop loving."

Molly hugged me again. "Let's go find some ice cream to cheer you up."

Molly was the perfect cheerleader in my life; her emotional disconnection from Tim allowed her to focus her energy on helping me look to the future. She cared about Tim, the poor guy robbed of life at a young age, but she also knew that her best friend needed to be told that she would carry on. It would be okay. Some ignorant people in my life brought me down, asking what I would do after he was gone. They asked it like I was dying too, but Molly spoke about the far-off future — the one in which I was strong again, moving on, stacking more and more days of grief behind me until I was able to smile, laugh, and hopefully find love again.

~

At work everyone tried to support me and lighten my load. My caring friends cleaned up the ER rooms after my patients were discharged or sent upstairs. I would come around the corner and find the beds already made and supplies restocked; I'd stomp off to find the guilty party. I knew they meant well, but their help was too much of a reminder that I was scarred. A scar that wasn't going to heal if I was trapped in the role of the mourning wife. I finally told them to stop; I needed the distraction, and I wanted to do my job.

When my twelve-hour shift ended I was exhausted, looking forward to bed and having the next day off to recuperate.

After returning home from work, I grabbed a quick dinner and climbed in bed with Clipper. Tim always had issues with Clipper sleeping in our bed, but with Tim gone, I was in control, so Clipper became my new bedmate. Some nights he would take over the majority of the bed, leaving me hanging over the edge, and I wondered why I'd started. I'd kick him off and send him to his doggy bed on the floor. It was the only way I could get any sleep.

My ability to sleep became somewhat of a mystery to me in the weeks following Tim's death. Some nights I would pass out and sleep until morning, but other nights I lay awake for hours, thinking about Tim and how much I missed him. On those nights, usually I'd cry myself to sleep.

I wasn't prepared for the haunting nightmares about my father's death, like the one I had the day after Tim died. My father stood in front of a burning building, the heat rising, flames rolling out the windows and doors. I could feel the hot fire. I could hear the men yelling to each other.

"Quick, get water over here! Put it on full blast through this window. Get the ladder truck up there, knock it down from above." Then my father said, "We're missing Dave! I'm going to get him."

No matter how the nightmares started, they always ended with my dad yelling the same thing: "I'm going in." My breathing became heavy. I'd begin to cry and yell, "No, Dad!"

Then I would wake and sit upright, drenched in sweat, as if I had been standing near the fire. Clipper would come to the side of the bed and rest his chin up on it to comfort me. I couldn't understand why I was dreaming about losing my father all over again instead of losing Tim.

Anyone driving by my house on those nights would see it was all lit up. The only way I could shake the images that haunted me was to go downstairs, switch every light on, make a cup tea, and sit in front of the television until I felt that I could sleep peacefully again. Some of those nights I got to watch the most beautiful sunrises, just me and Clipper.

~

STEADY AS YOU GO

On the last day of my first week back at work, I was busy checking on patients who had been brought in overnight. After a few hours, when everyone was content and resting, I grabbed my phone from my bag and noticed I had a new voicemail. I recognized the number, it was Will.

"Molly, I'm going to check this message. I'll be out back if anything happens." Molly had often covered for me if I needed to take a call or check in with Tim. Now she looked a bit surprised about why I was checking my phone. I knew she was curious about who had left a message.

The tenderness in his voice tickled my ear, like he was whispering in it. Warmth radiated through my body. Thank God I was leaning up against the wall for support.

"Hi, Maggie. It's Will. How are you holding up? I've been thinking about you being back at work and how hard it must be. Anyway, if I remember right, tomorrow is your day off, and I was wondering if you wanted to meet me for coffee or lunch, or maybe go for a run. Whatever you want to do, I would really like to see you. So, um, give me a call. Talk to you later. Bye."

My heart raced, and I think I was blushing. My cheeks were hot. Why was I responding this way to his voice? Why did Will want to see me? He was probably missing Tim. I had to meet him. After everything he'd done for me, it was the least I could do.

If I was to be honest with myself I missed being with Will and battled with my feelings for him. Over the past months I had really gotten to know him, and I enjoyed his company. He was probably the kindest person I had ever met—not that Tim wasn't kind, but in a different way. He was caring, but he didn't put himself out to help people like Will did. Tim and Will were very different people. I had enjoyed getting to know Will. Aside from me, Will was the only other person who had spent long hours with Tim and talked with him about dying. I figured he could help reassure me that Tim was truly at peace with dying and not faking it with me.

Molly practically jumped on me when I returned to the nurse's station. "Who was that on the phone?"

"Oh my goodness, Molly, calm down. It was just Will."

"Really? *Just Will*, then why are you blushing? And smiling?"

Suddenly my patient buzzed for me, and I left to respond without answering her.

~

Before driving home I sat in my car to return Will's call. I noticed my disappointment when he didn't answer. I left him a message and started for home while I pondered being in an empty house. I began to cry while I thought about being there all alone, without Tim.

As I rounded the corner onto my street and approached my driveway, I saw a truck parked there — Will's truck. My stomach flipped in delight – I couldn't believe my response. I'd just lost my husband a couple months ago, and now I reacted to seeing Will's truck like a baby bird that was being rescued after falling from its nest. Will was my rescuer. I shook my head. *Come on, Maggie — he's just being nice*. But I couldn't deny that there was something about the way I felt when I was with him that helped me to feel whole again and promised that someday I would be okay.

I pulled past his truck into my garage. In the rearview mirror I watch him walk in and stop behind my car.

"Hey, what are you doing here?" I opened the driver's door and retrieved my bags from the backseat.

He held up a bag. "I brought dinner." Then he flashed his killer smile. "I thought you could use some company and I have the night off. What do you say?"

I felt a smile expand across my face. "Come inside. I just need to clean up."

I unlocked the door, and Clipper greeted us.

"How long do you need? I'll take Clipper for a walk."

"You'd do that for me?" My spirits lifted a bit more. "The poor dog hasn't had many walks lately. I'm thinking of hiring a dog walker." I put my bags down, hugged Clipper and attached the leash, then handed it to Will.

"You don't have to do that. I'll come by and take him on my days off. Maybe he can play at my place while you're working. We'll figure something out. All you have to do is ask, you know. I'll do anything for you, okay?"

He stood facing me, his warm, safe eyes captivating me as Clipper circled around his feet, sniffing all the new scents Will brought in with him.

"I must be the luckiest widow ever." I turned to walk away, but then I turned back. "Did Tim hire you to babysit me? I wouldn't be surprised."

"I wouldn't accept the money." He shook his head and smiled. "We'll be back."

When Will and Clipper returned from their walk, we settled down at the kitchen table and shared dinner—Italian take-out, the perfect comfort food for a cold fall night.

"I got your message from earlier today. I was surprised to see your truck when I pulled in." I twisted long strands of pasta around my fork before taking my first bite; it was warm and satisfying after a long day.

"Oh, yeah. Well, it's been a while since I've seen you. I wanted to check on you and make sure you were feeling okay. After I left the message, I got this idea to bring you dinner, so I decided to surprise you. I'm just glad you came home. I was thinking I would have to eat all of this if you'd gone out after work." He smiled brightly at me.

I studied his face, trying to figure out why he was sticking around after Tim's death. Don't get me wrong; he was fun to be with, and with his charming good looks and strong muscular body, there was no reason not to want him around. His face was a wonderful place to rest my eyes.

"Oh, gosh, I never go out after work. Those days are far behind me. I'm too beat. I usually come straight home, especially now. Clipper needs me, now that Tim…" My throat closed off, and I couldn't speak. Tears spilled from my eyes. Will dropped his fork immediately and was by my side, his arms around me. I turned and rested my head on his shoulder and cried, my body shaking. I had survived my first week at work, but now the new reality of balancing life without Tim caught up with me. I realized how hard it was going to be to live life without him by my side. It was a lonely, heart-wrenching discovery.

The time I took off from work after his death was like a honeymoon period. I was allowed to hide in my house and let my parents and Tim's parents take care of me and do my laundry and shopping, but now that time had passed, I noticed people were backing off a bit. Maybe it was good that they were letting me come back to life slowly, but the emotions of the past week made my life without Tim too real. Now my emotions were boiling over.

"Oh, Maggie, it's okay. I'm here for you." Will turned my chair and wrapped me completely in his arms, stroking my hair.

After a few minutes I pulled back. "I'm so sorry. Sometimes I can't control my tears or emotions. They come out of nowhere. I think I'm doing fine and then *bam!* The floodgates open. I can't stop myself from crying." I looked down at his shirt. "I ruined your shirt again," I said with a half smile.

"Don't worry about the shirt. It'll dry. And don't worry about crying. You're still processing your new life. You won't need the tears some day. In time you'll be able to think about Tim and smile."

I held his hand in mine. "Thank you for being here. This would have been a lonely night for me."

"I'll always be here for you. I told you that before, and I meant it."

We sat holding each other's hands and looking into each other's eyes. I felt content when Will was around. He had a way of making everything feel bearable.

Will

AFTER WE FINISHED DINNER I STAYED WITH MAGGIE AND watched mindless television until she was too tired to keep her eyes open. She walked me to the door, but before I stepped out into the dark, chilly November night, I turned to her. "Did you decide on tomorrow? Will it be coffee, lunch, or a run?"

"Can I call you in the morning after I see how I feel?" She scrunched up her forehead, maybe worried I was looking for a different answer.

"Of course. No pressure. If you're not in the mood to go out, I understand." I patted her arm. "Good night and sweet dreams."

"Thank you for dinner and for your company. Good night, Will."

I heard the deadbolt lock. It was the same sound my heart was making – I ached for her. I hated to leave her alone, but I didn't think I could get away with sleeping in the guest room again. It was different now then from the beginning, when her family and I agreed she needed someone with her. I started the truck and began the lonely drive to my house.

The more time I spent with her, the harder it was becoming for me to be away from her. I tried to convince myself that Tim's dying wish was eating at me or that the rescuer in me wanted to protect her, but deep down in my soul I knew the reason—I was madly in love with her and incapable of acting on my feelings, which made me want her all the more. The only way I could satisfy my desire to see her was to check in with her to make sure she was managing life and not suffering alone. Some days at work I longed for a call to transport a victim to the hospital so that maybe I would bump into her there, but those calls never came.

I got the feeling that Maggie wasn't asking anyone for help, even though she'd told me her mother checked in with her every day. It seemed she was trudging through her days and coping with her emotions on her own, not wanting to be a burden to her family. As I pulled into my driveway, I decided I would keep reaching out to her, hoping she would come to see me as more than just the friend I had become.

~

The following morning I was leaving Sacred Grounds when my cell phone rang. It was Maggie.

"Hi. Good morning!"

"Hi, Will. Am I catching you in the middle of anything?" She seemed to be in a cheery mood.

"Not at all. I have a question for you. Just answer it and don't ask me any questions, okay?" She agreed. "What kind of coffee do you like?"

"French vanilla with a little skim milk."

"Okay, thanks." I turned and went back into the coffee shop. "What's on the agenda for today?"

"The weather forecast looks great, high fifties and clear skies. I don't think I have the energy to run, but would you be interested in a walk in the woods with me and Clipper?"

While she was talking I ordered her coffee.

"I think that sounds like a perfect day. Maybe a picnic lunch, too? We can cover all the ideas I had." I nodded to Terry when she handed me the coffee and whispered, "Thanks."

"Sounds like a plan. Do you want me to pick you up?" she asked.

"Nope. I can be there in ten minutes or is that too soon?"

"That should work. I'll leave the garage open and the door un-locked. Just come in."

I found it ironic that she'd called precisely as I was walking out of the same coffee shop where I'd met Tim. I looked up toward the sky and smiled. *Thanks, bro.*

Clipper greeted me as I walked in the house. His whole body vi-brated, his spring-loaded tail thumping against the wall. Maggie was in the kitchen, dressed in black yoga pants and Tim's oversized college sweatshirt. I recognized it because she'd worn it the day after Tim died.

She stood with her back to me, washing a dish in the sink. I walked behind her and reached around her to show her the coffee cup I held.

"Just how you like it."

She shut off the water and turned.

"Are you kidding me? You seriously stopped and got me a coffee?" She seemed shocked under her smile.

"It was nothing. I was just leaving the coffee shop when you called. It was very convenient to get one for you—I was right there." I chuck-led.

"Well, thank you."

"Are you guys ready? I see Tim's coming with us today." I tugged on the sweatshirt sleeve, teasing her.

"Oh, I know. I always wear this on my days off. I never knew how comfortable it was."

STEADY AS YOU GO

Or was she thinking how comforting it has become? Either way, she seemed happy and in a good mood, and that made me happy.

We got in my truck with Clipper in the back seat of the cab and headed toward the highway.

"Where are we headed? I thought this was my idea? You didn't ask *me* where I wanted to go." She grinned, and I knew she was kidding around.

"I knew right away where I wanted to take you when you said you wanted to go for a walk in the woods. I found this place years ago. I go there whenever I need to balance my mood and clear my head. It's especially therapeutic after a bad day on the job."

"Or maybe when your best buddy dies?" She looked at me. Was she trying to comfort me or perhaps get me to open up?

"Oh, a smart one, huh? Yes. I spent hours walking in these woods in the days following Tim's death." I gripped the steering wheel. "I never shared with you how I felt about losing Tim. Compared to what you were going through, my feelings seemed insignificant. I didn't need to lay them on you. Walking in nature helped set my thoughts straight."

I was surprised by how quickly she reached out to me, resting her hand on my arm.

"Will, you should never feel like your feelings over losing Tim don't matter to me. I saw how fast you and he formed your friendship. My God, your name was all I heard for weeks, maybe months, after you guys met. You and Tim had a special connection. He loved spending time with you, listening to your work stories. The way you lived was so different from how he lived and he admired you a lot. It looked to me like you were willing to show him more about life outside of his comfort zone and that you wanted him to break free from the security he'd built around himself."

She removed her hand, leaving behind a cold reminder that she had touched me. She looked out the window.

"That is a description of a true friend if I ever heard one."

I looked over. She tried to wipe a tear before I had a chance to see it, but it was too late. I reached over and rubbed her thigh just above her knee. "It's okay. We don't have to talk about it. I don't want to upset you."

"We have to talk about it or we will never heal. Tell me, what did you enjoy most about him?" She turned to face me.

"Oh, gosh…" I took a deep breath. "The way he analyzed his every move; I found that intriguing. I never knew anyone like him. I grew up in sunny California, the land of surfers and laid-back dudes, so someone like Tim appealed to me as a character I needed to get to know better — he lived a lifestyle foreign to mine."

"Funny, that's exactly why I fell in love with in him when we first met. He made me feel so safe. He never took risks or chances; he always considered his choices before making a decision. He told you that my father died when I was young, right?"

I nodded.

"After it happened, I saw my mother grieving every day over the loss of her husband, my father, and it had an impact on me. I convinced myself I could never, and would never, fall in love with a man who lived or worked in a dangerous or risky environment. I believed I had to protect myself from what my mother went through." She took a deep breath. "I was ten years old when I made that oath to myself. And look how it ended up for me. I fell in love a cautious man and he died from cancer. I guess you can't control what will happen in life, can you?"

I didn't know how to answer. She was right. No one has control over what actually becomes of their life. I see it every day at work. I have fought to save people with every fiber of my being, only to watch them slip away from me. But my heart sank when I heard her say she could never, would never, fall in love a risk-taker or a man with a dangerous job. I was just like her father. I didn't hold much hope that she would return my feelings for her.

"Maggie, sometimes I think we get what we need in life more than what we want. We usually discover that when it's too late. Ya know, my job as a firefighter — there's a lot of security in it. Your father shared the camaraderie of many men who would have given their lives save his. I can't picture some lawyer putting his neck on the line for his partner or a judge, but the whole structure of a firehouse means brothers would give their life for another member, regardless of rank or position, even if we have never met. I know my job, like your father's job, involves risks, but getting out of bed in the morning has risks, and you still do it, right?"

She turned back to the window. "I guess I never thought about it that way. I know men tried to stop my dad. The fire had grown ugly and the chief had called them back, but my dad went in to try to save his fallen brother. They never came out." She paused for a few seconds. "I miss him so much," she said softly.

We were approaching my special hiking spot, and I was thankful because the cab of the truck had become a tangled web of emotions.

"I'm sorry if I upset you. I didn't mean to."

"It's okay. Actually, since Tim died I have been having horrible nightmares about my father. In every dream he dies all over again. I don't know why that's happening, but it's so real that I have to get out of bed and go downstairs to watch television to try to clear my mind."

That's why her lights have been on at night when I've driven by for work.

"I figured I would have dreamed about Tim, so it's confusing me why I'm dreaming about my dad."

"Maybe you never completely healed from losing him. You were very young."

"I never spoke about it, either."

"Really?"

"My mother's pain was so intense, I couldn't bring myself to burden her. I heard her say to people that I was strong and I handled losing my dad well. She didn't know that I cried at night or on my way to school. I blocked her from all of it. That's why I tell you to talk about Tim and how you feel; I learned the hard way about trying to cover up emotions. They find their way out at some point."

I pulled into a parking spot and turned to face her. "That conversation was heavy. How about we leave it here and head out to the woods to clear our minds?" Clipper stood in the back seat with his head between us, blocking our view of each other. We ducked to see around him, and whenever we had a clear view he moved back in. We burst out laughing.

"I think Clipper agrees. Let's go," Maggie said.

We walked down the path to the trail entrance, the dead brown and yellow leaves crunching under our shoes.

"Do you want to know something interesting?" Maggie looked up at me. "These are the same woods I come to when I need to clear my mind. I wonder how many times I walked past you before I knew you."

"Really? I've been coming out here since I first moved here. I'm sure at some point we were here at the same time and never knew it." I put my arm around her shoulder. "I'm glad I can share this with you today."

"Me too."

When we got deeper into the woods, she let Clipper off his leash. He had his nose to the ground, enthusiastically tracking the animals that had been down the path.

"Have you thought about Thanksgiving Day and who you'll celebrate it with?"

"It's crossed my mind, but I haven't made any solid plans. I'm sure I'll end up at my mother's. It would have been our year to be with Tim's parents, but I can't imagine going without him; it would be too depressing. I think it'll be better for me to be with my family. Alison's coming back from Europe and her stories are always interesting — she'll be a good distraction. Maybe I should invite Tim's family to join us... Oh, I'm thinking out loud. Sorry. What are your plans?"

"Well, my mother wants me to come home, but I don't think I can make that work. Well, I *could* make it work, but I don't want to. I want to stay around here. I decided to take that shift and let someone with family have the day off."

"Aren't you a nice guy?" She patted my back.

"Oh, you're just figuring that out?" I looked at her out of the corner of my eye.

"Will you have to work all day? You could always have dinner with my family after your shift ends."

"Thank you, but I'll be there all day and night. If you want to serve turkey for breakfast, I'll swing by then." I smiled at her.

"Very funny. Maybe I could bring a plate to the station for you. Everyone has to eat a turkey dinner on Thanksgiving."

"That would be thoughtful of you, but I would rather you stay and enjoy your family. I'll be fine."

"I don't know... I may need a break from them and need a reason to leave."

We reached the clearing where I loved to sit and look over the pond. A picnic table waited off to the side, under a canopy of barren trees. I brushed the multicolored leaves from the top and set the picnic basket down. Maggie looked for a stick to throw for Clipper.

"Are you hungry? Do you want to eat now?" I asked.

"Not yet. I want to sit over here near the pond."

After she tossed the stick and sent Clipper off running, she went to sit on a boulder. Not just any boulder, but the boulder I always sat on when I came here.

"I love to look out over the water and watch the trees reflect off the surface of the water. When the wind glides over the surface, the trees look like they're dancing. Look at the way the blue sky outlines the trees; it reminds me of a photo negative — images and tones but no real color. I appreciate the beauty and find it inspiring. It's pure, like it was placed here just for me." She wrapped her arms around her knees.

She turned and looked up at me standing behind her. "What are you thinking?"

"The same thing... and that you're sitting on my rock!" I moved her aside and sat next to her. "This is the boulder I sit on when I come here. Sometimes I don't go any farther than this. I just sit here and think."

Clipper brought back the stick, and I picked it up and threw it farther away. I sat forward with my elbows on my knees, my fingertips touching.

"Do you think it's weird that our paths could have crossed when we were both here but didn't know each other?" I waited. "I met Tim, and then he was diagnosed with cancer and died, leaving us as friends. Have you ever thought about why things happen the way they do in life?" I turned to look at her.

She looked straight ahead. A flock of birds flew overhead, the lead bird calling out orders.

"I have, for sure. And sometimes I wonder why you and Tim met. You guys had such a strong friendship. He had many friends, but they distanced themselves when he got really sick. One by one they disappeared. Sure, some called or e-mailed, but none of them spent time with him like you did. For that, I am truly grateful, and I know Tim was."

"Yeah, I think about it too. I see the same people in the coffee shop almost every time I'm in there, yet I'm not friends with them, nor would I be interested in getting to know them. But with Tim it was different; we connected after a chance meeting, one that changed my life forever."

We sat in silence looking out over the pond, until we were interrupted by Clipper panting and barking for us to throw the stick again.

"Oh boy, someone has an addiction." I threw the stick again.

"You can thank Tim for that! That's all they did together when Clipper was a puppy, and he never outgrew it. I hope your arm can handle it."

"Don't you worry about me. I'll be fine." Clipper ran off to retrieve the stick.

We ate turkey sandwiches and shared our thoughts and feelings about random things, from our childhoods to our jobs. Then we walked deeper into the woods while Clipper ran ahead of us. The more time I spent with Maggie, the more clear it became that she was just the type of woman I had been looking for — loving, caring, and funny, yet serious about life — not like the party girls I often found myself with. And she was beautiful in a natural way that came from within, not artificial. Her eyes captivated me. The pure emotion in her gaze could stop me in my tracks. I was learning how to read her emotions from the looks she gave me.

When the color of her eyes was bright, she was either laughing or being playful; sometimes if the color deepened, she looked lost and sad. I knew she was asking to be held. Today was the type of day when her eye color shifted according to her emotions; lately that's how it had been.

After an enjoyable day walking through the trails and talking about our lives, I drove Clipper and Maggie home just before dinner. I walked with them into the house. I watched while Maggie prepared Clipper's dinner and I was sad to think I wouldn't see her until the following week. Before then I would be working overtime, filling in for a co-worker taking a vacation. When my shift ended on Wednesday morning, she would be starting her shift at the hospital.

"Maybe we'll see each other at the hospital; there's bound to be a call or two that will need medical attention." I leaned against her kitchen counter.

"Yeah, I'm sure we'll see each other. We can always chat on the phone, right?"

Clipper finished his dinner and stood next to her. She scratched him behind the ear, and he smiled blissfully.

"I'm worried about leaving you for five days. Are you sure you'll reach out to your mom or friends if you need support? You can't do it alone — it's okay to ask for help." A knot formed in my stomach.

"I'll be fine! Please don't worry about me — you have a whole town to worry about. I'm okay. I'll call my mom tomorrow and set up dinner plans, or maybe I'll call my sister and catch up. You have been so nice to me and more than helpful. You have no idea how much I appreciate your company. When I'm with you… I feel different. It's hard to put into words. Sometimes you say something that makes me miss Tim so much, but other times when we talk I feel like I'm normal again. My heart doesn't ache as much and the heaviness is lifted for just a moment." She looked at me. "Does that make sense?"

"Totally."

I reacted so fast my brain couldn't stop me; I pulled her into my arms. "Thank you for a wonderful day and for telling me that. I hope to see you at the hospital."

"Me too." She returned the embrace.

STEADY AS YOU GO

Outside, I opened the door to my truck, and a cloud of her perfume mixed with a little scent of Clipper hit me. I inhaled deeply, taking her scent deep into my soul, allowing it to comfort me. Five long days without seeing her — could I survive?

~

Maggie and I never did bump into each other at the hospital, even though the ambulance made trips there during my work day. I looked for her on her scheduled day but couldn't find her. We spoke a few times on the phone. She told me she had taken my advice and opened herself up to her family and to Tim's parents, who invited her to dinner. She went to the movies and shopping with her mom.

I tried to make plans on our first combined day off, but she told me she had committed to go shopping with her friend Molly. I had mixed emotions: I really wanted to see her, but I also wanted her to enjoy her time with her friend. With her permission I went by her house and took Clipper for a run and then brought him home with me for the rest of the day.

I returned Clipper around seven, hoping Maggie would be there, but the house was totally dark. *That's some shopping trip she's on*, I thought. I fed the dog. While he was eating, I closed the curtains and put the lights on, inside and out.

I left her a note.

> *Hi, Maggie,*
> *Clipper was a fantastic boy today. He had a long run, we played catch, and he watched me clean my house.*

I'm sorry I missed you. I brought him back at seven and hoped you would be here… I wonder if there are any clothes left at the mall!

I know you're working tomorrow, but I'm off, so if you have time, call me. I miss seeing you.

Your friend,

Will

She called around eight thirty. "Hi. I'm sorry I missed you." She sounded tired.

"I'm worried you bought everything in the mall—did you leave anything behind?"

"Yes." She seemed a little more alert now. "We shopped and ate and then had our nails done. Molly wanted to keep me out as long as she possible; she knows I don't like being alone at night."

"I wish she would have shared you with me. I feel like it's been too long since I've seen you." I couldn't believe I said that. I didn't want to seem envious, but it was the truth. I missed her terribly.

"It has been a long time. I'm off, you're working; you're working and I'm off—our schedules aren't aligned. I guess it'll be next week before I see you again. What's Clipper going to do with himself?"

"So he's the only one who will miss me? I find that hard to believe." Maybe I was pushing my luck, but I wanted to hear her say she missed me, the way I was missing her.

"Well, maybe I'll miss you a little. After all, now I'm going to have to exercise him." She laughed.

Ouch. Not the answer I was hoping for. I was forcing it—I needed to back off and give her time.

"I can swing by on Monday and take him for the day, if that will help."

"I was kidding! You don't need to do that. You spoil him, you know."

"He's a good dog and I enjoy his company. I'll grab him when you're at work, and he'll be back by the time you get home."

We talked more about setting up plans, but my schedule didn't line up with hers for the next two weeks; it seemed I wouldn't see her anytime soon. We agreed to call as often as we could to check in.

When we hung up my heart felt heavy. I missed her and there was nothing I could do about it.

~

Thanksgiving Day arrived. More calls for oven fires came in than I could ever remember. We tried to eat a Thanksgiving Day meal at the station, but it was no use. The calls poured in all day and by seven o'clock we were resigned to the fact that there would be no turkey for us.

I was cleaning up the station kitchen after our attempts to celebrate when I heard commotion coming from the garage bays. I dried my hands on a towel and walked out into the garage. Maggie, her mother and stepfather, and Tim's parents' arms were full of food. Maggie also carried a bouquet of Thanksgiving Day flowers. Jake circled them, trying to get at the food.

With a smile, I walked over and said hello to everyone. My brothers helped them carry the food and escorted everyone to the kitchen. Maggie stayed behind.

"What are you doing here? And what is with all that food? Did you guys cook two turkeys today?"

"Well, that's a fine 'hi, how do you do?' I haven't seen you in weeks and that's how you greet me!" She grinned. "Happy Thanksgiving." She gave me a big hug, the first hug Maggie ever gave me without tears or sad eyes. It felt wonderful to hold her in my arms. She was wearing the same delicate floral perfume she'd worn the day we went to the woods. I could inhale her all night long; in fact, I never wanted to stop smelling that scent.

"I'm sorry—happy Thanksgiving. I didn't mean it the way it sounded. I appreciate what you've done, and I know the guys are thrilled!"

"You have to remember that my mom is a firehouse widow. She knows the struggles you guys face during the holidays; your families are at home enjoying hearty meals without you while you're all here keeping the town safe. Tim's parents are so grateful for everything you did for Tim, and this is their way of saying thank you."

She released me. "We planned this after I told them you were working and couldn't come to dinner. Yes, they would have invited you, but you were working, so instead we came up with this surprise. We just cooked double; it was quite easy."

She made it seem so casual, but I knew it was more than that. The whole family had put love into the meal and I would be forever grateful for that.

"Okay then, let's go eat. I'm starving. We had turkey sandwiches instead of the real thing—they didn't come close to satisfying us. It smells amazing in here. Come on!" I grabbed her hand and led her into the kitchen.

There wasn't one dish they forgot to make. They brought all the fixings: green beans, butternut squash, mashed potatoes and sweet potatoes, cranberry sauce, stuffing, bread, gravy, and of course the turkey. They even brought homemade pies. The guys owed me big time for this feast.

"I would like to make a toast." I raised my glass of water. "To Maggie and her amazing family for bringing us this delicious meal. To the friends and family who are with us today, to those who couldn't be here, and to the loved ones who have left this world but will be with us again someday." I looked right into Maggie's eyes, and she looked right back at me with a smile. "Salute." Everyone cheered and clinked their glasses.

Maggie walked over to me. "Thank you. That was a very sincere toast. Happy Thanksgiving."

I looked down into her sparkling green eyes. "Happy Thanksgiving."

We were interrupted by Maggie's parents as they extended their holiday wishes. Tim's parents followed. "Too bad he couldn't have made it until today. This was his favorite holiday," Tim's dad murmured quietly.

I patted his back and told him I was sorry too.

There was a relaxed feeling in the air, as if we were all in someone's home enjoying a wonderful meal as friends and family. The laughter was different from the sounds we made as firefighters.

As we finished our plates, the alarm sounded and called us all to attention. I was thankful that we'd been able to eat without distractions, but peace doesn't usually last too long in a firehouse.

We were called to a house fire on the east side of town. My brothers stood up and ran from the room, and Maggie's family started putting the food away. Without a thought or a moment of hesitation, I grabbed Maggie's arm, turned her to face me, and kissed her, a soft kiss good-bye. I opened my eyes just as she opened hers. We both stared at each other, lost in another world. She took her lower lip into her mouth and chewed on it gently as she looked up at me. What had I done?

"I'm sorry, I don't know what came over me." Still looking into her eyes, I stepped back, hoping no one had seen. "I have to go." I ran to the door but stopped and turned around. "Thank you for dinner."

Maggie

WILL CHECKED IN WITH ME ON MOST DAYS. MY FEELINGS toward him were growing more intense, and it scared me. The kiss at the fire station on Thanksgiving Day caused a flurry of mixed emotions. He was Tim's best friend. It seemed like I was being unfaithful to Tim's memory. And Will reminded me of my father, which was comforting yet scary.

It had only been a couple of months since Tim's death, but the truth was that I had begun mourning Tim long before, the day we received the news about the prognosis. I had tried so hard to be upbeat with Tim, telling him a cure would be discovered or that a miracle would happen, but I had done my own research and I knew what the odds were. He was not going to get better. From that day forward, I slowly began saying good-bye to my loving husband as he slipped deeper and deeper into the clutches of cancer. I knew I had to let go of the life we had built, yet I was scared to imagine what my life would become.

But having Will in my life made me feel joy again. During the times when the sadness from missing Tim crept in, if Will was there I didn't feel so scared. Will reassured me that everything would be okay, and because he said it with such determination, I couldn't help but believe him.

We never got around to talking about the kiss he snuck in on Thanksgiving Day because our work schedules prevented us from seeing each other. When we spoke on the phone we had quick conversations about Clipper or when we would be finished with work and able to see each other. The days passed quickly and then it was mid-December. Finally we had two full compatible days off.

Will called me at work to confirm.

"I was wondering if you have plans for Saturday night. If you're available, would you like to go to dinner with me, a pre-Christmas celebration?"

"Will, are you asking me on a date?" I tried to sound proper, but I was grinning.

"I'm not sure we can consider it a date, but if *you* want to call it a date, I'll let you."

Oh, now he was playing me.

"No, I won't consider it a date — just two friends having dinner to celebrate the upcoming holiday." I was content with that.

"It's actually my work holiday party. I had forgotten all about it when we made plans for the weekend and I didn't have the heart to break our plans. So I was hoping you would come with me, as a friend, of course."

"Oh, I have to get dressed up, so it is a date. I couldn't possibly go in yoga pants, so that definitely makes it a date." I started laughing.

"Oh, man, you're not making this easy, are you?"

Had I cracked the cool façade that was Will Driscoll? I detected something different in the tone of his voice. Either he really wanted me to go with him or he was trying to get out of his obligation to me on Saturday. Either way, I had fun playing with him. He never stumbled like this; he always seemed to know the right thing to say or he kept quiet, hanging back and letting others do the talking.

"Do I sense nerves in your voice, Mr. Driscoll?" *This is too much fun.*

"Wow! You're laying it on hard today. What have I done to you that you're having so much fun messing with me? Barrett, it's a yes or no answer; what will it be?"

I continued to harass him. "I just enjoy listening to your voice fight to stay calm and chill—you know, the Will I've always known, the Southern California man—but I detect something else below the surface. An uneasiness. I'm not sure if ever heard it before, and we both know that throughout the last ten months we've talked a lot about many emotional things."

"You're enjoying this, aren't you?"

"Yeah, maybe a little bit." I paused. "Yes, I'll go with you, but you have to promise me one dance, okay?"

"You got it. You've never seen my moves though. I hope you're ready!"

And he was back, the cool Will I knew and was starting to fall for. I couldn't deny my feelings to myself any longer. I felt better with him than without. I remember those same feelings with Tim, and I was scared about it. Will was everything I had told myself to stay away from, but I could no longer deny that he had a way of relaxing me that I appreciated.

After I got off the phone with Will, our break ended. Molly came over, and we walked to the elevator.

"Who got you all flustered on the phone? I could tell something was going on. I haven't seen you act like that in a while. It was nice to see you smile."

"Oh my gosh, Molly, I'm really scared. I think I'm falling in love with Will." I looked at her, desperate for help.

"Good for you. At least one of us is."

"What? That's the advice you're going to give me?" The doors opened and we stepped inside the elevator. I was glad to see we were alone. "Shouldn't you say I'm crazy? My husband hasn't been gone for three months and I'm already moving on? Or, how about saying, 'No way! It's an emotional rebound.'" I leaned against the wall with my hands folded, anxiously rolling my thumbs over my palms. "Let's not overlook the fact that Will is everything I told myself to stay away from in life." I looked at her from the corner of my eye. "No, nothing like that; only *good for me!*"

"Look at you, Maggie! Clearly you like this guy. Who's to say when a person can move on to find love again? I didn't know there were deadlines for that. You're happy and smiling, and that's what I care about, not that it might be too soon." The doors opened at our floor. "I think you of all people should know that life is unpredictable, and if you have a chance at love, take it while you can. You chose a safe and secure man, and look what happened to him." She walked ahead of me and then turned. "Take a chance and see what happens. That's just my opinion." She kept walking and left me more confused than before.

My so-called date with Will was approaching fast, and I wasn't ready for it. Molly offered to go with me to the mall in search of the perfect dress. She was all giddy about dressing me. I kept trying to emphasize that it wasn't a date, more of an obligation, because Will and I had already made plans; he had just forgotten about the party. But she didn't want to hear it.

Poor Molly so desperately wanted a boyfriend, but she never kept anyone around longer than a few months. She was a romantic at heart, but I thought her standards were way too high. Even Prince Charming would have fallen short. When I first met Will, I had secretly hoped they would hit it off. But I learned Will wasn't attracted to girls like Molly; they were too high maintenance and needy. He was looking for a strong, easy-going woman who didn't need a man to give her confidence.

I started to wonder if he saw those traits in me.

After looking in a couple stores, I went back to the first dress I saw; it fit me the best. It was fancy but not over the top, and I loved it. I tried it on for a second time before deciding that it was the one. It was festive and complimentary to my red hair. It had three-quarter-length sleeves and a fitted red bodice with black lace overlay and a boat-neck neckline trimmed in small crushed rhinestones. With my hair, I couldn't wear certain shades of red, but the dress had the perfect pop of color. The high-waist black chiffon skirt fell a few inches above my knee. When I twirled it rose up and made me look like a ballerina.

As I changed back into my clothes, my emotions got the better of me. Despite my intentions, a sob escaped, and Molly whipped open the curtain.

"What happened?" She sounded disappointed.

"I don't know. I was feeling pretty, and then I started thinking that I should be going to Tim's holiday party in this dress. It's not fair that he isn't here with me. I miss him so much, and the holidays aren't helping."

"Oh, come here. Let it out. It was only a matter of time before this happened." She rocked me in her arms. "As a kid, I remember my grandfather was always crabby at the holidays and I wondered why he was such a downer. Then my mother explained that my grandmother had died right before the holidays, and after that he was never happy when Christmas came around." She pulled back to hold my face in her hands. She nodded. "Don't turn into my grandfather. You'll be okay. You have a hot date with a gorgeous man who I suspect thinks you're pretty great too. Please, for one night put down all the heaviness you carry for Tim, and live. Can you do that for me?"

"You make it sound so easy." I collapsed on the floor.

"No, it's not easy—I can see that. But having fun for a few hours isn't too much to ask, is it? Do you think Tim would prefer you crying alone at home or out hanging with his buddy?" She wiped my tears with her thumbs. "Hey, if you want to bail, I'm pretty sure this stunning dress will fit me. I have no plans on Saturday night, so I'm game. Just let me know." She grinned at me.

"I'm being ridiculous, I know. I'll go, but it won't be easy."

"No one ever said life is easy, Maggie." She pulled the curtain behind and left me to change.

~

I spent the better part of Saturday primping for my evening out. I remembered the last time I had a fancy party to go. It was Tim's holiday work party last year at the Copley. It had started out as a beautiful night, but we had to leave early because Tim didn't feel well. We thought it was the stress and fatigue from planning the event plus the approaching holidays. Little did we know it was the cancer slowly killing him.

Tonight would be different. Will and I were healthy, and it was sure to be a fun night. I kept telling myself that, hoping that I would start to believe it, but deep down I was jittery, my stomach nervous. How could I be doing this? It just seemed wrong. I needed advice.

"Hi, Mom. Are you busy?"

"Maggie, how are you, dear?"

"Well, not so good. I have plans with Will tonight. Sort of big plans—he asked me to his holiday party at work."

"That sounds like fun. I don't see what the problem is. Do you need to go shopping for a new dress?"

My mother was so practical; it was as if she'd never suffered the loss of my father.

"No, Mom, that's not it. I just feel sick about it—I feel guilty to be going out to a fancy party with another man."

"Oh, I see. Well, you're looking at it from the wrong angle. It seems straightforward to me. You are a beautiful single woman, and Will... let's face it, is *Will*. There's no need to even begin describing him. In my eyes, it only makes sense that he would invite you."

"But, Mom, I'm a widow. It hasn't even been three months since Tim died. Doesn't that seem wrong?" Why couldn't she see it from my perspective?

"Maggie, do you know how many dates I turned down after your father died? Too many. And every time I didn't go, I sat at home stewing because I hadn't gone. What a waste of time that was... Really, what was wrong with me? Your choice is to go or stay home; it's pretty simple."

"Well, when you put it like that."

"Margaret Emma,"—*oh boy, it was never good when she used my full name*—"you go out on that date and live it up. Have the time of your life. After what you've been through, you deserve it! You know, I wasn't going to bring it up before you, but I can't stand it anymore. I saw the kiss at the fire station."

I was speechless.

"I didn't want to pry. You know it's not my way. But, honey, he loves you. It was automatic for him to turn and kiss you good-bye. He's comfortable with you, and he cares *so* much about you. We can all see that."

I stopped her. "What do you mean, *we all*? Who all?"

"John and Alison—we've talked about it—and Edward and Betsy..." She trailed off.

"What! Wait a minute—what are you saying? You've all talked about me and Will? Was anyone going to talk to me about it?" I was mad.

"Oh, I think you're overreacting, Maggie. We didn't sit around and talk about it like you think. It's come up here and there. Do you really think a man like Will would look at a beautiful woman like you and not have feelings?"

"Yes, I do. I thought he was being nice because he's Tim's friend. Now all of you *crazies* think he's in love with me. Ugh! Another reason for me not to go tonight. I shouldn't lead him on."

"Oh, I don't think you're leading him on—quite the opposite. I think you have feelings for that gentleman and aren't ready to admit that or allow yourself to act on them. You called looking for my advice, right? Put yourself together in your party dress, go to the party, and knock him out! Make it a great night because you can, Maggie, and you should, as his friend." She had toned down her excitement and offered motherly advice; even though she could drive me crazy, I loved her more than she would ever know.

"Alright, Mom, I'll go for you—for all the dates you said no to because you didn't want to leave Alison and me home with a sitter. I'll go for you."

~

The front doorbell rang at seven o'clock on the nose. When I opened the door, Will took my breath away. He looked incredible. I was used to seeing him in jeans and casual shirts, not in a suit.

"Hi! You never use this door."

"Because we've never been on a date before." Will stepped over the threshold.

"So we are calling it a date then?"

179

"Let's see... I'm gonna take a stab and guess the dress is new?" He was waiting for me to answer and prove his point.

"Maybe... but if I changed into an old one, would that change anything?

"No, you'd still be the most beautiful woman in the room." There was that killer smile again, stirring up the butterflies.

"Come on, Romeo, I need to get my stuff in the kitchen."

We walked passed Clipper, who was waiting to be pat. After all the nurses and aides who came and went when Tim was sick, Clipper learned to wait to be greeted instead of pushing his way through legs and pestering the visitors. Will stopped to pat him for a moment while I gathered the important items from my big bag and transferred them into my black clutch.

I turned and watched him give Clipper wonderful attention; he was a good man. Maybe my mother was right. Maybe he was in love with me and I was too scared to admit my feelings for him.

"Ready?" I called out.

We said good-bye to Clipper and walked out the garage door.

Awkward is how I would describe the first thirty minutes at the party. We walked in with some other guests who were fashionably late. It felt like everyone convened on us before we got our jackets off.

Will's coworkers surrounded us, saying things like, "It's so great to finally meet you" and "You're Tim's wife. We've heard so much about him. Sorry for your loss."

One guy came out of nowhere, speaking Spanish to Will. His name was Diego. I admit that I thought he was handsome, but I would never tell him to his face because I got the feeling he already knew it.

"*Ella es una mujer hermosa,*" he kept repeating, and then he followed it up with, "*Más, más!*"

Will acknowledged him and directed me away.

"What was he saying?" I asked.

"He thinks you're beautiful. He's a flirt. Stay away from him. He's harmless, but he loves the ladies, if you know what I mean."

"Thanks for the warning."

We walked around the room, stopping to say hello to some of Will's coworkers. I recognized some of them from the hospital, but there were so many faces and names to remember I wasn't sure I would ever get them straight. The loud chatter in the room made it hard to hear my own voice. With every new person I met I became more and more overwhelmed. I excused myself and went to the bathroom so I could catch my breath. It had been a long time since I had been in a large crowd; I wasn't used to the noise and stimulation.

I wasn't sure I could go back out into the room full of strangers who were staring at me with pity in their eyes. I stood over the bathroom sink taking deep breaths. I laughed to myself because I was with the perfect crowd if I fainted. I realized then that I hadn't left my house much since Tim died, nor had I been in large crowds except for the trips to malls, and there it was easy to escape into department stores when I became overwhelmed. Coming to the party was a mistake. There were too many people, and too many of them knew about my loss. I couldn't hide from it. I held onto the sink with white knuckles.

A beautiful, tall blonde walked into the bathroom and stared at me. "Are you okay?" she asked. "Do you need help?"

"No, I'm fine, thank you. Just a bit dizzy. I'll be fine after I eat." I smiled, feeling like half the woman I had once been.

When I left the bathroom, Will was standing against the wall waiting for me with a drink in his hand.

"Are you okay? You were in there for a while." He seemed very concerned.

"Yeah, I'm sorry. I was just a bit taken back by the size of the crowd. I hadn't realized most of them knew about Tim. I wasn't prepared for it." I brushed my hands together. "I'll be fine." I smiled, trying to hide my true feelings.

"Okay, let me know if it's too much." He rubbed my arm.

"What? And ruin a perfectly good date?" I laughed.

"Come on, let's get some food, Ms. Comedian." He placed his hand on my lower back as we walked, and I felt some confidence return.

We ate and the evening passed more smoothly. It seemed the whole fire station was there. Will explained that other towns would cover for them during the party so they could all be together. I would never understand the bond among firefighters; no other profession supported each other the way they did. I was proud that my dad, and Will, belonged to that group of people.

The music kicked up after dinner and the dance floor was shoulder to shoulder with people. After watching for a while, Will looked at me and said, "You made me promise you a dance, so… may I have this dance?" He held his hand out to me.

I was a little hesitant because it was a serious up-tempo dance song, but I thought about my mother and the all dances she missed.

"Okay, let's go." So what if I made a fool out of myself. It was dark, and I didn't know anyone except Will.

We made our way to the dance floor. Just as Will started his college-era dance moves, the DJ switched it up and "At Last" by Etta James poured out through the speakers, her sultry voice a soothing contrast to the throbbing beats of the previous dance song.

Will stopped rocking and held his hand out. "Can I have this dance?" His expression was more serious.

"Sure." Before I knew it he took my hand and spun me around and then into in his arms; he was a good dancer, so I let him lead. We moved to the music. I rested my head on his shoulder and felt his body pressed against mine, his hand on my lower back, holding me close. I closed my eyes, enchanted by the intimacy. I inhaled his cologne, a clean, warm scent, and I felt at ease, content to be held by a man. Warm, captivating waves radiated throughout my body. It had been so long since I had been held in a close embrace.

I leaned back and looked up into his eyes. The allure of being held close to him caused my stomach to flip and my palms got sweaty.

He noticed my reaction and wearing a soft smile he whispered, "It's okay."

His words hung in the air as Etta's lyrics stirred more emotions in me. I stared into Will's eyes while she sang, "At last my love has come along, my lonely days are over and life is like a song." I smiled up at him; he smiled back and tucked me within his arms more closely. My ambivalence about loving him was triggered, and apprehension slowly expanded inside me. I began to question what was happening between us as we danced; it was as if we were the only two on the dance floor.

We moved together in unison and I felt every part of my body, every fiber of my being, buzz deep inside of me. My thoughts battled over what I was doing in another man's arms, allowing myself to feel the joy he brought to my life. My heart was beating fast, so I tried to slow my breathing down. Then Etta jolted my fears with the closing line: "You smiled and then the spell was cast and here we are in Heaven for you are mine... at last."

I broke from him and ran; I ran away and left him standing all alone on the dance floor. I needed air—I needed to get away. My emotions were too strong, and I was frightened to feel them.

By the time I reached the bottom of the staircase the next song had started, a fast one. I hoped no one had noticed me running away from Will, deserting him on the dance floor.

I ran through the doors into the cold night air without my coat. I shivered and started to cry. The deep indecision about my feelings for Will caused my makeup to run down my face. I wiped my cheeks and I tried to shake off my emotions, but I couldn't stop crying and I couldn't stop shaking. Then suddenly I felt a warm coat surround my shoulders and heard his sweet, tender voice.

"Come on, let's go. I'm bringing you home."

He'd rescued me again.

Will

WE DROVE HOME IN SILENCE. ALTHOUGH I WANTED TO REACH over and hold Maggie's hand to comfort her, I didn't want to upset her even more. I had never been in love with someone in a situation like Maggie's. She was still mourning her husband, yet I was ready to act on my feelings. I loved her more than I had loved anyone before, but I would need to be patient if I wanted this to work to our benefit — and Tim's, for that matter.

I was frustrated with Tim. Why hadn't he just talked to her about it? It would have saved her from the turmoil she was going through. She would have known that he blessed us being together, that it was what he wanted. I knew she cared for me. She couldn't hide it if she tried. The energy I felt radiating off her was electrifying, and in a different place and time I would have already made my move, but this was new territory for me, and for her.

We walked into the house and she didn't stop.

"I'm going to bed. Can you let Clipper out for me?" Her voice sounded sad and deflated, a far cry from the happy woman I'd picked up three hours ago.

"Maggie." I walked to her and reached for her hand, but she tried to close me out. "I'm sorry for whatever I did back there that upset you. I never meant to hurt you."

"It's not you, Will, it's me." Her voice was stronger. She turned to face me, whipping her hand from mine.

"Do you know hard it is for me to get through the day? No, because you didn't lose your husband." Her tone was intense and her voice was louder. "He was everything to me, but now he's left me, and I'm out tonight acting like it never happened." She turned away in disgust and then faced me again, tears falling from her eyes. "I love being with you. I have fun with you, and when we are together I can forget how terrible I feel inside. But then you leave me, taking with you the temporary joy you give me, and all my real feelings come back—the emptiness, the loneliness, the sadness, and the heartache."

Oh boy—I wished I had just let her to go bed.

I didn't know what to say to comfort her. I knew she was right; she had to mourn for Tim while she continued to live her life. She sat down on the stairs, holding her black heels by the straps with her fingers. She was silent, and she wiped a tear from her eye. She looked up at me and then shut me out again.

"I'm going to bed." She rose and walked up the stairs. I heard her bedroom door close.

I stood paralyzed at the bottom of the stairs. Clipper sat next to me, his tail wagging back and forth on the floor. His tail and my heart breaking were the only sounds I heard.

"Let's go, boy. I think we could both use a walk."

I walked in the crisp night air, vapor pouring from my mouth. The meteorologists had predicted a few inches of snowfall overnight. As I rounded the corner onto the main road flakes started to fall, quickly covering the dead leaves and coating the shades of brown the fall left behind. It was refreshing to walk in the snow; it cleansed my soul and cleared my mind. I had envisioned the night ending with me holding Maggie in my arms. Instead I was trying to find a way back into her heart. It was clear that she had feelings for me, but also that she was afraid to act on them. Maybe I should tell her about Tim's wish, tell her that he approved of us, but I couldn't. It would seem like I was trying to persuade her to do something she wasn't comfortable with.

Clipper and I returned to the house just as a thick band of snow began falling. I could hardly see in front of me. I settled him on his bed and made a choice I hoped I wouldn't regret; I got my overnight bag from my truck and headed to the guest room.

I often kept a change of clothes in my truck because sometimes after work I needed to change from my uniform. Earlier that day I'd tossed in a toothbrush, hoping Maggie would offer her guest room so I wouldn't have to drive home after a long night. I certainly had my hopes up about how the evening would go. I couldn't have imagined the actual ending. I hoped she wasn't mad in the morning when she woke and found me still there. But I would take that chance, because I couldn't leave her after the way things had turned out. And besides, we planned to spend the next day together.

I climbed into bed, thankful to be inside and warm. I imagined all the critters hunkering down in their nests and burrows to protect them from the storm. I drifted off to sleep and dreamed of Maggie and how beautiful she looked as we danced, everyone around us on the dance floor smiling at our joy and happiness.

And then I heard her yell.

"No, Dad! No, Dad!"

I jumped from the bed, wearing only my boxers, and ran into her bedroom. She was sitting up. I noticed Clipper resting his chin on the side of her bed; he'd got to her first. I switched the light on to see her better, and then I sat on her bed, holding her shoulders in my hands. She was breathing heavily.

"Maggie, it was just dream. You're okay."

She started crying.

I gathered her in my arms. Her body was warm. She wore a cream fitted thermal pajama top; it may not have been lingerie, but she still looked good to me.

"Why does this keep happening? When will they end?" She pulled back and looked at me with a confused expression. "Wait—what time is it? Why are you here, in your boxers?" She looked at her clock; it read one a.m.

"I thought I wouldn't have to answer that question until morning. Uh… well, we're hanging around together today, right? So I thought I'd get here early."

Smooth.

"You never left." She smiled.

"No, I couldn't leave you, not the way you were feeling when you went to bed." I brushed her hair off her face with my fingers. "I couldn't let you go that easy. I wanted to be here in the morning so we could talk. I hope you're not mad."

"No, it feels comforting to have you here after my nightmare. Now maybe I won't have to go watch television to clear my mind." She rubbed the back of my hand.

"Well, I'm sure we could find some old movie to entertain us if you want. I don't mind."

"No, I think I'll try to get back sleep. I'm really tired. Besides, I need energy for tomorrow. Who knows what you have in store for me?"

"Okay then. You think you can sleep now?"

"Yeah, thanks."

"Sweet dreams."

I returned to the guest room and climbed into bed. I lay there with my arm behind my head, the other resting across my stomach. Thoughts of how I could make her mine racing through my mind, I drifted back to sleep.

~

I woke up to a cold wet nose and a tongue bath.

"Oh, Clipper, what time is it?" I rolled over to look at the clock: 7:10. "Do you need to go out, boy?"

After I got dressed, I looked in Maggie's room. It was still dark, and I noticed the silhouette of her body in the bed. I quietly closed the door and went downstairs. The snow had stopped, leaving in its wake a scenic winter wonderland. The rising sun reflected off the trees and white ground; everything sparkled. The air was crisp and clean. Clipper and I were the first to leave tracks in the snow as we crunched our way around the neighborhood.

I was glad I'd started the coffee brewing before we left. The chill had made its way into my bones, and when I walked into the house the aroma hit me, suddenly relaxing every muscle in my body. I fed Clipper and poured a cup. After he finished eating we went into the family room.

The sunshine penetrated the windows and fell on the chocolate-colored throw rug in front of the fireplace where Clipper made his bed. I sat on the couch facing the fireplace and looked out the window toward the street at the freshly fallen snow. Remembering the chill in the air, I decided to light a fire; what else was there for me to do while Maggie slept?

Logs waited next to the fireplace, and I located the matches on the hearth. There were little wax candle cups to use as kindling that gave off the mixed scent of warm spices. On the mantle I saw a picture of Tim and Maggie taken on a vacation, maybe in Hawaii, because they were wearing leis. They looked happy together, smiling and hugging. *It's no wonder she misses him. They were happily married and had many dreams left to achieve together.*

I hoped Maggie would come down soon to enjoy the fire with me as she woke up. I could hold her in my arms and comfort her the way I knew how.

Instead I sat alone watching the first logs burn out and thought about how we could spend our day together. We could go holiday shopping or sledding or head back to the woods to our thoughtful spot, where we opened up and shared our feelings about Tim and how we all came together as one. Or better yet, we could get a Christmas tree. I noticed she didn't have any Christmas decorations out.

"Good morning." Her voice broke the silence and my planning for the day.

I stood and walked over to her. "Good morning. Did you sleep better after I left you? I didn't hear you call out again."

"Yeah, it was probably the best sleep I've had in months." She bent down to give love to Clipper. "It probably had something to do with a certain someone being down the hallway from me." She smiled up at me. "I am very sorry about last night. I'm glad you stayed so we can talk about it before too much time passes by. You didn't deserve what I said to you or how I treated you. You have been so kind to me, and I completely freaked out on you."

"Stop. Please don't worry. I get what you are going through. I've suffered loss, but not the magnitude that you have. I know the pain and fears that come with losing a love one. All I can tell you is that it will get better. Things will be different. You'll have to learn to accept that — it's going to take time."

She hugged me. "You're really the best! Thank you."

I could have held her all day.

"Is there more coffee for me? I would love to sit and enjoy this dying fire with you." She laughed.

"I'll add some logs. Go fetch your coffee."

I stoked the fire with new logs, and hot orange flames shot up the chimney. Just like the fire, the energy between us had changed; we could joke again.

~

I spoke with my mother on Sunday, a week before Christmas.

"I'm sorry, Mom, I'm staying here for the holiday. I know it's been two years since I celebrated with you."

She was not happy, "I don't like to hear that you chose to put work over Christmas, instead of taking time to come home. We miss having you here."

I missed the sun-filled days in California, and a break from the cold weather certainly wouldn't be a bad thing, but I wasn't willing to leave Maggie on her first Christmas. It would be a hard day for her, and I wanted to be close by if she needed me.

"Mom, maybe I'll take some time in January to come home or maybe you'd like to come out here?" Crazy question; my mother was not a fan of New England winters.

"That's a nice invitation, Will. Although I've never experienced winter in New England, I've heard all about them and nothing could make me want to go to Boston in January."

"Okay, I know. I'll figure out a good time to visit you and call you soon, love you."

"I love you, too."

I pulled into the tree lot as I finished my conversation with my mother. Maggie had planned on me picking her up to finish some Christmas shopping, or so she thought. I knew Maggie still hadn't bought a tree, and she was in for a surprise.

I called her as I was driving into her neighborhood.

"I'm right around the corner. Can you open your front door? I have something for you." I wondered if my excitement penetrated through the phone. I was like a little kid on Christmas morning. She was going to be blown away when saw the tree that I'd bought for her. It stood over eight feet and would fit nicely in her family room with its cathedral ceilings.

As I pulled into her driveway, I saw her standing in the front door, her arms wrapped around her body; the temperature was below freezing.

I called out and told her to wait for me in the family room. Carrying the tree up the front stairs and through the door was not an easy feat. It was no wonder she hadn't bought a tree; she would have had a hard time carrying one in alone.

"Close your eyes." Clipper was all over me and the tree, sniffing like crazy. "Can you call Clipper to you? Don't open your eyes yet. Give me a second."

I placed the bottom of the tree on the top of my boot to save the floor from getting dirty, and I surveyed the room, looking for the best spot for the tree. To the right of the fireplace in front of the oversized window seemed ideal; that way passers-by could appreciate its beauty.

I carried it there, kicked Clipper's bed aside, held it with one hand and rested the tree on top of my boot, and told her to open her eyes. I held my breath and waited.

"Oh my! Will, you got me a tree!"

Her tears started to fall. I think they were happy tears, because she was smiling through them.

"Thank you!" She walked over and wrapped her arms around me while I held the tree. "It's perfect."

And then I let my breath out.

"I hope you have enough decorations to cover this whole thing. I got you a big one!"

I lit a fire and Maggie put on Christmas music. We spent the entire morning and most of the afternoon retrieving decorations and decorating the tree and the house.

I was outside wrapping the light pole with garland and lights that afternoon when a neighbor passed by.

"Oh, it's nice to see Maggie getting in the holiday spirit; such a shame what happened to Tim."

Maggie was walking down the walkway, bringing me the extension cord.

The woman continued, "So are you her new boyfriend?"

I didn't know how to answer that. I looked to Maggie for direction.

"No, we are just friends. Will is helping me get the big jobs done for the holiday."

Okay, so now I knew I wasn't her boyfriend. *Glad to clear that up.*

"Well, I hope you have a lovely holiday. Merry Christmas."

"Thank you, Mrs. Wicket. You too."

Maggie turned to me. "Sorry about that. That woman is the neighborhood gossip. She would love nothing more than to shoot her mouth off if she thinks I'm hooking up with you — 'and oh so soon after Tim's death.'" She mimicked her and then started laughing.

I joined in; she did a really good impression of the busybody.

"Some people don't know when to mind their own business. I think we should have given her something to talk about, just for fun," I teased.

"Yeah, but you don't have to live here and face them every day."

"I suppose not."

I could understand what Maggie meant. It *was* too soon after Tim's death to move on to a relationship with another man; people really would have strong opinions about it. But I didn't care, because I knew Maggie, and I knew the depth of her love for Tim. There was no question in my mind that she loved him and wanted nothing more than to wake up from the frightening nightmare that had become her reality to find him next to her. I had also learned that life for those left behind goes on; she still had a lot of living to do.

After the garland and lights were hung, I let Maggie have the honor of plugging in the cord. We stood shoulder to shoulder, appreciating our hard work.

But quickly Maggie said, "Let's go get warm."

I was right behind her.

The fire was roaring, throwing out heat as Christmas carols rang out. Maggie lit candles that smelled like freshly baked cookies, and the mood was festive, even if Maggie was on the verge of crying at any given moment.

She was setting up her manger on a shelf near the Christmas tree when I walked up to her.

"How are you doing? There must be a lot of emotions inside of you right now. In every box you open there are reminders of Tim and memories from the past." I rubbed her arm.

"Aren't you brave to ask? I guess my crying fits don't affect you, huh?"

"Oh, they do—trust me. But I know this isn't easy. The Christmas after Melissa and Bobby left tore me up. One day when I was trying to get in the Christmas spirit by decorating, I opened a box and found a picture that Bobby had drawn for me. It wrecked me. I had to close the box and move on. I was a mess. We weren't together for very long, but I fell hard for her and for Bobby. He was a great kid. Seeing the picture stirred up all the old feelings, and it was like losing them all over again."

"That must have been hard for you." Maggie rubbed my back.

"Yeah, it was, but in time I got over it. I didn't fall in love after that. I never thought I would ever find someone who made me feel the way Melissa did." I looked at her sympathetically, trying to see if she understood that the situations were quite similar, except my girlfriend didn't die. She'd moved more than a thousand miles away, which felt like death to me.

"You still have time. You're young and quite handsome; you'll find some lady and make her quite happy. I'm sure of it." She smiled and patted my back.

"Maybe you're right. Maybe I'm closer than I think."

I headed to the kitchen to make us hot cocoa, letting her ponder what I had said. I learned that words with distance worked better than pouring it on too strong and adding physical touch. Slowly, I was discovering a way into her world. I could let her know I was interested, but also be patient because I had nowhere else to be.

Maggie

I WALKED INTO MY MOTHER'S HOUSE ON CHRISTMAS EVE, balancing bags of gifts in my hands and arms. "Merry Christmas, everyone!"

The kitchen was hopping with energy: my mom and John were preparing the hors d'oeuvres and Alison and Keith were arguing over the proper holiday music.

"No, we need classic holiday music, not rock-n-roll takes over Christmas." Alison had her hand on the play button.

"Come on, Al, this is going to put me to sleep." Keith sounded like he was losing the battle.

I set down the gifts I brought and walked over to Alison. I always had my sister's back. "It's two against one, Keith! Classic Christmas music it will be." I played the song and followed it up with, "Maybe later when we clean-up we can rock out." He smiled at me, knowing he had lost.

A couple of weeks earlier, my mother and I had discussed inviting Tim's family over for dinner; it would be nice for all of us to be together for the holiday. Betsy was overjoyed when I invited them.

When Tim's parents walked into my parent's house, it was harder than I thought it would be to see them. I had to stop myself from calling out to Tim to tell him they had arrived, as I had automatically done in the past. I thought no one noticed, but Alison had and she came over.

"You okay?" She put her arm around my shoulder.

"I think so. You saw that, huh?"

"I felt it more than I saw it. Old habits, that's all. Shake it off — you're doing really well. I know this must be extremely hard on you. I'm proud of you; you're a tough girl, Maggie."

"Thanks, Alison. This is tougher than anything I've had to do before. I thought nothing could be worse than losing Dad, but boy, was I wrong." I turned to hug her before I greeted Tim's parents.

"Hi, Betsy, Edward. Merry Christmas." I hugged them both.

"Merry Christmas, Maggie. Don't you look stunning?" Betsy was taking in the details of my dress; I could see she approved.

"Thanks." I wore the dress I bought for Will's holiday party; I was embarrassed and felt dishonest. I suddenly felt like I shouldn't have worn it; it was a dress from my new life, a life I was building without their son.

The evening passed pleasantly enough. I was gratified that I made it through with minimal tears, at least until after dessert, when I shared tea with my mother and Tim's mother in the living room. I sat next to my mother. Christmas carols were playing in the kitchen. I looked around at my mother's Christmas decorations on display and noticed my favorite one set up on the buffet table. It was a collection of white snow angels standing on a layer of fake snow with their hands folded and eyes shut; they were sprinkled with glitter and sparkled in the light. I smiled as I thought about past Christmases when I helped my mother decorate; it was one of my favorite times of the year.

Betsy said how much she enjoyed Will's company; she thought he would be joining us for Christmas. I explained that he was working to allow another firefighter to be at home with his young children.

"Oh, that Will is the nicest man I have ever met. He's so caring, isn't he?"

"Yeah, he certainly is."

"He has made himself quite available to you, hasn't he?" She sipped her tea.

What is she getting at? I looked at my mother, who sat quietly, looking straight ahead and sipping her tea.

"I think he is trying to help me because he was very fond of Tim. There's really nothing more to it, Betsy."

"Well, I hear about the many ways he has helped you through your grief, and I think it's commendable. I also think he's fond of you." She added and sipped from her teacup.

I thought I would die. "What? Have you two been talking?" I stared at my mother.

Betsy cut in. "There's nothing to talk about, Maggie. I saw the interaction between the two of you at the fire station on Thanksgiving. It's hard to miss love when it's staring you in the face."

"Betsy, I really wish you wouldn't talk about this. I miss Tim terribly and have a hard time envisioning my future without him." I took a deep breath and pushed the tears from my eyes. I felt my blood moving through my veins. I was in shock that I could be having a conversation like this with my deceased husband's mother.

"I'm just telling you that when you are ready, Will is a wonderful man, and I think Tim would be delighted to know you two are together. Will has had a positive effect on you, honey." She smiled at me as she spoke her warm and encouraging words.

I thought I was going to throw up. Had my mother put her up to this?

"Mom?"

"What, dear? I have nothing to do with this. I've already told you we notice how you are when Will is around and how you act when you talk about him. I think Betsy is giving you her blessing."

"She's right, Maggie. I don't want to intrude. I simply just wanted to let you know that I think it would be wonderful if you and Will were in a relationship."

My teacup began to rattle on the saucer. I set it down on the coffee table, stunned by their words. What was happening? Was everyone going mad? How could they even dream of me being with Will?

Or, maybe what was wrong with me that I couldn't allow myself to be with him?

~

Later, I was at the sink, barefoot, having abandoned my heels. Keith was beside me drying dishes, a job my sister put him up to I was sure.

"Maggie, I wanted to tell you that you look pretty tonight, and… it was weird not having Tim here."

At least he didn't mention Will.

Throughout the experience of Tim's dying, I'd learned that some-times people wanted to share their emotions over losing him, whether they were a friend or relative. I knew that was what Keith was doing. He wasn't trying to make me sad; he was sharing, in hopes of helping him feel better himself.

"Yeah, it must have been pretty boring for you without him here to listen to your stories and keep you company, but I think we all did just fine tonight."

"I'm surprised how much I miss him. I mean, we weren't that close, but we were family. He always loved my stories about tearing up the track on my bike. I don't know if you knew this, but he loved it when I sent him pictures from the events I was in, like the designs on the other bikes I was racing against or pictures of the arena; weird things like that. I can't tell you how often I reached for my phone at recent events, thinking 'Tim would love this,' only to stop and remind myself that he's gone."

"I didn't know that you did that." I turned my back to the sink and rested against the counter, trying to imagine Tim being interested in Keith's world. "I know it's hard. It hasn't been that long, but they say with time it gets easier. I don't know, though. Every morning I still roll over in bed thinking he'll be there, only to realize I'm alone."

I was surprised when Keith opened his arms and hugged me. "You'll never be alone, Maggie."

I thought about Keith telling me about how he had shared pictures with Tim, and it hurt, just like when his coworkers told me how he used to try sushi at lunch, hoping that just one time he would find a combination he enjoyed. I guess you can never know everything about a person, even when you're married.

~

I didn't hesitate when my mother suggested that I sleep over on Christmas Eve. Clipper and I didn't need to wake up alone on Christmas morning.

I was in my childhood bedroom buttoning up my red holiday pajamas when I heard a knock on my door.

"Come in."

Mom peeked around the door. "Hi, honey. I hope I'm not disturbing you."

"Not at all. Come on in. I was just getting more comfortable. What's up?"

"First, I wanted to tell you that you made it through the party with aplomb. I never once doubted that you were a strong woman, but tonight I watched you, and not once did I see you waver from your effort to remain strong under the circumstances. You're amazing to me, stronger than I ever was."

"Mom, your situation was very different from mine; you had two children and twelve years of marriage. Not to take away from my suffering, but you had a lot more to lose than I did. I love you, Mom." I hugged her.

"I love you too, so very much. I'm sorry if the conversation with Betsy upset you, but she wanted to let you know how she felt." We held each other and I was thankful to be here with my family for support.

"It came as a shock to me, that's all. I'll be okay."

"Oh, one more thing… Speaking about being shocked, you may want to go downstairs and save Will from John. I think he'll talk his ear off about the time the fire department went to his house when he was kid because a squirrel was stuck in his fireplace."

"What?" I pulled away. "Will's here? Like, right now, downstairs?" I pointed to the floor.

"Yup, and he has something for you. Better hurry, he's still working."

I ran downstairs thinking, *He can't just show up at my mother's house in the middle of his shift! What is he thinking? And what was I thinking when I packed my red one-piece Christmas pajamas with the button-up bottoms?* I would never live this down; I should have at least put on my bathrobe!

I walked into the family room, and John left to give us privacy.

"Hi. What are you doing here? Aren't you working?" I walked toward him, my arms folded in front of me, trying to hide my embarrassment about my pajamas.

He got up off the couch and handed me a gift box wrapped in red paper with a gold bow. He was so much taller than me, especially because I only had socks on. I felt safe with him near me, but I was still shocked that he was in my parents' family room.

"Merry Christmas." He kissed my cheek, and my body temperature rose. His eyes twinkled in the dim room, and he wore a smile that made my stomach flip.

"Thank you. Merry Christmas. What's this? You didn't have to get me a gift."

"I was Christmas shopping for my mother and when I saw it, I thought of you. It's not much, but I wanted to get it for you." He caressed my arm and I felt new energy swarm inside of me. "I can't stay. We're returning from a call in the neighborhood. But I wanted to at least come by and wish you a merry Christmas. Did you have a nice night?"

"Yeah, as good as I could have hoped for." I unwrapped the box as we spoke. I opened the lid, revealing the sentimental hand-painted ornament. I was speechless. I took the red surfboard ornament from the box and held it in my hands. It had the outline of a blue hydrangea painted on it and my name was written in blue letters. On the back were the words, 'steady as you go.' I squeezed his hand.

"I was walking around the mall and when I saw it, I thought of you." He smiled at me. "I thought you could find a nice spot for it on your tree."

The gift struck a tender spot inside of me. I appreciated his thoughtfulness and got choked up. I replied, "This is the most beautiful gift I have ever received. Thank you." I set it down on the table and hugged him.

"So I'll see you in a couple days, right?" We walked to the door. I wished he could have stayed longer, so I could enjoy the security I felt when I was with him. He had become the harbor in the storm of my life.

"Yeah, I'm looking forward to it." As he reached for the doorknob, he stopped and turned around. "Wait—you didn't really think I was going to leave without a comment about your pajamas, did you?"

"I was hoping." I hung my head.

"Where would someone buy something like them anyway? Not that I'm interested, but *wow*! Really?" He shook his head and chuckled.

"Okay—leave me alone. They're festive!" I slapped his arm.

"I guess." He kissed my cheek for the second time and looked into my eyes. "Good night."

"Good night. Thanks for stopping by." My insides stirred and I didn't want him to leave.

I laughed when I looked down the driveway and saw the huge fire engine parked at the end of it. I thought, *Only Will...*

~

On Monday when I went into work, Henrik Bauer, a very attractive German doctor who had recently started working in the ER, stopped me outside the elevator. I hadn't yet worked with him because our schedules didn't match up, but I had heard his name many times. All the young nurses were talking about his German accent, his blond hair cut short but long enough on top that you could see the waves; his eyes were ocean blue. Oh, if I heard about his blue eyes one more time I thought I'd go mad! Molly would have loved to be in my position when he walked up to me.

"Hi, Maggie. It's Maggie, right?" His accent made my name sound more formal.

I nodded.

"Hi, I'm Henrik, a doctor here in the ER. I don't think we've met." He reached out his hand.

"No, we haven't. We must be on a different rotation. It's nice to meet you." Thinking we were done, I started walking away.

"Wait, there's something I wanted to ask you." He caught up with me and walked beside me as I made my way to the nurses' station. "You caught my eye the other day in the cafeteria. A fellow doctor told me your name and encouraged me to invite you to his New Year's Eve party in Boston. I was hoping you would come with me, be my date."

I was hoping I'd misunderstood him because of his thick German accent, but the way he stood like a puppy dog waiting for me to give him a bone told me I'd heard him correctly. His eyebrows were raised, and his eyes glinted: *Come on, let me have it! Give me the bone.*

He was excited and not ready for rejection. I thought for a brief moment about my mother and the dates she had said no to and the regret she had about them. But this guy was not worth my time; he was too eager. I'd rather celebrate New Year's Eve alone at my house with Clipper beside me.

"I'm sorry, I'm not in the right place emotionally right now for dating. Perhaps you can ask someone else." I tried to walk away, but he stopped me.

"What do you mean? I am just asking for the night, not a commitment." His voice was soaked with privilege.

"Thanks, but I'm not ready." I picked up a chart and looked it over, hoping he would leave. Other nurses had gathered around, trying to make themselves look busy, but I knew they really wanted to hear what was going on. A rooster was in the hen house and all the hens were on guard. In my mind his persistence made him a cock.

"Really, no?" He looked confused. He wasn't leaving.

I looked him square in the eye. "Really, no." I walked away and didn't look back, but I heard the gasps, followed by several rounds of, "Hi, Dr. Bauer."

Uh, I think I'll puke! I wouldn't want a man like that if he was the last one on earth. What did the girls see in him besides his good looks? He was too assertive and self-absorbed for my liking.

We had a busy day before my shift ended, and I never laid eyes on Dr. Henrik Bauer again. Molly walked up to me as I was gathering my things to go home.

"Maggie, can I ask you something? Why did you turn down the most eligible bachelor in the hospital? Are you crazy, woman?" Her arms were folded on the top of the desk as she waited for my answer.

"Molly, I'm not ready. I know he is really good-looking. Maybe two years from now I'll kick my butt for saying no, but did you see how upset he got? Like he expected me to say yes. He's a bit pompous, not my type." I threw my bag over my shoulder. "Maybe you should ask him to the party. I think you like him," I kidded.

"Oh, I could never ask him. I'd be too afraid he'd say no."

"Then get him to ask you. Start hanging out near him when you're working, and get him to notice you. Or better yet, go to the party in a really sexy dress. He'll fall all over you and your sexy body. He just can't appreciate it under those scrubs," I teased.

"Will you come with me?"

"What, after I just shot him down? Are you crazy?" We headed outside and walked to our cars. "I can't handle crowds yet, especially the couple thing. It makes me too emotional. I told you about Will's holiday party and how I embarrassed myself, remember."

"I get it. Maybe Sue will come with me."

"She would be fun to party with. I think you should ask her." Molly loved going out and meeting new people.

"What are your plans?"

"Well, Will has the night off. We talked about hanging out, getting dinner, maybe watching some movies. I'm really not in the mood to go out. I love my house." I laughed.

"That sounds like a nice evening, very casual. How is Will?"

My cheeks burned, and I felt my expression soften. I was glad she couldn't see my face.

"He's good. Did I tell you he surprised me at my mother's on Christmas Eve with a beautiful hand-painted Christmas tree ornament? It was so thoughtful. I hung it on the front of my tree."

"What else happened?"

"He had to get back to work so he didn't stay long. When we talked on the phone on Christmas he told me he's going home to see his family in California the beginning of February."

We arrived at my car. "I'm kind of nervous about not having him around. He's been a nice distraction from my sadness and he's there when I need company."

"Just call me up. I'll keep you company." Molly winked before she started to walk over to her car. She called out, "Hey, wanna go shopping on Thursday and help me pick out a New Year's Eve dress to knock over Dr. Bauer? Come on, it'll be fun."

"Yeah, sounds good."

~

I called Will on my way home. He was already at my house, hanging out with Clipper.

"Hey, you're already there?"

"Yeah, well. I was off all day and I knew Clipper was here alone, so I came early. I started some dinner for us."

"Really?"

"Yeah, nothing too elaborate, just a roast, mashed potatoes, and green beans. It should be ready when you get here."

"You spoil me. Will I have time to jump in the shower? I want to clean up before we eat."

"Yeah, I think can I allow that." He laughed. "Drive safe."

I walked through the door and was greeted by the pleasant aroma of a homemade dinner; a fire was burning in the fireplace, and relaxing soft music played. All I needed was a hot shower to feel perfect. I quickly washed my hair and body, soaping the day off me until I felt refreshed. I felt like a new woman when I went back into the kitchen.

"Don't you look smashing? I wish I knew it was a dress-down dinner." He was smiling as he lit the candles on the table.

"What—did you expect a cocktail dress? Please, you know me by now; it's always yoga pants and a sweatshirt. I thought you were going to give me grief because I'm not wearing Tim's sweatshirt, not over my whole outfit."

I poured the drinks; it was the least I could do.

"Where is the sweatshirt? Did it turn back into thread?" He chuckled.

"No. I just decided that I would shake it up; I bought this on my last trip to the Cape with Tim, so it's still sentimental." It was hot pink, and white letters spelled out Cape Cod.

He held out the chair for me. "Well, it's very high fashion for our simple meal."

I noticed he was wearing dark jeans and light gray fitted sweater that accentuated his toned torso. And as he leaned next to me to push the chair in, I inhaled his cologne. A flash of heat washed over me.

I was definitely attracted to him; why wouldn't I be? He was gorgeous—tall, muscular, with dark brown hair and dark, warm, inviting eyes. It took willpower not to throw myself at him. It would have ruined our friendship if I did that. He meant too much to me to make our time together about remedial sex. And I wasn't entirely sure that's how Will would think of it; it would probably be more like pitiful sex, and that was worse. I figured Will would only be intimate because he felt bad for me. I was too old for that kind of relationship.

During dinner we talked about our day. I shared my run-in with Dr. Bauer, but Will didn't see the humor in it. He became defensive instead.

"He, what, followed you down the hallway? Go on—then what?" He took a bite of food and stared at me.

"He asked me out! Can you believe it? He actually asked me out for New Year's Eve!" I described how pushy he got and that he couldn't handle the rejection. I laughed as I told the story.

" I was so surprised! Every nurse in the place had their tongues out, drooling over him, and he picked me! Imagine—me." I shook my head. "Me over all those other beautiful, younger nurses. I've still got it!" I was acting all confident until I looked up from my plate at Will, expecting him to be grinning, but instead I saw a dark place between irritation and anger open on his face. It was not a typical Will reaction.

"Are you okay?" I asked.

"Yeah, I'm sorry. I hate hearing that a man would treat you like that. He didn't touch you, did he?"

"Will, be serious. There were five other nurses watching. No, he didn't touch me. Besides, I walked away as soon as I could."

"Well, what did you tell him?"

I heard hesitation in his voice.

"You don't honestly think I said yes, do you? Do I need to remind you that I couldn't even handle your holiday party? You think I'd say yes to a New Year's Eve party with a man I don't even know? You're crazier than him."

"Just checking. He is a doctor, after all, a single, available doctor. I know how women think." He took a bite of his roast, and his demeanor returned to normal. He seemed relieved.

I was pretty sure I had just witnessed a moment of jealousy. Maybe my mom was right; maybe he did have feelings for me. Why else would he react that way? It was reassuring to know Will cared that I was treated right by a man. I could never imagine Will treating a woman the way I was treated earlier today.

~

Will arrived at five on New Year's Eve dressed in jeans and a long sleeved tee-shirt under a fleece. I had warned him that it would be a dress-down evening: no fancy dress. In fact, the more cotton the better!

I greeted him at the door wearing my yoga pants and a light green fleece. I'd made an effort to not wear anything with a connection to Tim—well, nothing obvious. As strong as I tried to be, I always felt better wearing something that reminded me of Tim, so I settled on the undies he'd given me for Valentine's Day last year. Thank goodness my pants were black, because if they were white Will would see right through them to the red hearts.

"Hi! You ready to get the goods?"

"Sure am."

We left Clipper behind and headed to the grocery store.

I pushed the cart around as Will loaded it with our favorite snack foods.

"We are going to be sick if we eat all this," he said.

"We don't have to eat all of it tonight. We can settle for a snack plate with small helpings of everything we buy." I stopped so he could put a box of crackers in the cart.

"Yeah, because a plate of cheese and crackers, Doritos, a Hershey bar, Kalamata olives, and candy canes all complement each other so well. Sounds like a real nice snack, Barrett." He held up each food as he mentioned it.

I laughed. I liked the way he called me Barrett when he thought I was acting really crazy or silly. It was our thing, a secret playful exchange between the two of us.

"Everyone's taste buds are different, so suit yourself. I think it sounds heavenly, if you eat them in the right order, starting with the salty snacks and ending with the sweet ones. Seems perfect to me!"

"I'll take the Doritos, thanks."

We decided on steamed lobster for dinner. Will wanted to make me a special meal to celebrate the new year ahead and encourage me to welcome it with a revived attitude.

We finished our junk food shopping spree and walked to Will's truck. It was so easy to be with him. He kidded with me, which helped me relax, and he never let me get away with saying anything to deflate my sense of happiness or anything that he thought was untrue, like when I cried, saying my life would never be happy again, or "How can I go on living without Tim?" My mother and sister, and even Molly, just said "Oh, don't say that," but Will held me accountable and said things like, "Well if you keep telling yourself that, you're right. It won't." Or, "you're not the first one to go through something like this. Many people have, including your mother, and look how their lives have gone on. You'll be okay."

He wasn't afraid to be honest with me. Everyone else tip-toed around my feelings and treated me gently when I was sad, but I knew what Will was thinking. There were no invisible walls between us and that made it easier to be myself with him. Could I really have been so lucky as to have found two loves in one lifetime?

I ate too much junk food while we watched old movies. Just before midnight Will popped a bottle a champagne, poured it into crystal flute glasses, each holding a strawberry, and then made a toast.

"To Maggie, the fiery redhead in my life. You came into my life through my dear friend Tim. You were his gift to me, and I will always be thankful for meeting him. Together we have grieved for his loss. As much as I miss hanging out with him, you have filled the empty spot he left. I promise you, I will always be here for you, no matter what. You mean a lot to me." His eyes were focused and intense; he was honestly letting me know exactly how he felt. "I want this new year to be the best year of your life, because you deserve to have happiness and peace. Happy New Year."

"Happy New Year! Cheers."

How could I follow that toast? The truth he spoke to me made me emotional. I could barely swallow as I fought back tears. I stood looking up at his face with a small smile on mine. I found such comfort in his face. I pushed down the knot in my throat and dried my cheeks before speaking.

"Will, I feel like the luckiest girl having you in my life, supporting me through my grief and loneliness without Tim. I'm grateful that you two met and that he probably paid you to keep me company." I laughed. One of us had to lighten the mood a little. He shook his head and smirked. "Okay, all kidding aside, thank you for everything you've done for me. You'll never know how much it has meant to me. Happy New Year."

We sipped our champagne on the couch and watched the ball fall. He leaned over and whispered, "You know, they say you have to kiss the person you spend New Year's Eve with so you'll have love all year long." He puckered up. And he waited.

I stared at him; he looked like a fish.

"Really? So if I don't kiss you I'll be sad and lonely all year." He didn't flinch.

"Well, I might as well kiss you then, because I'm already sad and lonely most days. I can't imagine feeling this way every day for a year."

He maintained the expression on his face and didn't twitch or make any movement. *What a patient guy.*

I leaned in to peck his fish lips, and he opened his mouth on mine. Heat rose inside of me, and my heart raced. I kissed him back. It felt so good to express my feelings for him. Emotions poured through me like water through open flood gates. He pulled me into his arms and kissed me with more passion. He moved his hand up on the outside of my thigh. I stopped and pulled away. Breathing heavily, I rose from the couch and walked over to the fireplace.

"I can't do this. I'm sorry. It'll change everything between us, and I can't let that happen."

"Maggie, come on. You know how I feel about you. I would never hurt you." He stood by the couch, hesitant.

I cut him off. "Will, it's too soon, I just…" My words trailed off. "I just can't act on my feelings for you, not now. It's only been three months since Tim died. I can't disrespect his memory like that."

"I understand. I'll never force you to do anything you're uncomfortable with. I'm sorry I let that happen." He picked up the glasses and started to walk towards the kitchen.

"Will," I called out, "don't be sorry that it happened. You made me feel alive again. It was a very nice kiss. Happy New Year."

"Thanks. Happy New Year." A half smile and a remorseful expression spilled across his face.

~

Will and I continued to see each other as much as we could over the next few weeks, which was hard because his scheduled work days often fell on my days off. On the days he was off and I had to work, I would find him waiting for me at my house with a warm dinner and a tired dog. On those nights when I saw him for a few hours, my happiness increased.

We agreed that he would spend the nights in the guest room. We were both adults and in control of our emotions. I couldn't understand why he should have to drive across town to sleep when I had a bed for him in the guest room. I wish I could have told him that I honestly slept better with him in the house; on a subconscious level I could relax, knowing someone else was with me besides Clipper. But I didn't want him to think he had to devote his free nights to sleeping in my house. I thought I might have to a get a house-mate if I wanted to continue to sleep peacefully.

Our routine mostly mimicked my old routine with Tim; it was funny how it fell in line. Will would walk Clipper before bed. I would say good night to him as they left then I would get ready for bed. Tim would have come to bed and we would have made love before turning out the lights, but on the nights Will was there, after his walk with Clipper Will opened my door and let the dog in. Then I swear he waited outside my closed bedroom door. Some nights when I felt his presence there, I yearned to open the door and invite him in and ask him to hold me. I missed the security a man's embrace offered and the closeness of another human being; my mother always said I was a cuddle bug, while my sister couldn't get away fast enough.

~

I tossed and turned as images of my father played out in my head, deep, suppressed memories of him from vacations we took to the beach when I was younger. We were flying a butterfly kite as the sun warmed the air and sand; the wind blew my hair around. He was trying to keep Alison's kite from crossing mine, laughing. Then the images changed to the day he walked me and Alison to the bus stop. My sister and I hugged him good-bye and climbed the stairs into the bus. He blew us a good-bye kiss, and we chuckled in our seats. The imaged flashed to the day I rode my bike all by myself, and his words, "Steady as you go," rang in my ears as the wind whipped by me.

Then the images came faster and the edges became distorted like a freaky circus show: there was my childhood house the day he died, with hundreds of cars parked out front of it. I walked into my kitchen and everyone turned around. They were all wearing makeup. Sad clown faces stared at me and my sister, and when I turned to look at Alison, she was wearing a clown face too.

Next came images of the burning building. The fire lit up the night sky, and I could feel the heat. I was there, a little girl standing in my nightgown with bare feet. I could hear the fire crunching and hissing, eating its way through the wood and interior contents. Men's voices yelled to one another as the tension grew. Something was wrong—my breathing increased, my heart pounded. I looked around and yelled but no one could hear me; the words came out in a whisper. Then I saw him, my daddy.

"No, Daddy! Don't go in! Come home; come home."

He ran fast toward the building. "Stop, Daddy," I yelled, my chest tight. I couldn't hear myself.

"I need to get him!" he called out to the chief, and he ran into the building. I waited and waited before falling onto my knees. Then I felt light again; someone picked me up and carried me to my childhood bedroom and placed me in my bed. When I looked up at the face, I saw that it was Will.

He'd rescued me again.

I shot upright in bed and gasped for air. I had been yelling in my sleep. I switched on the light next to my bed. Clipper came to the side of my bed just as the door flew open. Will ran to my bed and tried to calm me.

"It's okay, I'm here." He held me and slowly rocked me. "Another nightmare, huh?"

I held on tight. I wanted to forget the images from my nightmare. His body was still warm from being wrapped up under the blankets of his bed. I found refuge in his arms from the horrible visions that plagued my mind. I shook, and his warm hands rubbed my back to calm me. Tears rolled down my cheeks onto his chest. Between sobs I said, "It's a good thing you're not wearing a shirt. I would be ruining it again."

"Oh, Maggie." I heard his compassion.

He released me to hold my face between his hands and wipe away my tears with his thumbs. I looked at his chest and saw the moisture my tears had left, and I started to wipe it away. His skin was soft under my fingers. I watched goosebumps appear where my fingers had been. I looked up into his eyes and saw protection in them. I was groggy and felt vulnerable, and I leaned in and offered him my lips. He returned my kiss and laid me on my back. My tank top strap fell off my shoulder and he kissed where it had been. My skin was exploding with heat, and I let out of soft moan. Shocked, I heard the sound I made, and I pushed Will away and gathered the sheets around my body.

"Will, I'm sorry. I can't. I know I started this, but I can't." I started bawling. "When will this feel right? When will I actually feel that it's okay to be with you?" I held my face in my hands. "I'm so sorry."

"I don't know, but I will wait for you." He paused. "Because I know that what we have is special." He kissed the top of my head.

After I reassured him I could sleep, he tucked in the side of my bed and left me, leaving the door slightly open. Clipper jumped up on the bed. I cried myself to sleep.

Will

OFTEN BEFORE I WENT OVER TO HANG OUT WITH MAGGIE, I would stop by the cemetery to talk to Tim. I was thankful that he and I had spoken before he died about what would become of Maggie after his death. My emotions toward her were more intense than I ever could have imagined. The caretaker inside me had awakened to a new level. All I wanted to do was to make her smile and feel happy. I wanted to show my love for her and have her return the love I knew she had for me, but every time we got close she pulled back.

When I was lost about how to break through Maggie's barriers of resistance, I would talk to Tim as if he were still alive.

"Hi, buddy. Some mess you left me in. Did you know it was going to go down like this? Is that why you were so adamant that I was not to leave her? She certainly is torn with anything more than a friendship." I crouched over, picking up and releasing fistfuls of cold fresh snow. "She is an amazing woman. I can see why you needed me to protect her; a couple of men have already asked her out." Aside from the doctor, Maggie told me a couple of other men who worked in the hospital had asked her to dinner and a young man who came to the ER with injuries invited her to his college frat house party. I was thankful she turned him down.

"Tim, I'm really trying man, but she is stubborn. She tells me it would never work between us because it's too soon and she doesn't want to disgrace your memory. I think these are excuses she uses to protect herself from feeling guilty about her feelings for me. No matter how much I try to make her see that living a *safe* life with you didn't end so well for her, she won't give into her feelings for me." I looked up to the sky. "Can you help me a little? You must have some pull from your vantage point."

A breeze kicked up from nowhere and blew the light snow around my feet. I think it was a sign from Tim.

I left the cemetery and I thought about Maggie as I drove. I would wait for her to become comfortable with her feelings toward me. I had to because nothing else felt as real in my life as the love I had for her. She had become part of me. I thought about her during every part of my day. Working distracted me from dreaming about her for a while, but then I would see something or someone that reminded me she was out there waiting for something or someone to save her from the pain and sadness that had taken over her days.

I always planned to be waiting for her at night when she came home from work; she had told me in the beginning that having me there when she walked in took away some of the desolation that she felt after Tim died. From that night on, whenever it was possible for me to be there, I was.

Loving Maggie was easy because our personalities fit each other so well. We balanced each other out. While I was more daring, she grounded me; she made me want to make better choices so I could be around for her. I still loved experiencing the thrill of life, and I always would. It was part of me, but she gave me a reason to think twice.

She was more reserved; I wanted her to embrace life, not hid from it. It was my challenge to encourage her to let go of the story she had been telling herself since she was a child about being afraid to take chances and always choosing safety over fun. I told her she had the power to make choices, safe or fun, and life would turn out the way it was meant to. She had to have learned that from losing her husband.

The give and take in our conversations was effortless. We laughed and enjoyed the ease between us. The more time we spent together talking, the deeper I fell in love with her. I only wished that the three of us, Tim, Maggie, and I, had talked together about Tim's dying wish; it would have made the circumstances between Maggie and me much clearer.

~

I pulled into Maggie's driveway as she was getting into Molly's car, so I parked on the road. Maggie got out and came to say hello.

"Hey, are you here for Clipper? He'll be happy to see you."

Even bundled up in her dark green winter coat she looked amazing; her hair was down and she was wearing her aviator sunglasses, which reflected the eager expression on my face. She was so beautiful. It was beginning to make me uncomfortable to look at her, because I couldn't be with her the way I wanted to. I needed to be patient, but all I really wanted was to take her in my arms and kiss her — and have her kiss me back.

Molly came over then. She was cute with long blonde hair. I couldn't understand why she was single; she seemed nice enough. Maggie had told me about her when we first met; I think she wanted to set me up with her. I'm glad we never went out. Molly seemed like the type of girl I would have had fun with, but nothing more would have come from it. She wasn't what I was looking for in a girlfriend.

"Hi, Will. Do you mind if I take Maggie for the day?" Molly smiled at me.

"Oh, no I am here to get Clipper. We have a date to go for a walk in the woods!" I headed for the house. "You can keep Maggie all day," I joked. "Have fun."

"Thanks! He is so cute!"

I think she meant to whisper it, but it came out loud enough for me to hear. I smiled and chuckled.

I drove out to my favorite place, the place Maggie and I shared, to walk with Clipper and clear my mind. I let him off the leash, and he tore through the snow, kicking it up as he ran. Dogs and snow — it was like crack to them! He made me laugh, and I wondered if he and Jake would get along. Poor Jake. He was so jealous when I showed up at work after spending the day with Clipper; his scent was all over me, and after Jake got a snout full he would retreat to someone else's side.

We walked past the pond, now slightly frozen, not yet solid enough to support any weight. I hoped the kids knew to stay off it. I walked the whole woods that day, hoping to make peace with my new life. It was a new year, and I had an amazing woman to share it with. Even if she wasn't committed to me, I was committed to her. I was the sap in the relationship, willing to do anything to make her happy.

We came out of the woods at dusk and headed to Maggie's, but first I wanted to make a stop.

The house was dark when I pulled up, and I noted my disappointment. Clipper and I went in, and I put on the necessary lights before I fed him.

"She's out late tonight, boy, isn't she?"

I left my surprise on the table with a note that read:

I fed Clipper.
Sweet dreams,
Will

I looked around at the house Tim and Maggie had made their own. It was beautiful and comforting, a true home. I wouldn't mind sharing it with Maggie. I prayed that one day I would.

The drive back to my place was lonely. I sat in my lifeless house watching the end of the Bruins game. My phone rang; caller ID showed Maggie's number.

"Hello."

"Hi. Thank you, Will—they're beautiful. Tulips are my favorite flower."

Her soft voice soothed my soul and filled my ears with rich emotions. Speaking with her on the phone, having her voice so close to my ear, increased my desire to be with her. It was as if her essence was entering my body.

"I know." I sounded confident.

"How did you know that?" She was not buying it.

"I have a good memory. Do you remember when you had me over to dinner last summer? I gave you pink tulips. I'll never forget the look on your face. It was the first time I noticed how beautiful you are. A man doesn't forget a day like that."

"Will, I think I'm blushing." She laughed.

"If I know you as well as I think I do, I'm sure of it."

We spoke on the phone for hours, finally having to say good-bye because she dozed off one too many times. She needed to be up early for work, and I felt guilty for keeping her up so late. It would be too long for me before we saw each other again, and only for one day at that, because I was leaving for California to visit my family.

"So I'll pick you up next Thursday morning, right?" I confirmed.

"Shoot, I forgot."

"What—did you make plans with another admirer?" I teased.

"Mary Ellen asked if I would cover her night shift on Wednesday night and I said yes. I've been feeling guilty about not helping out more. She covered so many shifts for me after Tim died. So when she asked, I felt I owed it to her. I'm sharing it with Molly, and I won't finish 'til one in the morning. I'm sorry. Maybe we can do dinner as a compromise?" I could tell she felt awful that she forgot.

"Yeah, that's fine. I'll take what I can get. Do you want me to cook, or would you rather go out?"

"Let's go out; you're always cooking for me. My treat!"

"Okay, I'll see you next Thursday evening. Take care, you."

I hung up, rolled over, and had fantastic dreams about her all night long.

~

My shifts at work involved the usual tedious winter calls: no heat, carbon-monoxide alarms, chimney fires, car spin-outs, and the rest of the issues that we had to respond to. I loved my job, but sometimes people were just plain stupid. They were in a hurry, racing to get somewhere, speeding in their cars, or lax about leaving food unattended on the stove or in the oven. Some of the calls we responded to made me shake my head.

The call we received early Wednesday morning was anything but tedious, the kind of call that went down as a "good job" that winter. We had been practicing our whole careers for that call.

Dispatch reported smoke from an abandoned building by the river, called in by a woman walking her dog. She smelled it first, and when she made the bend she saw smoke coming out from a broken window on the third floor; there were four floors, not including the basement.

We jumped from our beds, ran to the trucks, dressed in our bunker gear that lay prepared for us, and loaded the fire engines. It was too early in the morning for the sirens. No one was driving on the road near the station, but as we drove along the traffic got thicker, so we alerted the commuters we were coming.

We pulled onto the scene with lights flashing and sirens blaring. Smoke was billowing out from the third-floor window of the abandoned brick building, creating a gray halo around the sky just above the roof. It had been about ten minutes since the call came in. After we stopped the sirens I noticed there were no other alarms; it was an old building and not equipped with smoke alarms. We were lucky the lady had walked by when she did or it could have gotten out of control before we arrived.

First, we needed to check for people or victims. Clearly this fire had been set — arson. I wondered what had been left behind when the previous tenants left the building and hoped we weren't in for any surprises. The main door was boarded up, so Al used the ax to clear an opening. I was the first guy in the building. We performed a search using the thermal imaging camera. We cleared the first floor and made our way up to the second, continuing the search. Finally, we reached the third floor to get as close to the smoldering fire as possible. We found no bodies and no victims.

We saw the fire burning; heavy smoke filled the room. We broke the appropriate windows to ensure the fire would have a place to burn out through and escape. If we could get water on the fire fast, we could put it out in no time. We continued up the staircase to the fourth floor to systematically break windows and vent the building.

When we finished on the fourth floor I turned to my partner, Brian, and pointed that we should go; no one was in the building. As we made our way down to the second floor I noticed the smoke become heavier. I reached for Brian's arm, and we quickly moved down the rest of the stairs. At the bottom I had to remember to keep the wall on my right side, which would lead us out. I was relieved to see Al at the door with a flashlight.

Two went in and two came out; I was relieved.

I told the deputy chief that the smoke was getting heavier and we needed to get water on it fast. He relayed to me that the building was once used to make chemicals for paint products, which made sense given the evidence of leftover chemicals near the entrance and around the building, but before I could tell the chief about the collection of containers I'd noticed in various places, we heard glass shatter.

"Get the water on it now!"

This was not going to be as easy as I'd thought. Just behind the building, on the other side of the tree line, was a new neighborhood containing multimillion dollar homes that concerned the deputy chief. Dead leaves hung on some of the surrounding oak trees; if the wind carried a spark, he worried the trees would burn next.

The deputy chief made a plan to send four guys in with a hose to fight it from within and to lift the ladder truck to approach it from outside. I was sent into the building with Brian, Al, and Jack. We had our orders and by then the smoke that poured out of the windows had turned into angry orange flames rolling outside and up the building, spreading, looking to eat anything in the fire's path. More smoke began to pour out of the adjacent windows. One whole side of the building was swallowed by smoke. Soon fire would be raging through those windows.

We checked our tanks and our gear, and just before we went in I remembered to say a quick prayer to God to watch over us. *Four went in,* I said to myself.

Inside the building, sounds were different from outside. I heard snapping and whistling. Everything was muffled. To me, the most haunting sound was my air flow; I knew it would keep me alive as the smoke expanded around me. Despite my anxiety, I slowed my breathing to conserve my air — slow, even breaths would ensure that my air would last longer. I stayed focused on putting the fire out and not making any mistakes.

We walked through the first floor in a tandem formation, feeling our way against the left wall. I was second in line, with Brian leading the way. Brian held the nozzle of the hose, and we carried it through the door, clearing the first floor. As we felt our way to the second floor the smoke became black and dense. I could hardly make out where we were. The scene had completely changed from when we were in before, but we kept walking and found the stairs on our left. I turned, using the thermal camera, and saw the guys were still behind us. *Four went in.*

Halfway up the stairs Brian stopped and reached his hand back to stop the rest of us. The fire had begun eating its way along the ceiling at the top of the stairs; it spread out like a sheet, covering the ceiling with orange and red waves of color before it crept down the walls. Less intimidating flames flickered around the corner, licking the floor. The fire was coming at us; we had to fight it from below. We backed up and directed the water flow to the top of the stairs. We wouldn't be able to get access to the fire from our vantage point if we lost the stair-case.

Smoke and flames stared down on us; we sprayed water at them, back and forth, winning and losing as the fire lunged at us. It had more strength behind it, forcing it toward us and giving it life. The heat was intense. Sweat dripped down my back.

We stayed in the building as long as we could. I wasn't sure we'd made progress, but we kept the second floor from burning. I was hoping the crew on the ladder was having more success fighting it from outside.

We made our way out through the smoke, and four new guys went in. *Four came out.* It was a huge relief to remove my mask and inhale natural air. I filled my lungs and coughed.

We received treatment at the rehab truck: we got rehydrated, had our blood pressure checked, and rested before returning to the burning building. Dawn had broken a long time before, and the sky became lighter as the sun moved up the horizon. At this time on most other work days I would be on my way home. In the distance, behind us through a clearing, I could see the brightness in the sky expand, but the sky around us was filled with thick smoke. The red lights from the trucks flashed off it creating red smog.

I said to Brian, "That's some fire. It's pissed off." He was a veteran firefighter and had seen many fires in his career. I was thankful to have him as my partner today.

"You ever fought one like this before?" He took a drink of water.

"No, I've watched a lot of videos and done the reenactments, but I've never been to anything this involved. I heard Chief say it's a three-alarm; they had to call in the neighboring towns. We have our whole force here fighting it plus coverage back at the main station by another town. Newspapers are gonna love this story." I snickered.

"Hopefully we'll get it out before they have too much to report on. At least no one was in there."

"Yeah." I sat without speaking and finished my water.

After fifteen minutes we pulled up our suspenders and dressed, collected new air bottles, and were ready to go back into the building. The chief was relieved that the fire had been contained to the building so far.

As I walked over and waited for the signal to enter, I couldn't help notice that the size of the fire had changed drastically. The third floor was fully engulfed, and smoke poured from the fourth floor. Two ladder trucks were dousing the building from outside; shades of orange raged behind the intact windows, and flames shot out through the broken windows. Heavy gray smoke filled the sky around the top of building. It was the biggest fire I had ever scene.

I entered through the same doors for the third time that morning and offered the same prayer for God to watch over us; *four went in.* The previous crew had kept the raging fire from taking over the second floor, as we had done; the top of the staircase looked open and available for an attempt to approach the fire. Brian and I walked up, testing each tread before putting our full weight on it. Brian held me back when a flame flickered around the corner, teasing us; he blasted water at it.

We successfully cleared the stairs and now fought to keep the fire on the main section of the third floor. We held our position, annihilating the fire and smoke with a steady stream of water, while the guys outside fought it, giving it all they had.

We were settled in position, keeping the fire at bay. Suddenly I sensed that something was wrong, and then I heard it — an increased snapping and crackling off in the distance. The floor still felt stable under my feet. I heard it again and tapped Brian's shoulder. We had to retreat. When he turned around to look at me, it was the last thing I saw before the *boom*!

Maggie

I HAD AN AWFUL NIGHT, BUT NOT BECAUSE OF THE NIGHTMARES that haunted my sleep or the loneliness I felt when the light faded and the darkness crept in. This time the guilty party was a skunk that had sprayed outside the house. Every time Clipper smelled it he went ballistic and wouldn't stop barking. Just when I thought he had settled down he would start up again and then I had an even harder time trying to fall back to sleep. So at four thirty I decided to get up and start the coffee. I curled up on the couch with a book until I had to shower for work.

I drove into work Wednesday morning dreading the eighteen-hour shift ahead of me, but thankful that Molly had agreed to split Mary Ellen's shift with me. I pulled into a parking spot in the hospital garage. Off in the distance I noticed smoke flooding the sky. It was coming from the area of town that used to have active mills. Most had been remodeled into apartments, but a couple were abandoned. Nothing had been done to update them. I looked at my watch, hoping that Will's shift had ended before the fire started and that he was home, and not at the fire scene. I wasn't even in a relationship with him and I still worried about him at work. If he was my boyfriend, I imagined how worried I would be every day when he left me to go to work.

I put my stuff away and walk to the nurses' station holding my travel coffee mug; it was one of those rare days that I brought coffee to work with me because I was so tired. Nancy sat behind the desk look-ing over her charts and organizing them on the computer.

"Busy night?" I asked as I sat down beside her.

"Oh, the crazies were in here last night. Hopefully, the day shift will be quieter for you." She turned her chair to face me.

"I hope so. I'm beat. My dog had me up all night barking at a dumb skunk." I stretched my arms overhead and yawned. I looked at the list of patients I would be caring for. I had two; not a bad start. One was waiting to be admitted, and the other was awaiting an ultrasound test for possible kidney stones.

I introduced myself to both and asked if they needed anything, I was relieved when they told me they didn't. Before leaving, I told them to call for me if they did.

I walked out of the last room as two janitors walked by. I overheard them saying something about a three-alarm fire burning at the old abandoned chemical building. That explained the smoke I'd seen saw earlier. Will, the adrenaline junkie, would for sure be mad that his shift had ended before the fire started. I, on the other hand, was glad.

I was relieved to know it was an abandoned building. At least there would be no causalities or victims coming into the ER and because the site was abandoned I figured it would be a cinch to put out the fire. Like Nancy said, all the crazies were in last night, and so far the day was off to good start.

An hour later a nurse's aide arrived from the fourth floor for my patient; the room he was waiting for was available. I said good-bye to the sweet old man and his daughter and wished him better health. Then I wheeled my other patient over to the radiology department, and I felt the ground shake. I thought, *that's weird — was that a mini earthquake?* My patient didn't seem to notice it, so I shrugged it off and didn't say anything.

The assistant in the radiology department planned to return my patient to the ER after her test was finished, so I left her. As I walked back through the ER doors I noticed the energy had changed in the short time I was gone — typical in an ER, but not what I wanted today. Nurses were hustling to prepare beds and stock rooms with burn treatments, cloth, and gauze.

The energy level was just below panic; it had to have something to do with the vibration I felt.

"Nancy, what is happening? What's going on? What are you prepping for?"

On the brink of a calamity, she stood at the desk with her arms folded across her chest.

"Did you feel the floor shake? There was an explosion in the building at the fire scene. We just got the call that they are transporting four firefighters."

"What? No." I broke into a cold sweat. *The families.*

"Two critical, two non-life-threatening." She shook her head.

The doors thrust open. Suddenly EMTs were yelling orders at the doctors and nurses. The head nurse, Janet, directed patients into various rooms. That day I was covering rooms five and six; my patient who was in radiology had come from room five, so room six was available.

"You, room six," Janet directed the EMT, pointing at the room.

That was me. I was on.

My patient was semiconscious. I was perturbed that I had to assist Dr. Bauer, but I refocused my thoughts on caring for the patient. After I cut all his clothing off, Dr. Bauer and I assessed his exterior. He hadn't suffered any severe burns, but he did have some superficial cuts; I cleansed them right away. He had a significant gash on his head that would require stitches. I cleaned and prepped the area for Dr. Bauer as he stood by, practically breathing down my neck. I gestured to let him know I was finished, and he moved in, wearing his surgical glasses. With steady hands he stitched the laceration. As he rhythmically closed the wound, he explained the firefighter's injuries.

"There are four different classes of blast injuries. The farther a person is from the source of the explosion, the less damage will be done. This patient and one other one were farther away, so they suffered less than the other two." He took his time to close the skin perfectly.

As I assisted Dr. Bauer I could hear commotion in the other rooms; the noise sometimes escalated and became frantic. I was glad my patient wasn't as bad off as the others. After the doctor finished stitching him, I stared at his face, trying to recognize him from the holiday party, but his face was blackened and covered in soot, his hair matted to his head.

We medicated him for pain, and I proceeded to clean his face and hands. I saw his features better once the first layer of soot was off. I checked his paperwork and read his name: Jack Bolton. He was young, only twenty-four years old. I was glad he would heal and not suffer life-long injuries. I vaguely remember Will saying he worked with a "probie" and this must be who he had been talking about.

I made Jack comfortable in the bed under blankets and checked on his IV drip. When I went to chart my work I noticed my other patient was back from radiology. I checked in with her and she told me she was fine; thank God, because I needed a few minutes to pull myself together. I was tired and felt the emotional stress of tending Jack.

I sat at the nurses' station in the center of the ER filling in Jack's information. Suddenly I heard a doctor yell, "Come on, Will, stay with us." I jumped up and ran to room seven, stopping in the doorway. I saw his body on the gurney. His pants were still on, but his boots were off and his chest was exposed. His face was beneath an oxygen mask. I knew it was him — my Will.

"No!" I yelled.

Not missing a beat, the doctor placed the paddles on Will's chest. "Clear!"

I saw Will's still body jolt off the bed and land. Tears flooded my eyes. *What happened to him?*

I looked at the monitor and saw the green line go up. *Thank God*, I thought. I stood paralyzed, like I was frozen stiff. Shock waves of fear radiated through me and I couldn't think. Janet took me by the shoulders and redirected me to the nurses' station.

"We have a serious situation here. Are you going to be able to pull it together?" She stared me in the eye.

I was shaking. "I don't know. I don't know… I know him—is he going to die?" I was a mess, a torment of tears flowing down my chin. I looked past her into Will's room at the monitor screen; his heart was beating.

"Not if we can help it. The doctor is working to stabilize him; his injuries shouldn't be life-threatening, but he is in critical condition. His partner in room one was hit the worst; we've lost him twice already. Are you sure you can do your job and stay clear-minded today?"

"Janet, I wish I could say yes, but I don't think I can. Look at me. I'm shaking. This is stirring up everything I have been trying to heal from. Can we call someone in?"

"We have enough coverage for now. Your patient in room five will be discharged soon. Just watch over the other firefighter in six. We'll try to keep your load light. That's the best I can do for now."

"Thank you. Please don't let him die," I called after her as she walked away, tears dripping down my cheeks. I couldn't lose Will.

I checked on my patients, who were resting comfortably. I called Molly.

"Can you come in for me today?

"What's going on? Aren't you already there?"

"Will was brought in—he's in critical care. I'm a wreck. I don't think I can finish my shift."

"Oh my God. What happened to him?"

"He got hurt fighting a fire." I started bawling; it was like losing my dad and Tim all over again.

"I'm coming in. I'll figure out Mary Ellen's coverage for you, don't worry."

"Thank you. I can't believe this is happening to me again." I sniffled. It was hard to catch my breath.

"I'll be there as soon as I can."

I walked back into Jack's room to check on him; he was still resting, so I headed to check on my other patient. I stopped short in the doorway when I heard Janet giving her the doctor's discharge orders and smiled in relief. She'd stepped in to help me.

The next room was Will's. I hadn't gone in since I'd seen him being resuscitated, and I was nervous about what I would see when I rounded the corner.

He lay on the bed attached to many wires and had an IV needle in his arm. His eyes were shut. Vanessa worked to clean his face.

"Excuse me." I forced strength in my voice. "Did the doctor stabilize the patient?" I remained in the doorway.

"Yes, we have him on some meds and an IV drip. I think he's going to be okay. He suffered some lacerations and cuts, but nothing deep enough for stitches. Aside from the minor internal injuries from the blast, I think he'll be good as new once he wakes up."

"Vanessa, I want to finish cleaning him up."

"Of course. He's your boyfriend, right?"

"No, we're just friends, but he's a special man and very important to me." I wiped a lonely tear.

She left me alone to finish. She had cleaned the right side of his face, which faced away from the chair, so I started on his left side, working around the oxygen mask. I dipped the cloth into the basin of warm water and moved it over his cheek. A lonely tear rolled off my cheek and landed onto Will's. I wiped it away with the cloth.

I leaned down and I whispered in his ear, "I need you, Will Driscoll. You can't leave me; you can't."

I carefully swabbed the skin around his eyes and recalled how his eyes had captivated me the first time I met him. Lately when I felt sad and lost, I found reassurance and comfort in them.

"You just have to pull through."

I moved the warm cloth over his forehead, wiping away every trace of the fire.

"Will, can you hear me? I've never known for sure whether unconscious patients can hear family members talk to them, but I always encourage them to talk. And now I hope you can hear me. I love you." As I touched his cheek with my fingers, I blushed and felt my emotions rolling down my cheeks.

It felt natural to say the words, and I meant them. But as soon as they left my mouth, I wanted to take them back. How could I love him? I loved Tim and had for eight years, and although it wasn't supposed to be that way, Tim had died, leaving me alone to find love again. I was meant to grow old with Tim and enjoy life with him by my side, but he was gone and now Will was in my life. Looking down at his sleeping face, it was clear to me he was a man I also loved, even though I was deeply confused about opening up to him about my true feelings.

I made another pass over his handsome face, making sure I cleaned off all the soot and debris. Vanessa had cleaned his body; his chest was exposed, wires attached to it. His sleeping face looked different from those nights when I'd snuck into the guest room to stand over the bed and watch him drifting in sleep, it was then that I discovered that I loved him. He had become my guardian angel, but I hadn't been ready to bare my inner feelings to him.

I stood over the hospital bed that held the body and life of the third man to steal my heart, and I prayed to God to save him, to allow him to live, so that we could be together. Knowing how close I had come to losing him made me finally realize what I had to tell him when he woke up: I needed him and wanted him to be mine and only mine.

When Molly arrived later she came straight into Will's room.

"Maggie."

I felt someone shake my shoulders.

"Maggie."

I sat up in the chair, gradually becoming aware I'd fallen asleep with my head on the bed. My neck crunched when I rolled it. "What happened?" I asked.

"Are you okay?" she whispered. She rubbed my back.

"I can't believe I fell asleep. What time is it?"

"It's just about noon."

"Oh good—I wasn't out for too long. Thanks for coming in." I hugged her.

"Any changes?" She pointed at Will in the hospital bed.

"He's going to make it. The tests came back and indicated the shock wave from the explosion caused internal injuries, but they're not life threatening. He has a few gashes and some cuts, but none need stitches. I would say he got lucky."

"Are you okay? This can't be easy for you?" She stroked my arm.

Emotional tears suddenly emptied from my eyes. I was glad Molly was here to talk to.

"Do you know how many times he tried to make it easy for me to love him?" I didn't wait for an answer. "Every time we were together, every time he made me dinner or walked Clipper. He's been there for me every time I've needed him since Tim passed. I joked that Tim must have paid him." We both chuckled quietly.

"It wouldn't surprise me," Molly observed. "Tim loved you very much. I could tell because he always watched out for you. You're lucky to have found two men to love you in one lifetime." She smiled at me.

I know she was thinking she'd love to find just one.

"I guess I am. I almost let this one get away."

Molly put her arm around my shoulder, and we stood staring at Will's body in the bed. Then Janet popped in and asked Molly to follow her, and I left to go check on Jack. He wasn't my patient anymore, but I wanted to make sure he was okay.

He was awake when I went in.

"Hi there, I'm Maggie. I helped take care of you when you first came in. Can I get you anything?"

He smiled. "You're Will's Maggie, aren't you?" His eyes had a glint in them.

I was caught by surprise. "Yes, I know Will." I nervously smoothed my scrubs down.

"I knew because of your hair—no one else here has red hair. The boys always tease Will about the cute redhead ER nurse he flirts with." He grinned.

I blushed.

"Well, I guess that's me!" I tried to sound casual, but I was uncomfortable. "Do you need anything?"

"Can I get a report about my brothers? From what I remember the situation didn't seem very good. I was in and out of awareness pretty quickly, but everyone seemed really worried."

"Will is unconscious, but the doctors feel pretty confident that he'll make a full recovery. Al is probably awake by now. I think he fared as well as you did — a few stitches and cuts. Brian had the hardest time. They lost him twice. He's on life support now; they think the shock of the blast affected his lungs. I believe he's going to make it, but it will be a longer road to recovery for him."

Jack considered the news. As he looked out the door another nurse walked past.

"Do you guys have families?" I inquired.

"I don't, but Al and Brian do. They're married, and with a couple kids."

"I noticed people sitting in their rooms wearing heavy expressions on their faces. Families are important at times like these." I recalled the emotions of my childhood, "I hate your job." Quickly I jumped back in. "I'm sorry — that sounded awful. It's just that my dad was a firefighter, and I lost him when I was ten."

"That sucks. Sorry."

"Thanks. It's hard. I really care about Will, and this accident is bringing back all of those old emotions about losing my dad. Seeing Will confined to a bed, attached to wires, is disturbing. I just want him to wake up." My honesty with this guy I didn't even know shocked me, but I guess in the turmoil I was rambling to anyone who would listen.

"Will's the toughest guy in the department. Don't worry about him. He was made to be a firefighter. Besides, he knows he has your pretty face to come back to! I guarantee he's fighting hard to wake up." Jack's grin was huge.

"You think so, huh?" I blushed again.

"I know so. Our families give us the desire to survive." He looked at me. "Go to him, I'm fine."

"Thanks, Jack."

As I walked around the corner to Will's room I thought about what Jack said about families. Then it hit me—Will's family didn't even know what had happened.

I called the fire department dispatcher and pleaded for Will's parent's phone number. The fact that the phone number that came up on the station's caller ID was a hospital line probably was persuasive enough, because the dispatcher gave it to me, and I wrote the number down.

I looked at my watch; it was about nine-thirty in California, and everyone should be awake. I dialed.

"Hello?" An older woman's voice answered, probably Will's mom. My heart sank because I had to tell her of Will's accident.

"Hi. Mrs. Driscoll?"

"Yes?"

"This is Maggie Barrett—"

"Oh, hi, Maggie. How are you?"

She knew who I was? How could she know me? I started to smile. Will must have told her about me. *He talked to his mother about me!*

"Maggie? Are you there, dear?"

"Oh, I'm sorry. The reason that I'm calling is because Will was in an accident. I think he's going to be okay, but I thought I should call you."

Silence.

"Hello, Mrs. Driscoll?"

"Hello, who is this?" A man's voice pounded down the phone line. It had to be Mr. Driscoll.

"Hi, Mr. Driscoll, I'm Maggie, a friend of Will's."

"Hi, Maggie. It's nice to hear your voice. What's going on? Helen just handed the phone to me and sat down on the couch."

Oh boy, she's in shock.

"I'm sorry to tell you, but Will's been in an accident. I don't know much except that he was fighting a fire and there was an explosion. He's in the hospital."

"Okay, thank you for calling." He took a deep breath; he reminded me of how Tim would react, calculating his next move. "We'll be on the next plane out. It's early enough that we should be there before morning."

"Mr. Driscoll, please tell Mrs. Driscoll he's going to be okay. I'll make sure of it. I don't want her to worry."

"I will. Thanks, Maggie."

I gave him the details for finding Will and my cell number and then hung up with mixed emotions. While I didn't like being the one to inform Will's parents about the accident, at the same time I'd received welcome news—Will had told his parent's about me. *They know my name and who I am.* I smiled and walked into his room. Vanessa was checking on him.

"How is he?"

"No change. It'll take some time. Did you eat?"

"I grabbed a quick snack a minute ago, thanks." I sat in the chair next to the bed.

"So, he's your friend, right?"

I nodded.

"He's really good-looking. Does he have a girlfriend?" She was checking the connection between the electrodes on his chest and the heart monitor wires.

A rush of jealousy rose inside of me. I hadn't expected this feeling of ownership with Will; there was no way another girl was going to get him in her clutches. Vanessa struck as me the type who would go out of her way to fluff his pillow extra-special to make sure he noticed her.

"He's had a few. A lot of them were heartbreakers, so he's sworn off girls. That's what he told me anyhow." I touched his hair, proving that I could touch him in ways she could only dream about. "He's not in the market for a girlfriend, and after this accident I'm sure it'll be awhile before he wants a girlfriend."

"Too bad because I'm available. I just broke up with my boyfriend." She finished with the wires and walked to the door. "Oh well, there are more fish in the sea, right?" She shrugged her shoulders.

Nope, none that I can see myself settling down with.

I was thankful she left. I pulled the chair closer to his bed, rubbed his shoulder, and told him that I'd called his parents.

"They are leaving today and should be here in the morning, if not sooner." I played with his hair and felt the soot in it. "It was interesting that they knew who I was. I don't suppose someone talked to them about me." I looked at his face. I wanted him to wake up right now. It had only been a day since we last spoke but I missed hearing his voice. Between losing my dad and then Tim, I was learning not to take anything in life for granted; it was too precious.

I decided to wash Will's hair and clean him up before his parents arrived; they didn't need to see him looking disheveled.

It wasn't a thorough shampoo, but the results were an improvement. I felt useful, able to do something to help him feel better, to be able to touch his hair, to move my fingers through it and feel the softness tickle my fingers, just like I had dreamed when I watched him sleep. I wanted to touch his face. I wanted to look into his caring eyes and kiss his soft lips again with no guilt. I hoped someday I would have all of that with him.

I reached into my pocket for my lip balm. I swiped my finger across the top and moved it over his lips; they soaked up the moisture. I stared at his perfect mouth as I traced my finger over his lips, his desirable lips. I leaned over and touched my lips to his. They were warm but unresponsive. When he woke up I would try again, and then I would feel his love.

I sat by his side all day, caring for him and waiting for him to wake up. At dinnertime Molly came by to urge me to eat, but I couldn't. It amazed me how little appetite I had when I was nervous.

"I'll get some food from my bag," I promised her. "I don't want to be away if he wakes up. Will you wait with him?" Molly nodded and sat in the chair.

I grabbed a yogurt and my water and I called my mother. I told her what had happened and asked her to take care of Clipper for me. She offered to come to the hospital to support me, but I held her off, waiting until I really needed her. For now I needed her help with Clipper.

I returned to the room in under ten minutes, carrying my snack.

"I'm back — anything?"

"Seriously, you could have taken longer, Maggie. You need a break. You can't sit here all night."

"Watch me! I'm not leaving his side ever again. I'm not losing him, Molls — no way. If I have to sit here all night and all day and all night again, I'm never leaving. Not without him." I sat in the chair next to his bed; I had no plans to go home.

Through the course of the day no changes came. By eleven at night I was exhausted. I laid my head on the side of the bed and closed my eyes. The next thing I remember was a hand rubbing my back and someone calling my name. I opened my eyes and realized I had fallen asleep with my head and arms resting on the bed. I sat up, stretched, and turned to see two older people standing next to me, smiling. *Oh my gosh, Will's parents.* He looked like a mixture of them both, sharing their good looks.

"Mr. and Mrs. Driscoll, I'm so sorry. I must have fallen asleep." I stood to hug them and offered my chair to Will's mother.

"Sit with him; talk to him. He might hear you."

Will's dad put his arm around my shoulder and squeezed.

"You are a resilient woman. Thanks for taking care of him." Then he kissed the top of my head. It's no wonder Will is so courteous and affectionate. With his dad for a role model, he couldn't help but turn out to be the caring guy that he was.

"Thanks, Mr. Driscoll. It's very easy to take care of Will. He's been there for me in my darkest days. I owe him a lot."

It was a relief to have Will's parents to sit with and talk to — it softened my mood to have company. As a bonus I got to hear the backstory of Will's life — and he couldn't stop them from telling me everything. I heard stories about when he was little and pretending to be a firefighter. Sometimes he would tie his sister up and then act like a superhero and *save the day*. He seemed like a cute little boy in the stories, not too different from the Will I knew today. I smiled at him as they told me story after story.

I offered to get coffee and left Will's parents, allowing them some time alone with their son. I walked to the cafeteria, which was closed at that hour, but there was a Keurig machine. Taking my time, I walked slowly down the corridors, pausing to look at the pictures of the people who made substantial donations or were somehow affiliated with the hospital, but I wanted to be next to Will so badly that I surprised myself by how quickly I returned.

"I'm back." I rounded the corner. Will's mother was crying in her husband's arms, and I felt awful for interrupting. She pulled away from him and tried to pretend nothing was wrong, but it was too late. I had seen her crying and holding onto her husband.

"I'm sorry. Do you want me to give you some privacy?"

"No, honey, come sit with us. It'll be a welcome distraction," Mr. Driscoll said.

We kept vigil next to Will's bed all night. Molly came by to check on Will, and I introduced her to his parents. After Vanessa's shift ended, Molly was assigned to Will's care, and I was happy that I didn't need to defend my position in his life. Molly knew to back off.

Will's dad went to check on the other firefighters, reporting back that Jack and Al had been released, but Brian was still in tough shape.

"I spoke to his wife and his father, who was also once a firefighter. They said that the doctors were hoping as the day moves on he will make progress, and if not, they'll move him up to the ICU. If the doctors are hopeful about Brian's progress we should be optimistic that Will be getting better by then too." He rubbed Helen's back.

"Oh, I hope so." She held Will's hand.

"Will's strong. He'll pull out of this; I know it." I wanted to be positive for his mother and hoped I was right. "The first twenty-four hours are the most crucial, and we've made it through eighteen of them with no setbacks, so that counts for something."

"I like the way you think, Maggie." Will's dad smiled at me. "Is this the hospital you work in?"

"Yeah, I was on when he came in, but I didn't realize he was here for awhile. When I heard his name it shocked me. Did Will tell you about my late husband?" I was uncertain if I should bring it up, but it seemed odd not to acknowledge it.

Will's dad spoke first "Yes, he did. I'm awfully sorry for what you had to go through. It must be very hard on you."

"He talked to me about it as well. I'm sorry for your loss," Mrs. Driscoll added.

"Thanks. I'm not sure I would be standing here today if not for your son's support. He's been a real friend to me, as he was to Tim."

"Will has a big heart, always has," his mom said with pride. Then she covered her mouth with a hand, and her eyebrows raised in alarm. "Oh, Wayne, we need to call Ellen! She wanted an update. She should still be up. Will you come with me?" I described the area with the best cell service, and when they left I pulled the chair close to the bed and held Will's hand.

"Superman, huh? I am not surprised! Always looking for someone to rescue, aren't you? Well, big guy, I think this time you need rescuing. When are you going to wake up? I miss you, Will."

I stayed by his side, hoping he'd heard me and would open his eyes, but he didn't.

I kept talking. "Will, I have been thinking about something. On New Year's Eve you kissed me, and I felt something shift inside me that I hadn't felt before, but I was too scared to allow myself to go with it." I swallowed, thankful that he was unable to comment on what I was about to say. I needed to get it off my chest and sit with it without judgment. I was experiencing new feelings, and I wanted to make sure that they were real, hoping they weren't just an emotional response to Will's accident.

"Almost losing you today made me realize something. Tim is gone and he is not coming back. No matter how much I mourn for him and the life we shared, it will never return. It can't be. I know you are what's real. You are here, and you have love to give me. So please, Will, come back to me and let's start again. I will try to be open with my feelings to you, okay? Can you wake up now?" I sat back and waited, certain it wouldn't be that easy.

In the morning, Will's mother encouraged me to grab a quick breakfast when the café opened. I bought scrambled eggs and toast, which was all my stomach could tolerate. I ate quickly and returned to Will so his parents could eat too.

I chatted with Molly in Will's room near the door; the poor thing had three more hours on her shift before her relief came in, and she looked exhausted. I thanked her over and over for helping me, and she brushed it off. "It's what friends do." She said she looked forward to having the next two days off, not to mention her paycheck. Suddenly she moved to the bed.

"Did you see that?" She bent closer to Will's face. "Will, it's Molly—can you hear me?"

"Did he move? Did you see him move?" I stepped next to the bed.

"I don't know. I thought so. I thought I saw something from the corner of my eye. I guess not. Sorry." She frowned.

"That's okay. It has to happen at some point, right?" I rubbed his arm.

"Don't get down. You have a good attitude. Keep it up. I'm going to check on my other patient."

It was just before lunchtime when I saw Will's foot twitch.

Will's parents had decided to take a walk outside to get their blood flowing. I called them on my cell phone.

"I think he's waking up!"

Will's dad assured me they were on their way with relief in his voice.

I held Will's hand and talked to him. I did believe the patient could hear voices when they began to return, as if they were waking from a dream.

"Will, I'm right here. Your parents will be back in a minute. They went outside to get fresh air. Will, turn to my voice. Can you hear me?"

I patiently waited for him to do something: move, talk, something. *This takes time, Maggie,* I reminded myself.

His parents returned with hope on their faces. His mother took the seat across from me and held his other hand.

"Will, it's Mom. I'm here and so is Dad." We looked at each other and waited... Nothing.

"I swear I saw his foot move."

"We believe you. It's okay, Maggie. He'll do it."

We held his hands and talked to him, encouraging him to open his eyes. The oxygen mask had been removed; a nose piece was now providing oxygen, so I could see his whole face. His whiskers made him look even more attractive to me. He began to grimace and twitch.

"Mrs. Driscoll, look at his face!"

"I see it! Will, wake up, honey." Will's mom loudly encouraged him.

I put my lips next to his ear. "Will, I'm right here. Baby, come on. You can do it! Open your eyes."

I heard him moan.

"What? Say it again."

He tried again and again, each time louder and more clear, but I couldn't understand what he meant. I looked back at his father.

"He said, 'Four in.'" He smiled and nodded, as if he knew what Will meant.

"Four in; what does that mean?" I looked at Will's father, confused.

"It means he's going to be all right." He grabbed his son's leg and gave it a shake. "Four in, four out."

Will's eyes were closed, but he was smiling from ear to ear.

Then I recalled the simple, yet powerful rule used at most fire stations. If four firefighters go in, then four need to come out. It's how they kept track of each other. It was just like my dad was doing the day he died, when he went back for his brother.

Will

THE LAST IMAGE I REMEMBERED WAS BRIAN'S FACE, BUT I when opened my eyes Maggie was smiling above me. *I survived.* I turned and saw my mother on the other side of me and my father at the end of the bed near my feet.

"Oh, I see you've met Maggie. How long was I out for?" My head ached when I tried to lift it from the pillow, and my voice was raspy and dry.

Maggie spoke first. "They brought you in after nine yesterday morning. I have been by your side ever since."

She held my hand in her left hand and stroked my hair and my face with the other. Her eyes were alive, intense, and full of excitement, in contrast to the confused looks I often received when she was this close to me.

"Will, Maggie called us, and we came out right away." My mother held my other hand. "I never thought I'd be in New England in January—only you could get me here. I couldn't stay home with you in the hospital."

I smiled at her. "Thanks for coming, Mom. I love you."

"I'm proud of you, son. I talked to the chief. He said you did a fine job fighting that fire. It took them another five hours to knock it down after the explosion."

"God, I'm lucky to be here," I said.

"Yes, you are," Maggie said, smiling. She kissed the back of my hand, all the while looking into my eyes.

She had never been this free with physical contact before. I stared at her in confusion. Then it dawned on me: she thought she was going to lose me and that I was going to die. *Oh my God, what have I put her through?*

I released both hands and told Maggie, "Come here." I gathered her into my arms, careful not to pull on the IVs. "I'm so sorry for what this did to you." I kissed the top of her head.

She looked at me, smiling with tears in her eyes. "I'm just relieved to hear your voice. I really missed it."

"Wayne, let's go call Ellen and give her the good news." I was sure Mom sensed I was looking for privacy with Maggie.

"Thanks, Mom." They both smiled and gave little waves as they headed to the corridor.

Maggie sat next to me on the bed. I lifted myself against the pillows to see her better.

"Your parents are very nice. We spent most of the night talking. I got to hear about you when you were a little boy. It was quite fascinating."

"Oh gosh, really?" I scrunched my eyebrows. "I can only imagine what they told you. Should I be embarrassed?"

"Never with me." She smiled and picked up my hand again. "I really thought that I was going to lose you when you first came in; you flat-lined and I heard them call your name."

"That must have been awful. I'm sorry." I could imagine her shock.

"No, you couldn't control it. You were just doing your job. I can't think about what might have been. You are here now and that's just how I want it." She leaned in and kissed my cheek, leaving a warm imprint.

I left the hospital the following day with some aches and pains, but mostly I felt appreciation for being alive. Brian came to shortly after I did and was admitted for observation, but I was told he would make a full recovery.

~

Maggie decided I should stay with her at her house while my parents stayed at mine; I wasn't about to fight the arrangement that would allow me to be with her all day and night.

She walked me to the couch while Clipper followed behind. She insisted I sit while she fixed me lunch. Our roles were reversed; now Maggie was taking care of me. While it felt nice to have her tending to me, I wanted to be taking care of her, reassuring her that I was okay and would be okay. I hated to think of the pain and suffering my accident caused her, but whatever she'd suffered must have caused an awakening because every time she looked at me I felt admiration flow through her eyes.

She brought me a sandwich. "I can eat in the kitchen, you know. I can walk, I don't have broken legs," I joked.

"I know, but I want to take care of you and keep you comfortable." She fluffed the pillows behind my back.

"I'm comfortable just being with you." I took a bite of my sandwich. "Are you okay after all this? You seem different."

She took a deep breath and sat down next to me. "I'm fine. When you were hurt and lying unconscious in the hospital I had time to think about my life, your life, and everything that has happened between us." She paused, playing with a loose thread on her blue sweater, "I realized that I am happier with you than without you. I want you to be in my life and I want to be in yours." I knew she meant the words she was struggling to free, but there was still some hesitation behind them. "I need time to be comfortable moving ahead in a relationship with you, but almost losing you showed me that I need you more than anything in my life."

I put down the plate and took her in arms and held her, appreciating that she had finally said she needed me, but better than that, she had finally told me she *wanted* me in her life.

"Maggie, I will never let you go. I always want to be in your life." I hugged her tight. "Thank you for telling me that. I feel better already, knowing that I have a future with you." I kissed her head.

I spent the afternoon resting, and later my parents arrived and brought dinner with them.

"So this is Clipper." My dad rubbed between his ears.

Maggie looked at me as if she was thinking, *How does he know about Clipper?* "What can I say? I'm close to my parents. I tell them a lot because they're not here to see it," I whispered.

She smiled.

They stayed for a few hours before it was time to return to my house to catch up on lost sleep.

I walked them to the door. My father went outside first, but my mother stopped.

"Will, don't lose this girl. She is fantastic for you, and I think she can keep you on your toes. I adore her, and from what I saw at the hospital, she adores you." She kissed my cheek and turned to leave.

"Thanks, Ma."

I closed the door and walked into the kitchen as Maggie cleaned up the remaining dishes.

"You made a great impression." I walked up behind her at the sink and put my arms around her. She turned around to get closer to me.

"Really? Good to know." She nodded like she was real proud of herself. "They made a good impression, too." She kissed my nose and returned to her chores.

We argued over which of us would walk Clipper; I lost, but she promised she wouldn't go far.

I got ready for bed when she left and hoped she would invite me to sleep with her now that our couple status had been revised, but I wasn't about to push my luck. I prepared my bed in the guest room, thinking, *At this point it should be renamed Will's room.*

I thought about the changes that had occurred in only a couple of days. I climbed between the sheets and recalled my visit to Tim's grave. I wondered if he had anything to do with the events that played out with the fire, but I would never know.

When Maggie and Clipper came to say goodnight, Clipper jumped up on the bed and made himself cozy next to me.

"I guess he missed me too," I said.

"I guess so. I can leave him if you want?" She sat on the side of the bed.

"Maybe for a while, but I'd rather he go with you. I know you sleep better with him."

"I don't think anything could keep me awake tonight. I'm beat emotionally and physically." As if on cue, a yawn grew and escaped. "See? I'll keep both our doors open. Clipper can come to me when he's had enough of your snoring."

Then she poked at me.

"Oh yeah?" I pulled her down on top of me and tickled her before a sizable pain shot through my body. I let out a yell.

"Are you okay?" She shot upright.

I breathed heavily and waited for the pain to subside. "Phew—I guess I still need to heal. I didn't see that coming. But I'll be all right."

"I guess I need to do a better job taking care of you then. First order: sleep. You'll feel much better in the morning. Good night, Will." She smiled at me and kissed my cheek.

"Good night, Maggie." I squeezed her hand and winked at her. "See you in the morning."

~

When I woke, sunlight was creeping in behind the shades. I rolled over to check the time: ten o'clock. Wow, I hadn't sleep so late in a long time. I reached with my hand, in search of Clipper, but he was gone. Suddenly I could smell coffee. Oh, I imagined how good a cup of coffee would taste. I moved to sit up and felt like every muscle in my body was glued together.

As I climbed out of bed, Maggie appeared in the doorway holding a coffee mug. "What are you doing? Get back in that bed," she ordered.

"Oh, I need to stretch. My body aches and feels so tight." Slowly I moved my legs over the side of the bed and stood upright. *So far, so good.* Then I moved my torso from side to side, feeling my muscles release. I bent down to touch my toes and felt my spine lengthen. It felt good.

"Get back in bed and I'll help you feel better."

I liked the sound of that. "Yes, ma'am!"

She held out the mug so I could take a sip. Oh, it tasted good. Then she told me to roll over. She sat down next to me and began moving her warm hands all over my back. Tension was released as every muscle under my skin relaxed to her touch. The blood pumped through my veins faster; I was getting excited. She massaged down my arms, and when she got to my hands I tightened mine around hers and flipped over on my back; seduction poured from my eyes. She kept on rubbing my chest, exciting me even more. I closed my eyes, and she moved her hands over my bare chest. I let out a soft moan and then she stopped.

I lifted my head. "Ah, what happened? That was feeling really good."

"I got nervous. I was only trying to relax your muscles. I don't want to send the wrong message." She seemed nervous.

"No, it was great. It felt amazing to be touched by you. I know it was for therapeutic reasons, not sexual. I just couldn't hold back the feeling when you released my tension." I hugged her and longed for the day when she could touch me and I could feel her naked body on mine.

"I'm sorry, Will. Just give me time to sort through all my emotions and be comfortable with this. I want to be with you. You have no idea how badly I want it, but I'm still struggling with my guilt about diminishing my commitment to Tim."

"Maggie, he's not here anymore. It's okay to move on." I rubbed her arm.

"Just give me time, please." She got up and walked away.

I let out a sigh. I was disappointed with myself for pushing her and with her for her inability to let go of her emotional restraints.

Maggie

WILL'S PARENTS INVITED US TO A BRUINS GAME AT THE GARDEN; the Los Angeles Kings were in town, and his parents thought it would be beneficial to Will to get out of the house for the night.

As we approached the city, the buildings grew tall looking like they could reach to the sky. I was excited about watching the hockey game. I had only been to one in my life; my dad took me when I was eight years old. The Bruins played against the Canadiens that time. All I remember is that it was crowded, there was a lot of yelling, and I could only see the legs of the fans when we walked around the Garden.

Will's dad was right; Will needed a night out. I could tell he was having a blast. It wasn't too strenuous or stimulating for him, just a nice relaxing night. We had an early dinner in the North End before walking in the brisk night air to the Garden. Will's parents were easy-going and fun to be with, and it was evident that they missed their son. During dinner they took every opportunity to tell him how proud they were of him and how they missed him. They asked if he ever thought of moving back home. My stomach flipped when his mother pleaded her case; I couldn't imagine my life without Will in it, and I certainly wasn't moving to California and leaving my family behind.

He explained that he was happy in New England, that it had become his new home, a place where he was able to enjoy a mixture of seasons and activities. He put his hand on my knee under the table and squeezed it. "Besides, I have met too many people out here I would miss too much. I couldn't leave, even if I wanted to."

My stomach settled.

I gathered his mom had argued with him about this in the past because she let it go after that, rolling her eyes and repositioning herself in her seat, resigned to the fact that her son would never move back to California.

When we got to the Garden after dinner, I noticed the hockey crowds had changed from what I could remember as a child; they were less rude and boisterous. Most of them were mellow. However, as Will and I followed his parents to our seats a couple of drunken men crashed into me. The younger one slammed me with enough force that my handbag was knocked down, spilling some of the contents on the floor. They kept walking, and laughed about it. The young guy brushed it off without so much as a "sorry." Will's expression made it clear he was pissed.

The men went to stand in line at the concession stand for another round as I picked my stuff up. Out of the corner of my eye, I saw Will walk up to them. He was much taller than either of them. Apparently, he told the one who had bumped me that he needed to apologize. The guy walked over to me, said he was sorry, and helped me pick up the rest of my stuff.

In the aisle leading to our seats, I stopped to ask Will what he'd said to the younger guy.

"I told him he was rude and if he didn't want my fist down his throat he would turn around and say sorry to the pretty lady he almost bowled over." He grinned and rubbed my arm. "I need to defend you, you know."

"No, really. What did you tell him?"

"I just told him that he needed to apologize to you, that it was rude to knock a woman over and keep going. Then I asked him, 'What if someone did that to someone *you* love?'"

I stared at him—was he for real? I searched his face for a clue to whether he was joking or telling the truth, but he smiled, kissed my cheek, and walked away. I watched him walk to his seat, repeating his words over in my mind: "someone you love." I felt a wave of warmth roll over me. Will just told me he loved me, even if it was in a round-about way.

~

I took care of Will for the remainder of the week. We both returned to work more connected than before. The notion of almost losing Will too, made me realize what I had in my life, and that I wasn't willing to let it go. I tried to give myself permission to love Will, to throw out all the worries I had about loving a risk-taking man and moving on so soon after Tim died. I had to convince myself that it was okay to love again.

We'd shared some physical moments when it would have been natural to move forward and let the moment carry us, but I got cold feet and pulled away. Will was patient with me and never got upset; he understood how I felt. He would hold me and say, "It's okay. In time you'll feel better about moving forward." I appreciated him so much in those moments because I knew he must have been very frustrated, but he never showed it. He allowed me time to heal without worrying about hurting him in the process.

I was at home on a snowy Saturday, the day before Valentine's Day, with nothing to do. I thought about the approaching tax season. Tim had been very disciplined about starting our taxes early, usually just after the new year, but I was behind. We were creeping deeper into February, and I hadn't even thought about getting all the paper-work together.

Will was at work and it was the perfect time to start organizing the past year's receipts and documents. Clipper followed as I walked upstairs to the door of Tim's office. I usually kept it closed because seeing the room was too much of a reminder that he was gone. I opened the door and walked in, inhaling the scent of Tim's memory. Clipper stayed at the threshold. I turned around and told him, "Come on," and patted my leg; he just looked at me and lied down. *Poor dog*, I thought.

Being in Tim's office was like being in his embrace. Everywhere I looked I saw him and felt his presence. Someday I would have to clean away his memory and make this my office to run the household from, but I wasn't ready to say good-bye to the room Tim had decorated; he still existed in here. This room was like a broken-in, cozy pair of sweatpants that I couldn't throw out.

I opened the file cabinet and started moving through the tabs on the files, looking for the one titled Tax documents. I was thankful that Tim was so organized; it would make my job a lot easier. I sat at his desk, opened the file, and began separating the paperwork into piles. Then I came upon an envelope addressed to me in Tim's handwriting. *This is weird. What's this?*

My heart was beating so fast I could feel it pounding beneath my chest, like it would pop free. I took a deep breath, trying to calm my nerves, but my hands were shaking and I couldn't open the seal. I reached for the letter opener, and then I carefully removed the paper from the envelope as if it was Tim's life in my hands. This was all I had left of him, a final letter.

Old sentiments grew inside of me and my eyes filled with tears as I read the opening line.

My dearest loving wife Maggie...

The cursive letters looked like a weak old man had written them. Tim left me a letter before he died. He took the time to tell me how much he loved me. I sat and cried before continuing. Tim was always a thoughtful, considerate man, but this was the most generous thing he had ever done for me.

I took a deep breath and I continued reading.

> *This letter has found its way into your life at pre-cisely the right time. My battle with cancer has ended, and I have moved on to bigger and better places. I want you to know that my final days were filled with love, laughter, family, and friends. I thank you for making that happen.*

I had to stop reading because I couldn't see the page for the tears were pooling in my eyes. My nose ran, and my lungs fought for air. I moved to the couch and curled up in the corner.

> *I'm sorry that the life we planned for didn't hap-pen; I think that is what hurts me the most. You wanted a life of security and I thought I could give that to you, but in the end I hurt you and left you, just like when your father died. I never wanted it to be this way for you. You deserve more.*

I frowned and wiped away the tears and took another breath.

> *Your love filled me more than anything else in my life; my life was better because I got to wake up next to you every morning and lay my head down next to you every night. You encompass love, Maggie. I have never met anyone who loves*

life and people like you do. I know that's why you are a nurse — the best one ever!

I thought, *Thanks, Tim.*

I spoke to you tonight about carrying on in life without me. You must, Maggie. You can't let this cancer kill you too. Allow it to only take me from you, not steal your life from you. You are too pre-cious to stop loving and sharing yourself with the world. I know your dreams always included hav-ing a family. Boy, did I mess that up. If only there was a way I could have known before it was too late, I would have done anything to leave you the mother of our child, so that you could always carry my memory with you in life, but it wasn't meant to be, not with me anyway.

My brain couldn't believe what I was reading.

Maggie, you need to allow yourself to expand your limits; allow people, even men, in, even though you told yourself so many years ago you would not. Will is a great guy, probably better than me in some ways. Yet I know he is exactly what you told yourself you didn't want in a man. But look at what you got from the type of man you wanted — a safe man who avoided risks. I got cancer and died. You can't foresee a person's fu-ture from how they live their life. I played it safe, and my life was cut too short.

He was giving me his blessing to be with Will; my heart raced even faster. *Does Will know about this?*

Please turn to Will. Allow him to comfort you.
You may be surprised by how he can lift your
spirits. He, like you, is a lover of life who can of-
fer you richness and bring security to your future.
I have talked to him, so he is aware of my dying
wish: that he love and take care of you. Don't
turn away from him. You are everything he al-
ways wanted in a woman. Even before I told him
about my wish for the two of you, I could see the
way he looked at you. He showed his love for you
in his eyes long before I asked him to love you for
me. I simply gave him permission and my bless-
ing.

I thought, *Will did know... But why didn't he tell me that*
Tim wanted it this way?

My sweet Maggie, I want you to be happy and
not carry pain and grief until your dying day;
that would kill you too soon. I will see you again
someday. When it's your time, mine will be the
first face you see, but until that day live like
you've never lived before. Throw caution to the
wind. I'll catch it and throw love and protection
back to you. You are my one and only love; so
please fulfill my dying wish. Continue loving
and living the life you were given.

Until we meet again, your loving husband,
Tim

My hands shook. I dropped the letter into my lap and I looked up.
Clipper sat in front of me with his ears tight against his head. "It's okay,
buddy, I'm all right."

261

Tim must have written the letter on one of his last nights alive. I remember the night I cuddled with him, when he told me to continue to live after he died. I'd gone into the hall and cried in Will's arms; it was the first time I had ever been held by Will. I remember the security I felt in his strong arms, the sense that everything would be okay.

But if Will knew about this agreement, why didn't he ever mention it? A mixture of love and joy, disappointment and anger bubbled up inside of me. I needed to talk to the only person who could answer my questions. I looked out the window as the snow fell; the roads were barely covered.

I called Will on the phone. "Are you at the station? Can I come by?"

Panic was evident in his voice. "Are you okay? Is everything all right?"

"I need to talk to you — it's very important. This can't wait."

"Sure, Maggie. Come on over."

As I pulled into the visitor's parking lot, big snowflakes started to fall. I walked up to the door of the fire station, which Will held open.

I kissed him passionately and pulled away.

"Is that what couldn't wait?" His face expressed an eager smile.

Then I smacked him across the face because he knew about Tim's dream for me, while I didn't.

"Geez, what's that for?" He rubbed his cheek.

All of sudden I felt awful. *How could I have hit him?* "I'm so sorry." I rubbed his cheek for him and kissed it. I was many inches shorter than Will; if he had wanted to he could have had me under his control in a second, but he just stood there.

"What's gotten into you?" he asked me.

I pushed past him into the station, which appeared deserted. Will followed and shut the door. I handed him the letter and told him to read it. After he finished it, he brought me into a small room in the corner of the station that held extra supplies.

"Maggie, I'm sorry. I know how this seems. I have to be honest with you. First of all, from the first time I met you at the coffee shop I knew I loved you, but I could never act on those feelings because you were married to my good friend and I'm not that kind of guy. Secondly, when Tim talked to me about this I thought he was crazy. I wish he added that detail to the letter." He brushed his hand through his hair, choosing his next words carefully.

"Tim and I spoke many times about this. I tried to tell him you wouldn't go along with it; I wasn't your type. Tim could tell I liked you and said that you may begin to overlook my lifestyle and learn to love me over time. And that happened a lot faster than I thought it would; we have a connection, you and me." He held my hands. "When I'm with you, nothing else matters, and when we are apart you're all that matters, and I can't wait 'til I can see you again. Maggie, please don't think I was being deceitful." He looked away and then back at me. "I love you with all my heart and want nothing in this world except to be with you."

I felt his words wrap around my heart and tears ran down my cheeks, and he wiped them away.

I threw myself into his arms and cried so hard I couldn't breathe while my emotions poured out. He held me close, brushing my hair with his hands. I never I thought I could love again after Tim died; how would I find another man to treat me the way he had? Even in his dying days Tim had gone out of his way and found a man for me, better than any man I could have found, and brought him into my life to take care of me. He chose Will for me. It was his idea, his dying wish; he wanted me to be with Will, and he'd blessed our relationship.

"I love you, Will." I squeezed him tight and felt his muscles through his shirt; he would always protect me.

"Maggie, I've been waiting to hear you say that. I love you, too."

He lifted my chin, and we shared a passionate kiss. Then he looked into my eyes.

"I knew it would happen. I knew you felt the same way for me that I felt for you, but you were too nervous. Now's there's nothing to be afraid of—it's all out."

"I will always love Tim, and I love him even more now for bringing you into my life."

We stood in silence looking at each other, enjoying the easiness between us. We were free—I was free to share my feelings with Will.

Then the alarm tones sounded, and suddenly the strongest reason I hadn't wanted a relationship with Will intruded.

"I'll be okay." He held my face in his hands, deep determination in his eyes, reassuring me of his safety. Then he kissed me with tender lips.

I held onto his hands, not wanting to let go. "Please be safe. I can't lose you."

"I gotta go. I'll see you soon."

~

Driving home in what was now a snowstorm, I replayed the events of my day. In the end, what I thought would kill me ended up bringing me to love another man—as much, if not more, than I loved Tim. Being in love with Tim taught me how to love another person and trust that I would be safe. With Will, I would be able to build on my experiences with Tim and I believed that I would love Will more deeply than I had ever loved. I appreciated the depths of our relationship and cherished it because I knew at any time love could slip through my hands again; there were no guarantees in life, no matter how safe you played it.

Clipper was waiting for me at the door. I walked into the kitchen with an armful of groceries. I had patiently made my way around the store with all the other last-minute shoppers who braved the storm for needed items. The forecast was for up to a foot of snow to fall by morning.

I was walking on air, in love and finally at peace with myself, ready to feel it.

"Hi, Clipper. You have a new daddy, but you probably already knew that, didn't you?"

I'd bought a full spread to cook for Will on Valentine's Day to celebrate finding Tim's letter. I planned to prepare a pot roast and bake an apple pie for dessert, Will's favorite. I even bought vanilla ice cream to scoop on top. I put the food away and organized the kitchen while soft melodic music playing in the background enhanced my mood. I was in love, and it felt wonderful. I heard my phone chime. When I picked it up, I saw I had a text from Will.

Back at the station; car slid off road. See you in the morning. I love you.

I can do this, I told myself. I smiled and typed, Thanks for letting me know. I love you too.

It felt wonderful to be open about my feelings with Will. He deserved to know it; he had been so loving and helpful to me when I mourned for Tim. Even before Tim died, I could turn to him for help. What a lucky girl I was.

While the apple pie baked in the oven, I took a shower. As I washed my body, I thought about the sensation of Will's hands on my skin and feeling his warm skin beneath my hands. Will had the stereotypical firefighter's physique, with broad shoulders, rippling stomach muscles, and bulging biceps; his chest was a sanctuary that would keep me safe. He was hot and sexy, and he was mine. I smiled.

As much as I dreamed about touching Will and having him touch me, I wasn't ready to be with another man yet. So many changes had happened in my life, and I couldn't rush into it. But I did want him to spend all of his nights off with me, and I understood for the first time I wanted him to sleep in my bed with me. Oh, I couldn't wait to cuddle up next to him. Then maybe my nightmares would finally end. If not, at least he would be right by my side to hold me.

I made it downstairs just as the timer for the pie went off. *What timing!* The aroma of warm apples and cinnamon swirled through the house as the snowfall outside accelerated. I set the pie on the counter and decided to build a fire in the fireplace. Tim had wanted to install a gas fireplace when we remodeled the house, but I had put my foot down and demanded a real fireplace. I loved the allure of a cozy fire. I guess I was like my dad.

I was reading when my phone rang. Butterflies swarmed my middle when I saw Will's name. I felt like a teenager in love for the first time.

"I wanted to say good night while I could. I love you, Maggie."

It was so comforting to hear him speak those words to me. Even though he wasn't with me, it was as if he'd given my hug. When I heard his voice I felt relief from all my insecurities.

"I love you, too. See you in the morning?"

"Yes. I'll head over right after work, and we'll spend all day together."

We said our good nights. I watched the fire burn out. I was in love—the fear and loneliness I felt after Tim died were replaced with peace and wonder. My life had changed incredibly in the past year: from being content with Tim, to feeling hopeless about his death, to worrying that I would never be happy again, to feeling this new magnitude of love. Through all of it Will had been there with me.

STEADY AS YOU GO

Will had once explained to me that there was a lesson for me to learn from Tim's death. He said, "You get a second chance to live, to open your eyes and mind and rethink how you are living. Maggie, you don't have to accept things the way they are. You can change how you view your life."

As I pondered my life's choices, I realized that I'd thought I had been living, but in reality I had been hiding from life. Will's outlook on life had influenced mine and reassured me that the life I loved living would be fuller if I could admit more experiences into it instead of denying them.

~

I woke early the following morning to a winter wonderland. Snow blew around my neighborhood. The minutes ticked by as I waited for Will to come home from work. The cinnamon-scented candle on the kitchen table refreshed the aroma of the apple pie that I had baked. I hoped it would penetrate Will's senses when he walked in the door after a long shift at work and it would relax him. I heard Will's truck plow through the snow in the driveway and stop in front of the garage. I wished I had sold Tim's car before the winter started so Will wouldn't have to park outside. Yet he never complained.

I ran to the mudroom door. When Will stepped through I wrapped my arms around him and greeted him with a big kiss that I wished would never end. But Clipper was eager to greet him too and kept trying to squeeze between us, pushing us apart. We finally had to acknowledge him.

"Hi, Clipper. How ya doing?" Will patted his head and Clipper was satisfied.

Then Will enclosed me in his arms and kissed me again, with more passion than I've ever experienced. My body tingled in his embrace. I never wanted him to stop, but my lips were getting sore. It had been awhile since I'd kissed anyone for that long.

"Wow, someone missed me!" I tried to slow him down, but he kept on kissing me. He picked me up in his arms and carried me to the couch. He laid me down on my back.

"You smell so good, but you taste even better. Do you have vanilla lip gloss on? It's driving me mad."

I couldn't talk because he had his mouth on mine and then on the side of my neck and then my ear. I could hear him breathing heavily and along with my breath I thought I would burst from excitement. I breathed in and out hard. I wanted him and clearly he wanted me. I reached down to take his tee-shirt off, touching his strong stomach, it felt like a rock. I had to have him. My hormones were in overdrive, racing around my body. The past four months were the longest fore-play I had known in my life. I needed him now.

Then my phone rang. When I tried to climb out from under him, he pulled me back. "Where are you going? Get back here." He was smiling.

Between kisses I said, "I need to check who's calling. What if someone needs me?" I gave him a big push that didn't produce any movement; he was too solid.

"You're gonna have to push harder than that if you want me off you." He laughed.

I knew I could never push him off me; my only other strategy was tickling. I recalled he'd told me he was very ticklish on his neck where the muscle meets the collarbone. I managed to free my hand, acting like I was going to caress his face, but instead I teased my fingers along the muscle and tendons on his neck. He shot up and swatted my hand away. I came at him with my other hand and got him again, but then he grabbed that hand too and held them above my head. I was done. He was too strong for me. I started laughing when he tickled me on the stomach and my underarms — everywhere he could reach without releasing my hands. I could hardly breathe. "Stop! Mercy!" I gasped between breaths. "I give up, you got me."

"You're right I got you." He kissed my mouth. "And I'm never letting go." He stared down into my eyes, penetrating them with his love.

I reached up and kissed him back. "Please don't."

He released me to check the missed call. He followed me to the kitchen and told me he wanted to shower. I offered to get his bag from the truck and bring it up to him.

I retrieved the bag, set my snowy boots on the mat, headed upstairs, and knocked on the bathroom door.

"Coming back for more, are you?"

"No, I have your bag."

He peeked out from behind the curtain, his hair wet. Water dripped along his muscles. I prayed he couldn't see me drool through the steam; he had the most spectacular body I had ever seen. I stood, frozen.

"Maggie. Maggie?"

I heard him the second time. "What?" I looked up to meet his eyes.

"I said you can put it down next to the cabinet. You girls are all alike — you see a naked man and you can't think anymore. It's all right, I don't bite. Well, sometimes I do, but it's playful." He started laughing at his own joke.

"Well, I think men are the same way," and I pushed the cold, wet shower curtain against him. He yelled when he felt it touch his skin.

"I'll wait for you downstairs."

I started a fire while I waited for him to finish, put some coffee on to brew, and sat on the couch, watching the storm rage outside.

Will joined me on the couch, his hair still wet. He smelled like a crisp spring day. We held our mugs of coffee and watched the flames swirl and rise off the logs in the fireplace.

"I wish I could thank Tim for writing that letter to you."

"I know. It was so like Tim to do that, you know. He always thought ahead and planned things out that he needed to be prepared for. And look—after he's gone, he still managed to arrange things for me. He was such a great guy." I smiled.

"Yeah, he certainly was. You know, I don't know if I could have done what he did, arranging for a man to fall in love with you. I think it would kill me to know another man would take my place."

"I don't look at it that way, and I don't think Tim did either. It's not like you are taking his place; no one else could be Tim. He was protecting me, and that's all he ever wanted to do. When he learned his future would be cut short, he needed to know I would be taken care of so that he could leave me peacefully." I started to weep.

"Oh, I didn't mean to upset you." Will put his mug on the coffee table and held me.

"I'm not upset. I'm confused that I can love two men at once. I love you for being here with me, but I love Tim, too. Because of him we are together." I sat up and pulled his face down to meet mine and kissed him.

We separated slowly, gazing into each other's eyes and feeling the energy moving between us. He reached out and I put my hand against his, locking our fingers together.

"Well, when you put it like that… maybe I could do what Tim did. It was very unselfish."

Before I could agree, Will pulled me under him on my back, he on his side leaning over me. We kissed while the snow fell and the fire crackled.

STEADY AS YOU GO

CHERYL MURNANE

When Clipper decided it was time to go out, he came over and started licking our faces and sniffing. We tried to push him away, but he kept coming back.

"Do you ever feel like Tim has come back through Clipper to interrupt us at the perfect time?" Will asked.

"Yeah, I do. Yesterday when I found the letter, he came and sat in front of me with an expression on his face that said, 'What do you think, will you give it try?' It was like he was channeling Tim." I chuckled.

Later that evening, the snow stopped. I cleaned up the dessert plates as Will prepared Clipper for a walk.

"It'll a beautiful night for a walk. The moon is out, the skies are clear. Come with us?"

Clipper sat next to Will, alert. The two of them stared at me — how could I say no?

"Let's go."

Will was right. The air was crisp and clean. The snow sparkled in the moonlight and our feet crunched on the compacted snow; it was the only sound I could hear. I held Will's hand as we walked around the neighborhood. It felt revitalizing to be out after a storm. The blanket of snow had created a new path for me to walk on in my new life.

When we got back home, Will and I walked upstairs as we had so many times before. At the top of the stairs Will turned to me.

"Well. All right, good night. I'll see you in the morning."

I stopped him, took his hand in mine, and looked up at him.

"I was thinking…" I paused, playfully touching his tee-shirt with my fingertip. "With the permission we received yesterday, maybe you would like to sleep in my bed tonight."

He leaned in, kissing my neck, hot and heavy.

"Wait." I pushed him away. "Not that kind of sleeping—just in the bed with me, as opposed to being alone in the guest room."

"I know. I'm just messing with you." He smiled at me. "I would love to sleep in your bed with you tonight, and every night from here on out." He picked me up in his arms and walked down the hallway to my bedroom. Clipper followed at his feet.

The relief I felt climbing into bed with Will was immeasurable. I hadn't had the company of another person in my bed in many months. I couldn't wait to sleep. I wasn't alone anymore, and it felt wonderful.

Clipper curled up on his bed. I touched Will's bare chest and told him, "I find it very hard to control myself with you. You are very sexy. When I'm with you I feel alive, but I want it to feel right between us. I don't want to rush into it."

He took my hand in his, kissed it, and replied, "Don't worry about it. I'm not going anywhere. We will both know when the time is right. I just love being able to hold you in my arms. I've been dreaming about this night for a long time, and I want to savor it." He kissed the tip of my nose.

I turned to shut my light off and then turned back to be held by my new love.

In the middle of the night I started dreaming of my dad and a burning building. I must have been thrashing around. I suddenly woke up, my legs tangled in the sheets, and I felt Will's arms around me. "It's okay, I have you."

I snuggled down, and a tear rolled down my cheek. I never had to be alone or scared again. I had Will.

As dawn approached, visions of me sitting in a chair on my patio on a warm spring afternoon swirled in my mind. I was looking up at the sky, feeling the warmth of the sun on my skin. A few birds flew overhead, and butterflies began to flutter around me—all different varieties, with beautiful patterns and colors, some big and some small. In the sky, off in the distance, I saw an image begin to form in the clouds and take shape; it was distorted in the dream, but I knew it was Tim's beautiful, calm face wearing a warm smile. He spoke a few words, but I only remembered hearing him say, "It's okay." He smiled as his words echoed, and then he slowly faded away.

I sat up with a jolt, breathing heavily. I looked over at Will, who was sound asleep on his side, facing me. He looked like an angel. I pulled the covers up over my body and curled up next to him, content to try to fall back to sleep in the arms of the man my husband chose as my new lover, knowing I had his blessing to move on.

Will

AFTER THE DISCOVERY OF TIM'S NOTE, OUR RELATIONSHIP SOARED to new levels. Maggie learned to let her guard down and allow me in her life as her romantic partner. I felt liberated after that. She could now be my girlfriend, and we could move on to discover deeper emotions in our relationship. The feelings I experienced with Maggie were like no other feelings I had felt in my lifetime. Even with the crazy things I had done in my life, like skydiving and rock climbing, nothing could compare to the deep feeling of being in love with another person. My heart raced, my stomach flipped, and my palms got moist whenever I looked at her or held her. No one I had met was equal or even close to Maggie. Her thoughtful, loving, caring ways gleamed through her when she tended to people, and her generous and honest heart allowed many people to feel her love. As a bonus, she had a smoking hot body. I saw her as a perfect woman.

The more I got to know Maggie, the more I witnessed how much she loved life and she appreciated the small things that life offered and the things I did, like walk Clipper and surprise her with dinner or a roaring fire in the fireplace. It was because she loved the simple things in life that I loved her even more. She didn't treasure materialistic things like some of my other girlfriends had. She knew what mattered most in life and that was *love*.

A couple weeks after Maggie shared Tim's note, I went to the cemetery to talk to him.

"Hi, man. I have got to say thank you. The last time I was here, I prayed for a sign and you did not let me down. But was sending me into a burning building and almost killing me really necessary? I guess that's what it took for Maggie to realize what she had in her life and what she was willing to do in order to keep it."

The sun began to melt the snow that had whitewashed the town overnight. I pushed it around with my feet.

"Seriously, if you can hear me, *thank you*. Thank you for asking me to take care of Maggie and giving me the opportunity to find love. She is amazing—everything I ever wanted in a woman. I'm just sorry it took losing you in order for me to be able to love her. I will not disappoint you, Tim. I will honor my word and your dying wish. I will make sure she is taken care of. I miss you and your *perfectness*." I laughed. "I loved the letter—nice touch! Although I wish you had told me about it. It may have prevented the remorse Maggie felt about her feelings for me."

I stopped talking when I heard a car pull down the lane; it was Maggie's car. *Funny, I thought she went to the grocery store.*

She walked up to me, bundled in her winter coat and smiling. "What are you doing here?"

"Hi." I kissed her. "I'm wondering the same thing."

"I needed to talk to Tim. I always feel like he really hears me when I'm here. You?"

"Same thing. I came to thank him."

"For what?"

"For you, that's what!" I hugged her close. She fit so nicely in my arms that I never wanted to let go.

"Oh, right." She grinned.

"What are you here to tell him?"

"Well, I wanted to tell him that I miss him so much…" She pulled away and stared up at me. "And thank him for the letter and for giving us his consent and freeing me to move on without him." She stood on her tippy toes, and I bent down so she could kiss my nose.

"Yes, that letter was more than reassuring to you, wasn't it? I'm thankful he had the strength and awareness to do it. He certainly was a smart man."

"Yes, he was." She hugged me. I offered to leave her in peace to talk to Tim, but she told me she just had, and we walked away arm in arm.

~

I spent every night at Maggie's from that point forward. Because we didn't need two homes, in the spring I sold my house to a fellow firefighter who was ready to buy his first home.

The last time I walked through my house I remembered the times Melissa and Bobby had stayed over and how they made it feel like a home. After they moved to Florida, it had become a shell for me to hide in, a retreat from the loveless world in which I lived. When Melissa left me, I broke in two. I never thought I would find a love like ours again. Then I met Tim. He changed my life. Maggie lost him and found me. Our lives were intertwined. Our love was even stronger than the love I shared with Melissa.

I locked the house up. When I turned the key I repaired my broken heart. I said good-bye to one chapter of my life. As I walked to my truck, where Maggie and Clipper waited for me, I looked forward to the next chapters.

~

On a warm spring afternoon after I returned from a walk with Clipper, Maggie greeted me in the kitchen with a glass of iced tea.

"Thanks."

"I thought that you and I could go to dinner tonight in the city. We've been so busy with work, I feel like I haven't seen much of you."

"I think that sounds great! I miss you too." I kissed her cheek.

Later, as Maggie got ready for dinner, I sat in the chair in our bedroom enjoying one of the best benefits of living with her — watching her get dressed. I would pretend to read while I sat in the corner chair and she didn't seem to mind that I stayed in the room, but secretly I watched her walk around in her underwear and bra while searching for the right outfit.

That night was no different, except I wasn't hiding my longing. I sat in the chair ogling and whistling at her as she walked from her closet to the mirror and back, again and again. I watched her legs move and her muscles tighten under her skin and noticed how her butt rose just a bit before her leg came forward. She had the roundest, tightest ass. I just wanted to grab it. She was driving me mad.

She looked at me with a giggle. "Are you enjoying yourself?"

"Well, yes, I am. You're very sexy, and I find your body very intriguing." I walked up to her and held her body in my arms. I couldn't hold back on my cravings to have her, all of her, I reached around and squeezed her butt in my hands.

"We're never going to make it to dinner if you start that." She swatted my hand away.

"Who says we have to go to dinner? We can stay here and enjoy ourselves, and I can go get us something later." I kissed her neck and continued to grip her butt.

"But we have reservations, and they are…" Her voice trailed off when I started kissing her mouth.

Reservations or not, I was taking advantage of this situation. Dinner could wait, but I couldn't wait any longer. The desire to have Maggie all to myself was too intense to resist. For the first time she wasn't prohibiting my hunger to have her.

I pulled away. "Don't worry about the reservations. Someone else will take our table."

"I can't not show up, it would be unfair. I need to call them and tell them we'll be late."

"Tell them we aren't coming at all." She looked up at me, and I cocked my eyebrows and smiled.

"Will?" She looked shocked.

"Come on, Maggie, be adventurous. I want you so badly right now. We'll eat later. Remember, this night is about being together. Forget going out. I want to be with you now." I kissed her neck and slowly moved my lips down to her shoulders.

"How can I resist you any longer?"

"You can't." I held her gaze and lowered the bra strap off her shoulder with my finger, allowing my fingertip to gently slide over her skin.

"I know. Hold on—let me call them. I'll feel better." She grabbed her phone and made the call.

On the nights when I had laid awake envisioning the first time I had sex with Maggie, I imagined burning candles and soft music. A romantic night was what she deserved. But tonight was spur of moment, and it felt right. I couldn't let it pass us by.

I stood behind her as she spoke to the hostess on the phone. I caressed her body and moved my lips over her skin. I chuckled when she let out a soft moan as I sucked on her ear lobe. I could sense her body relaxing as I continued to explore her skin with my lips. I unhooked her bra and reached around to feel her breasts.

She hung up the phone and swatted me. "You had to do that, didn't you? I'm embarrassed," she said with a playful smile.

"Oh, you'll never see her or talk to her again. Don't worry about it." I said with a snicker.

I took her face in my hands and kissed her lips slowly but with passion, tickling her tongue with mine just a bit. She returned the kiss with desire, and I felt my body temperature rise. I had waited so long for this night I couldn't wait to get started. At the same time I wanted to stay in the early moments of the first time we discovered each other's bodies.

Maggie stood naked in my arms. As she lifted my shirt over my head, her breast brushed up against my chest, exciting me even more. I held her breast in my hand as she unbuckled my pants. They fell to the floor.

"Commando, huh?" She looked up at me.

"What can I say? I like the freedom."

She didn't need to work hard to get me stiff. I had waited so long for this experience with her, and now I wanted to explore all of her body before I felt her around me.

I carried her to the bed and laid her on top of it. Clipper walked into the room.

"Would you mind if I kicked him out and shut the door? He makes me feel like we have an audience."

"Not at all."

When I returned to her, she was propped up on the pillows, waiting to begin where we had left off.

I kissed every inch of her body that night, taking my time to explore. My heart raced when she combed her fingers through my hair as I stimulated her body with my lips. It had only been in my fantasies that I was able kiss her in places she guided me to. Her fingers touched my skin, stroking up my arms, across my back and chest stirring my desires. When I couldn't take it more, I rolled her over and got on top and entered her. I moved slowly, holding back on my craving to release myself inside of her. It felt so right to move with her. As I got closer to the end I whispered in her ear, "I love you, Maggie."

Before she could answer she moaned and screamed as her muscles contracted around me; I echoed her moans and pushed deeper inside of her. I felt sweat on my forehead as I gasped for air; making love to Maggie was better than I had imagined.

After I rolled off of her, I held her in my arms, our hands intertwined, and kissed her lips softly. My body was relaxed. I already looked forward to when I could feel that way again with her. It was pure passion.

"You're so beautiful. Thank you for making love to me. That was amazing."

"You weren't disappointed?" She looked up at me with a half smile, her eyebrows lifted.

"You could never disappoint me." I kissed the tip of her nose. "Although I'm still waiting for a reply." I raised myself up on my elbow and hovered over her, sweeping her hair off her forehead.

"Did you say something? I didn't hear you." She was playing with me.

"Oh, I think you heard it *and* felt it, Barrettt." I nodded.

She pushed me over and crawled on top of me; I enjoyed feeling her on top. She ran her fingers through my hair as she studied my face without speaking. I enjoyed the peace between us as we held each other's naked bodies and looked at each other's faces. I was observing Maggie's features from a new angle. She was even more beautiful. She hadn't applied makeup before I attacked her, and her natural being shined through her bare face.

"When Tim got his cancer diagnosis I thought my life ended. I couldn't imagine living life without him in it. When he was sick and getting sicker, parts of me were dying with him. Losing him stirred up all the painful feelings I had lived through when I lost my dad. I knew I had to be strong for Tim, but all I wanted was to curl into a ball and hide away alone somewhere; it was all too real for me.

"Then this guy's name started popping up, and he started coming around. I think his name was Will."

I smiled as she toyed with me, but I remained quiet, allowing her to speak about her feelings.

"Anyhow, he stirred a new life in my husband and together they conquered Tim's fears about being adventurous and he experienced a few thrills before he became too weak. All the while this… *Will guy* was breathing life back into me because he became a source of great joy and pleasure. The days when I was filled with worry, regret, and sadness changed whenever I saw Will's truck in the driveway. My nerves would relax, and I breathed a sigh of relief."

She looked me deep in the eye. "You see, Will, long before you even knew it, I loved you. I loved you because you took take care of Tim. You brought so much happiness and joy to his life when it mattered the most. I will never forget how you made him feel and then, like a ripple effect, how you made me feel."

She sat up on top of me, tugged me up so we were face to face, and held my face hands in her hands.

"Will, I don't know if I've ever sincerely loved anyone more than I love you." She kissed my lips with purpose, and I felt her love pour into me. With one last brush of her lips, she sat back.

"You are the best thing that happened in my life when everything else was falling apart. You are like the sunshine after the storm. I found warmth and life in you. I never want to live a day without appreciating how full you've made my life. I have learned that I can't control what happens in life. I've lost two great men, but I lived through the pain and came out stronger. I know I can't create a safe world to live in, but I appreciate what I have because I could lose it at any time."

She hugged me tight.

"I love you so much." Our words echoed.

Maggie

I POURED MY HEART OUT TO WILL THE FIRST TIME WE MADE love; it was a vulnerable moment. I needed to confide in him and share all my thoughts and feelings about our relationship. It was the right time to reveal the magnitude of love and respect I had for him so we could move forward to create a life together.

We would talk on the phone during our work days and the days he worked and I was off I would visit him at the station. On the nights when he didn't have to work, having him in bed with me kept the nightmares away. I found safety in his arms and peace in my dreams. We made love most nights to make up for all the lost time when we'd been in separate beds dreaming of being together. I found a new life with Will. He was everything Tim wasn't and that was okay. I was learning that it was refreshing to be with a man who was always up for an adventure, even if it meant getting hurt or coming close to it. I loved the safety Tim provided, but with Will I had come to learn that life was for living and experiencing, not hiding.

One warm, sunny summer day Will loaded me in the truck without telling me where he was taking me, except that it would take a while to get there. As we approached the destination he pulled the truck over and blindfolded me so that I couldn't see where we going.

When he started driving again, I said that he was being ridiculous. I could have just closed my eyes, but he said, "It wouldn't be as much fun as being blindfolded; it's all part of the adventure." Will lived for adventures, and he especially enjoyed getting people to join him. It was more fun to share it with someone, he said.

When the truck stopped he told me to sit still and not to peek. I heard my door open and felt Will take my hand in his. He helped me down from the truck, and then we walked a short distance and stopped. He turned me to face him and said, "I know you are going to be afraid, but trust me. It will be the greatest thrill you've ever had." Then he pulled the blindfold from my eyes and turned me to face the sign: Skydive.

"Oh, man, Will, I can't do this. Are you crazy?" I shook my head, and my palms filled with sweat.

"Oh, yes you can! If your husband did it, then you can do it. Let's go!" He was acting like a kid, and truth be told, I kind of liked it. I never thought in a million years I would ever jump from a plane, but Will made me see my life differently—he was teaching me to expand my comfort zone. I had lived many years avoiding danger, but Will thrust me into it, and as long as he was by my side, I was willing to try to be brave.

He directed me into the building by my shoulders.

"I can't believe I'm letting you make me do this. I love that you're adventurous, but that doesn't mean I need to be."

"Come on, chicken. We're going. You're gonna love it!" He sounded way too enthusiastic for my liking. *What kind of person have I fallen in love with?*

We watched a video and signed our lives away after being told many times that there was a possibility we could die, and then we loaded into the plane and prepared for the jump. I turned to Will, hoping I could back out, but I got side-tracked because he looked really hot in the form-fitting jumpsuit that showed off his physique. I realized there was no way he would let me back down. He was teaching me to live and not hide behind my fears.

"If I die before this is over, just remember I love you!" I whispered in his ear.

"You're not going to die." He kissed me. "I'm right behind you, okay? I'll see you on the ground. Relax and enjoy it." He smiled at me, that smile that melted my heart.

I stood at the door of the plane harnessed to my instructor. He started counting down and then we were airborne. We sailed through the sky, free falling. Air streamed passed my face as the ground raced up to us. When he pulled the cord, we slowly sailed through the air and everything turned quiet. My heart pounded in my chest and adrenaline raced through my veins; I felt more alive than I ever had. I imagined Tim floating through the air like this, the knowledge that he was dying accompanying him. Did he experience the same thrill I sensed inside? I wondered if he felt truly alive and awake on so many different levels.

We approached and dropped to the ground smoothly. The instructor and I detached the harness and waited for Will to finish his jump. I watched as his body fell closer, larger, until he was on the ground. He released his harness from his instructor's.

I ran up to him and jumped in his arms. "That was amazing!"

He threw his head back and laughed. "I knew you would love it."

"I want to do it again!"

"Slow down, Ms. Fearless! There are so many other crazy things we can do..." He pulled away and looked down into my eyes. "If you are willing."

"I am!" I never knew I carried a daredevil inside of me until I met Will and started experiencing all the daring adventures he enjoyed in his life. Shortly after our skydiving experience, Will found us a zipline adventure in the woods up north. After so many years of sheltering myself from sadness and loss, I found pushing myself and letting go was liberating. I had already experienced a life of fear; now I was ready to start over.

Will told me he was breaking me in for a bungee-jump outing; I wasn't sure I was up for that venture, but somehow being with Will reassured me that nothing bad could happen, so I told him I would keep an open mind, but no promises.

~

When the longer and warmer days of the summer arrived, Will and I enjoyed our days off together at the beach. He surprised me with my own surfboard and encouraged me to spend more time practicing. He taught me how to balance and position myself, how to read the waves, and showed me when to paddle with them and pop up, and when it was too late to get on. He was patient with me while I was learning. I always deflected to humor when I was done trying.

After practicing awhile, my legs burned, so I sat on the beach and watched Will surf. He moved on the water with grace. He knew exactly how to position himself to flow with the wave to the shore and then he would paddle back out and do it again, patiently sitting and waiting for the right wave to come along. After he had had enough, he walked up to me, his wetsuit unzipped, water dripping off his muscular body. Goose bumps rose on his skin.

"That was awesome! The best surfing is always after a storm. Look at those waves crash!" He shook his hair spraying water around.

"Yeah, that was fun." I stood up. "But I have to admit, I'd rather sit here and watch you." I kissed him. "You look hot out there; it kinda turns me on."

"Oh, yeah! Hold that image in your mind for later." He kissed me back.

We stayed at the beach all day, enjoying the sun, playing in and out of the water; time passed faster than I liked. I started to gather our things. Will dug around in his bag and asked me to sit with him for a moment and watch the waves. I couldn't resist the opportunity to sit between his legs with his body surrounding me, feeling his naked chest on my back when I leaned my head on his shoulder.

"I love the beach," I said. "I love the openness and the sounds of the wind and the crashing waves. I love how it can be quiet until suddenly a wave meets the shore and *splash*, it creates sound." A flock of birds flew over the ocean. "And the birds that hover when you eat and the ones flying over the sea looking for food or for freedom to just spread their wings and fly. I love playing with the sand between my toes."

He interrupted. "I love that you love the beach because this is my happy place. With all the crazy things I love in my life, I love the beach the most."

"Me too."

We sat listening to the waves and the birds calling to each other. The sun began to descend, and soft pinks and yellows lit the sky. I wanted this moment to never end. I wished I could have bottled it.

"Maggie, I need to ask you something."

"What is it?"

He turned to sit next to me, and I turned to face him.

"I love you with all my heart and soul. I have never asked a woman this question before, and I hope I don't have to again because you are the only woman I ever want to be with." He held my eyes with his. "Will you marry me?" He rambled. "I know it hasn't been that long…"

"Yes!" I interrupted. "A thousand times yes! Don't say anything else. It would make me so happy to be your wife. I love you."

"Here, hold on…" He dug in his swimsuit pocket. "I know it's here."

"Don't tell me you lost the ring in the sand!"

He reached into his other pocket and pulled out a black velvet box and smiled. "I had to mess with you a little bit." I swatted him and he laughed.

"Maggie Emma O'Brien Barrett, will you marry me?"

He opened the box. I put my hand over my mouth and gasped when I saw the ring he'd bought me. Tim and I were young we got engaged and didn't have a lot of money, so I had a modest engagement ring, but Will had a stable career and had lived a simple life during the many years he was a bachelor.

"Yes! You don't have to keep asking me. Yes, yes, yes!" I was so excited. The ring sparkled in the lingering sun, the rays reflecting off the large round center diamond that was surrounded by a wreath of smaller diamonds. Instead of a solid platinum band, this delicate braid band featured diamonds. It was the most spectacular ring I had ever seen.

"Here, put it on me." I held my hand out.

It fit perfectly. I stared at it and started to cry.

"I haven't seen those in a long time," he said, and he wiped my tears away.

"I know. That's because having you in my life makes me the happiest woman ever. Thank you for asking me to marry you. I love you so much."

I wrapped my arms around him and held him close. I never wanted to let him go.

"I thank God for you every day," Will told me. "You've made me so happy. Just when I was beginning to give up on love, I met you." He took my arms from around his neck and held my hands in his. "Thank you for saying yes."

He moved his lips over mine and I felt the energy of our love flowing between us. In that moment the world paused. There were just the two of us, sitting on the beach, kissing, sharing our love for each other.

~

After discussing and weighing our many options, Will and I agreed on a short engagement and a backyard wedding in September at what had become *our* house. We would share our day with our families and closest friends.

I had already had a big, formal wedding and worn an elaborate gown, and now I wanted a simple elegant second wedding. Will, the relaxed California guy, was happy to wear a taupe suit and ivory tie, not a tuxedo. I wore a sleeveless ivory dress with a lace bodice and a flowing organza skirt that fell just below my knees. My hair was styled with waves and curls cascading below my shoulders.

I asked my mother to be my matron of honor, a role I felt she deserved the most because of what we had experienced in life. I knew that without her as a role model, without her support, I couldn't have carried on after Tim's death.

Clipper would escort me down the aisle.

Will had a harder time choosing his best man. Candidates included cousins and many of his firehouse brothers, but in the end he asked his father to stand up for him because he had been the greatest role model in his life. I knew his father was proud to be by his son's side the day he took his wedding vows.

Wayne's face was the first I saw as I approached because Will was talking to the officiate. His father jabbed his arm and pointed my way.

Will turned and flashed that killer smile of his, and I thought I would fall down in the aisle. His eyes assured me that I would make it to his side. He waited for me to join him and adjusted his hands. When Clipper ran up to stand by his side I smiled at him. I maintained my pace, steady as I went — just like my dad taught me.

I reached Will's side and handed my simple bouquet of orange calla lilies to my mother and kissed her cheek. I turned back to Will and held his open hand. He didn't speak but mouthed the words, "You look stunning."

I smiled and mouthed, "You do too." I squeezed his hand.

In the short ceremony we professed our love for each other and made promises to always love and support each other. When the time came, Will gathered me in his arms and, with one hand on my cheek, he kissed me more passionately than he had ever kissed me. I kissed him back with great delight. Everyone stood and cheered. Finally we broke apart and laughed. It was the happiest day of my life, surrounded by family and friends celebrating our love. It was a far cry from what we were experiencing one year earlier.

We ate and danced into the night. I wanted the day to never end. Will and I danced to our wedding song: "At Last" by Etta James. During that song at Will's holiday party I'd realized I was truly in love with him; it had become our song. Almost all the couples were on the dance floor, holding each other close. Everyone was enjoying the celebration, including Molly. Out of the corner of my eye I saw her dancing with a man. She had arrived alone because her latest boyfriend failed to meet her expectations and she'd dumped him.

I didn't recognize the man she was dancing with. Will told me his name was Andy; he had started at the department less than a year ago. He was easygoing and up for anything; Will described him as a cool guy. I hoped he could make Molly happy; from the looks of it he already had. I watched them dance close together, seeming very content.

Will held me in his arms as we moved around the dance floor. I was overcome with joy and appreciation for how my life turned out after losing Tim. I was pushed out of my comfort zone and forced to reexamine the loss I thought I had healed from. Through Tim's death I'd learned to live life. He'd given me the best gift, the opportunity to create a new life. I knew I couldn't create my own safe world to live in — in order to really live, I had to take chances.

Will was my knight in shining armor, my salvation, and so often my rescuer that I couldn't remember each instance. I did remember that he was always there when I needed him. The night we became husband and wife I longed for our life together. I never wanted to be without him, but I knew that there were no guarantees in life. We would love and cherish each other for as long as we both should live.

Epilogue
Two Years Later

Maggie

OUR LOVE STORY GREW AND IT SEEMED WE FELL DEEPER AND deeper in love every day. We enriched each other's lives and shared many laughs at our new discoveries. As the years went by, fewer tears were shed on Tim's anniversary and more appreciation was shared for what had come before so that Will and I could become what was.

We sometimes traveled to California to be with Will's family. The first time we went was in the spring after we found Tim's letter. I had booked the flight for a spring vacation, thrilling Will's mother. Will teased me that I had done it for brownie points, but I really did it because I knew he would never go without me.

Each time we traveled there, I enjoyed listening to the stories his family shared about him growing up. Will would always leave the room when he got embarrassed, and I would follow him, drag him back in, and make him sit with me to listen to his childhood as told by his parents. I appreciated this gift that his parents could share. I only got to hear one side of my childhood story, so I made sure Will appreciated having both his parents there to tell him their memories of his adventures and the trouble he got into.

Will's dad and I got along very well. I sat and listened to his stories about being a firefighter and wondered if my dad had experienced anything like he had. I'm sure in some ways they had, but I would never know all the experiences that my dad lived through.

Will's parents' marriage was the type of marriage I prayed for, rich in love, commitment, and support.

Although I was still learning how to be more adventurous, I wouldn't allow my fears to prevent Will from being the adrenaline junkie he was—the more life-threatening the adventure, the better it was to him. We celebrated our one year wedding anniversary in California. While we were there we went to visit Alison and Keith at the arena where Keith's motocross tour was racing that evening.

After a bunch of hugs and high-fives, Will turned to me and said, "I'll be back in a while; stay with Alison." He kissed me and ran away like a little kid.

"Wait, where are you going?" I yelled.

"Keith invited me to ride. Look for me out there." He pointed to the track.

I turned to my sister. "Oh, I don't know if I'll ever get used to this. He could kill himself out there."

She looked at me sympathetically and said, "He could also kill himself out there." She pointed to the world beyond the arena doors. "Come on, let's get closer and watch. You'll love it."

We walked down the bleacher aisle to get a better view. Will put on some protective gear and a helmet; if nothing else he certainly looked sexy to me. He turned and looked at me, giving me a thumbs-up, and I returned the gesture.

He straddled the bike and pulled back on the throttle, revving the motor. *Oh God, he's going to kill himself,* I thought.

He rode around the track twice before pulling over to check in with Keith. They spoke for a minute before he was off again. I watched my husband the daredevil with a smile on my face. He'd discovered a great friend in Keith when we spent time together; they fed off each other. Alison and I laughed at how similar they were. I fell for a risk-taker after all, just like my twin sister.

When he was finished playing, he rode up to us and told me to get on.

"No way. You can play, but not me. No thank you." I held my hands up.

My sister pushed me. "Go on."

Will held his hand out. "I won't let anything happen to you." He nodded at the empty space behind him.

"Fine, but I'm only doing this to make you happy." I took a helmet from smiling Keith and strapped it on. I got on the back of the bike and wrapped my arms around Will.

"Go slow, please."

He revved the throttle. "Fast? Did I hear you say 'go fast'?" He took off. I held on tighter and ducked my face behind his back.

After the first turn, he slowed down for the remainder of the turns and managed to sneak in some small jumps. He brought me back to where we started, where Alison and Keith were clapping and smiling for me.

We got off the bike and took our helmets off. Will leaned down to kiss me.

"You're my hero," he told me.

"No, you're my hero." I kissed him back.

~

STEADY AS YOU GO

Life with Will was never boring—that was guaranteed. Weeks after our vacation to California, Will came home to tell me he had booked us on a bungee-jump adventure. He had been waiting for me to become more comfortable with my new adventurous lifestyle, and apparently he thought I was ready.

"Next month we are doing this." He handed me a brochure. "We'll take a road trip, drive down, and jump off the bridge. It's gonna be epic. I can't wait to see your face! I know you're gonna love it."

He hugged me, and I could feel his excitement. I hated to disappoint him.

"Will, I can't do it," I said. Then I waited.

"What do you mean? I know you're ready. You can handle it! Come on, don't be nervous. You'll be strapped..."

I cut him off. "No, you don't understand." I reached over to the counter and picked up the clear bag that protected the white plastic stick inside. I walked back over and placed it in his hands.

"What's this?" He turned it over and over.

I stood opposite him and waited for it to register.

"Holy shit, Maggie, are you pregnant?" I wished I had a camera to capture the look of pure surprise mixed with elation on his face.

I nodded, a huge smile on my face. He picked me up in his arms and spun me in a circle.

"Oh my God, we're gonna have a baby! I'm gonna be a dad, and you're going to be the most beautiful and caring mother ever." Tears pooled in his eyes.

He put me down and kissed me sensually.

"Oh, Maggie, I'm so happy." He placed his strong hands on my belly and said, "It's okay. You two don't have to go bungee jumping."

I laughed and kissed him again.

~

My contractions started soon after Will left for work. I held off calling him for as long as I could, but when they became too intense hours later, I wanted him with me.

"I need you home. I'm in labor. My water just broke." I breathed through a contraction. They were getting stronger.

"I'm coming in the ambulance. We'll transport you to the hospital. I can't take a chance that something will happen to you. Stay on the phone with me. We'll be right there."

I stayed on the phone and huffed with each contraction. I tried to stay focused while Will talked me through them. Clipper was by my side and I explained to him between contractions that his life was about to change again, but this time it was going to be more hectic and loud. The poor dog had no idea what I was saying.

I had set my bags by the door, ready to go, before Will ran into the house.

"Maggie, let's go! Maggie!" he yelled.

"I'm in here." I had moved to the couch in the family room; I needed to lie down.

Will found me.

"I have to push, I can't hold back." I looked up at him with hesitant tears in my eyes, knowing this wasn't how it was supposed to be. I should be at the hospital with doctors, but it came on too fast.

He radioed out to Seth in the ambulance. "Get in here! We're having a baby!"

Seth ran in the room carrying a bag. He opened it and pulled out a clean sheet, gloves, and a towel. Clipper remained on his bed in the corner of the room, watching the commotion.

"Are you ready, Maggie?" Will asked me. "I can see the baby's head." He had tears in his eyes. "Come on, Momma! Give me a big push on your next contraction."

I looked up at him. "I love you." Then the big one came, and I pushed and kept pushing until I felt intense pressure and then relief. I heard a cry. I opened my eyes and saw my loving, caring husband holding our newborn baby. I panted heavily.

"Oh my God, Will, we did it! And you too, Seth." I laughed. "What is it? What do we have?"

Will held up the baby and said, "It's a boy. We have a son." Joyful tears rolled down his cheeks.

After Will cleaned him and wrapped him in a clean towel, I reached out to hold my baby.

"Hi, baby. I'm your mommy." I stared at my newborn and looked up at Will, tears flowing from my eyes. "Thank you. You rescued me again. I love you."

He sat on the floor next to the couch and curled up next to me.

"I can't believe I just delivered my baby, our baby—we have a son! Maggie, I love you." He brushed my hair off and kissed my forehead.

"Are we still in agreement about our baby name, William Timothy Driscoll?" My father and Will's first name, plus Tim's name for his middle name—the three loves of my life rolled together in a perfect baby boy.

"Absolutely!" Will beamed.

Will held Billy—we decided to call him Bill after my father—as Seth loaded me onto the stretcher, and then Will placed our new baby in my arms. Seth drove us to the hospital. Will sat in the back with me and Billy, and we stared at our baby's face. A face and life that our love created.

After the doctor's gave Billy a complete check-up at the hospital, I held him in my arms and I shared my thoughts about the day's events with Will.

"I was thinking about how all of this happened today, how quickly labor came on, preventing us from getting to the hospital. I don't feel that it was a coincidence that I delivered Billy in the same room Tim died in. I feel Tim's blessing in this? Do you?"

"I thought of that too when I came into the room and saw you in labor. What a story we have to tell. I love you, Mommy." He kissed me.

"I love you too, Daddy." I kissed him back.

~

A few months after Billy was born, Will and I took Billy and Clipper for a walk to our special place in the woods on Tim's birthday. We walked to the spot where we could see the pond, and Will began to throw sticks for Clipper. I sat on the same boulder I always did. Will came over to check on Billy, who was sleeping in a front carrier, and made sure there was enough shade on his face.

A friendly dog, a chocolate Lab with rare brilliant blue eyes, approached. We started petting him while his owner made his way around the bend. Clipper returned with his stick. He dropped it when he saw the other dog and froze.

"I'm so sorry, he took off from me," the owner apologized.

"It's okay. He seems really friendly," I said. The dog sat next to me. "Isn't he cute?" I petted his head. Clipper came over to sniff him and then sat down next to us.

"That's weird. He's never done that before. He must like you guys," the owner said, and then he called the dog.

"Come on, Timmy, let's go."

I looked up at Will with a startled look and then at the dog. He hadn't moved. The dog looked at me and then at Will. Stood, sniffed Clipper, and then with his head held high, he walked alongside his owner with a pep in his step and a wag in his tail.

Will and I stared at each other and looked up to the sky. At the same moment we said, "Thank you."

Acknowledgements

The first time I wrote a book I had no idea what I was doing. I had taken a writing course and poured through the internet looking for insight and direction. In the end I did what I always do. I followed my heart. I have had many occurrences in life in where I let my heart lead me and in those times I found some of the most fulfilling experiences. My approach to writing this second book wasn't too different except for the fact that the path had been worn and I had some direction. As I walked down that road, I met people, learned the art and tucked away knowledge to be used during the writing process. Some things never left me, like my desire to tell a story…I think I will always have a book in me! Some things came back to me with me with ease. While some of the issues I had struggled with before were there the second time around, the knowledge I had gained pushed me to try harder, writing and re-writing until my brain cramped. Education is power. Power is freeing. To be free in a story is the sweet spot! I thank my characters for bringing me on a ride of a life-time! I cried with them, laughed with them, and got mad with them. All for the love of writing! I can't explain how these fictitious people climb into my brain and my daily life emerging when I least expect them! You have to try writing to experience it and once you do…you're hooked!

This story of Tim, Maggie, and Will came to me through seeing the same people in my life week after week and wondering who they were and how they lived their lives. In some cases I see them more than I see my extended family. I began to wonder what would happen if we struck up a friendship? How far would it go? What impact would they have in my life? All questions that I needed to answer for the love of the story!

To my readers and followers, thank you! It had been a great pleasure to meet some of you and have your support on the rocky ride of being an author! The joy I feel when I hear someone has read *During the Fall* fills me with gratitude and appreciation that I may entertain and hopefully offer hope to my readers. It's truly an honor.

I was so fortunate to work with my editor, Sue Ducharme of TextWorks-EquiText again. With her help we dusted off the webs and enriched the life in the story! She brought her sparkle again with her amazing editing talents. Thank you, Sue.

To my amazing beta-readers who grew in numbers! Juliet, Liz, and Sandra thank you again for your time, honesty, and questioning to fine-tune my thoughts and expressions! To my new additions Emily, Kate, and Michelle! I know the time you all poured into the manuscript and I thank you from the bottom of my heart for searching for the errors of my ways!

Thank you to a special Fire Lieutenant who sat through an interview that ran over into a Patriots game; even though I had told you it wouldn't! I couldn't have timed it any better to be present for the many calls that came in and bear witness to the men and women who bravely run into unknown emergencies all for the sake of human life! God bless all of you!

Props to my make-up artist, Christine Galatis, for transforming me for my photos. My amazing photographer, Cristen Farrell at Cristenfarrellphotography.com, created beautiful images in her sunny studio. My cover artist, Gabrielle Prendergast at coveryourdreams.net, had enormous patience to extract what I couldn't see but that was hidden inside of me. Thank you! Guido Henkel, at Guidohenkel.com, formatted the manuscript for the e-book and paperback, and did an amazing job, again!

To my extremely supportive family Mike, Abby, and Brendan, you poured many cups of coffee to keep me going, left me alone to hang out with my imagination and dream on my laptop, and never once told me what I was doing was a waste of time! Your encouragement means the world to me! I can't say where we're headed, but that wherever it is, we will be together! I love you guys!

I can't close without thanking my God, my spiritual advisor. For, without your guidance there would be no book! You have made many of my dreams come true. I can't even grasp the thought that *During the Fall* has been sold world-wide in countries like England, India, and New Zealand! I could not have done that alone! The journey still lies ahead of us. Lead and I will follow; let's keep this thing growing! Amen!

About the Author

CHERYL MURNANE lives in a suburb of Boston with her husband, two children, and dog, Mitzi. Cheryl is also the author of her debut novel *During the Fall*. As a practitioner of yoga, she lives a disciplined life, balanced by faith and family, and she believes that everything happens for reasons we may not always understand. Cheryl loves to hear from fans at www.facebook.com/cherylmurnaneauthor or at her website www.cherylmurnane.com

Made in the USA
Middletown, DE
28 August 2016